Pearl of Fire

C. Chancy

Cover Art by tasgart.
http://art.tagbooks.net

Manufactured in the United States of America
ISBN-13: 9781793120175
Library of Congress Control Number: 2019900142

Chapter One

Fire-bolts cracked, tearing air apart. Water-bolts hissed in return volleys, arcing cold between the two groups of deadly serious men.

Crouched low behind a wooden crate, splinters digging into her jacket, Shane Redstone kept her head down and her eyes closed. A familiar gummy sweetness tainted the air; half-cooked serpent venom, stabilized with some kind of agave syrup.

Riparian, or I'm a seared snowflake.

Which meant the water-bolts weren't just enough deadly elemental force to punch a fist-sized hole through flesh. They were poisoned. Even if she didn't get hit, poisonous drops misting into open eyes could drop her just as dead. It'd just take longer.

I'm probably the only person in this warehouse who's been in worse situations before. Oh, the irony.

Not that long before, even. The flying strike on Richter's Pass, eight months ago; that'd been a pure hair-on-end from crashing start to fiery pullout.

Eight months ago. Two months before-

Firefight. Here. Now. Think! You've really screwed up this time, Flame. Royally and by the numbers. You followed armed men into a confined space without backup - and you missed whoever had them under observation. If Erastus were here, he'd-

But Strike Leader Erastus Elizier wasn't here. She'd never hear his steadying voice again.

Don't need his voice, need his tactics. How would he handle this?

Besides not leading his team into a warehouse full of rod-happy lunatics without a plan in the first place?

Besides that, Shane thought dryly, fingering the steel-scale bracelet on her left wrist. The smooth ripples of metal calmed her breath; a physical anchor to old oaths. *Observe, look for an opening, get the hell out of here and call for backup.*

Risking the spray, she opened her eyes, straining to make out any differences between light and dark.

Nothing. A spark-strewn blur, all she'd known for the past half-year. Dark enough that she knew she was out of full sun. Beyond that....

Damn them all.

Closing her eyes again - what was the point? - Shane rested her fingers on the crate she hoped concealed her, and listened. Echoes rang metallic from above; the warehouse must be mostly empty for the girders to be so exposed. Shuffle of footsteps from two areas; either these two bunches were the only people in here, or any warehouse personnel were huddled as low and quiet as she was. Not likely. Grunts and bitten-off swears on both sides; she thought she heard an accent that wasn't *quite* Riparian, but the echoes made it confusing-

"Caldera City Watch! Put your weapons down!"

Another volley of water hissed back; five, no at least six by that swift rise-and-fall of chill slicing air. The enemy was silent, the enemy was disciplined....

And if her elemental sense was true, then despite their water-bolts, the enemy had traces of bound Fire clinging to their auras. Not civilian grade. At all.

Here's hoping they don't have a Fire-Worker.

Deep breath; in through the nose, slowly out through the mouth. It'd been years since she'd needed to make herself calm to sense Fire, but with all her nerves screaming she was alone and outnumbered, no team watching her back-

Because they're dead, and you're not, and you don't get to give up and die that easily, Shane snarled at herself. *So use the desert-lost basics and breathe, damn it.*

She felt her heartbeat, pulsing against the ever-burning heat of the Fire-pearl inside. Took another breath. And *reached*.

That way, four stored rod-cores of Fire, thrumming as the Watch shot back. The more diffuse sense of the officers' body heat, raised by adrenaline. To her left and a bit behind, more body heat, streaked with the cold of Water; just as determined, just as angry. Just as controlled.

Professionals. Ah, damn.

And behind them, lower down - on the floor? - a glass-slick knot of bound Fire. *Tightly* knotted, with a familiar twist that-

Sweet Handmaid of Mercy.

Cane in hand, Shane vaulted over the crate, and struck.

Crunch. Not *crack*.

Shoulder, not arm, he'll be on me any second-

"Hell, where did she- Hold your fire!"

Too late. There were bolts already coming.

Perfect.

A clutch of fingers, and fire-bolts veered; one flaring in her attacker's face to drive him screeching back, the rest arcing around her to sweep into the chill of envenomed water.

Blind-fighting. Always hated it-!

Her eyes might be shot, but her ears still worked. She ducked a punch, twisted away from a rushing body, hit the floor and grabbed-

Metal box. Steel from the way it vibrated at her touch; Fire locked inside, linked to something fragile.

Not in my city. Not in my *city!* "Get out!" Shane yelled, sweep of hand and cane raising a searing shield of Fire around her. "It's a bomb!"

I hate civilians, Inspector Allen Helleson thought fervently, making himself a calm center of Spirit even as he ducked another venom-shot. It wasn't easy. The poisonous green swirl in blasting water would have been more than unnerving, but he was just skilled enough with Spirit to feel vaporized venom trying to claw its way into his body.

Are they crazy, or do they have some kind of antidote?

The knot in his gut leaned toward crazy, and a fervent wish that Army Intelligence had snatched this file out of Watch hands before it ever got near Captain Mason. But it'd seemed like an ordinary city-securing assignment. Their Watch squad had tracked this group of Riparian operatives for the past few weeks, cleaning up the usual mix of sabotage, blackmail, and attempted security breaches. Yet the Riparians' operation had been *off* for that, somehow; and when they'd put the pieces together and realized the spies were focusing on this half-empty airship warehouse, for some ungodly reason-

We're right above one of the main lava-Wards.

High above; Calderans weren't stupid. Layers of welded tuff, air, and water armored the space between this floor and the Ward. It should be secure. Riparians used poison, not bombs. They were Water-Workers, with the rare Spirit born into their nation-

And who in the cold deserts was the blonde? Brown denim jacket, loose light shirt and pants, tough walking shoes - she'd have been a scandal and a hissing back in Waycross, but here in the city he'd only noticed her for the chastity bracelet... and the ironwood cane. Street-legal, but perfectly capable of giving a mugger, or an unwary Watch officer, a very bad day.

Of the two, the bracelet was weirder. Allen was used to the shimmer of steel from under young Orthodox sleeves, or older widows content to spend the rest of their lives as Aunts and Grandmas. On a woman in ordinary city clothes?

That, and the way she'd just appeared on one of the operatives' tails as his squad closed in for what should have been a simple arrest, somehow scooting out of sight as it all went down....

A Fire-Worker. Did they recruit an agent? And who throws Fire near a bomb?!?

Well, outside of his team. Not that they had much choice.

Not an agent, maybe, Allen thought wryly, as three of the seven Riparians started firing desperately at the shield of flames.

And if she wasn't an agent, yet had the Fire-Working skill to slam up a wall like that - Master-level, or he'd eat his Orthodox hat-

Then she needs help. Fire won't stop everything - and even a Master can't hold a Fire-shield long. "Callie!"

"Yeah?" Tucked up behind a pillar for cover, the brunette inspector was chewing gum, apparently oblivious to the bolts punching out rivet-sized dribbles of steel.

Maybe he hadn't been in Caldera City that long, but Allen knew this was nowhere near a normal day. And even his best Spirit-calming couldn't be that effective. Callie was bluffing. Why?

No time. Ask later! "Take over."

"Got it." She popped a bubble, pushed gum to the side and spoke into the Air-Worked silver shell. "Keep 'em busy, people."

Fire blazed bright lines across the warehouse; Allen gripped his rod, but didn't fire, deliberately switching it to his off hand. He wasn't a major Worker; he hadn't been born with that strong a gift. But the Spirit he had was sure and stable, he wasn't trying to get *through* the Warded warehouse wall, he could do this....

Tracing the intricate rune from memory, whispering the chant, he fixed *here* and *there* in his head - as *there* had been, moments before the flames rose-

Power poured through him like starlight.

He stumbled inside the fiery wall, still not good enough at teleports to step from *here* to *there* on the level-

The blonde's hand snatched his, cane clattering to the concrete. "Who are you?"

"Inspector Helleson." His eyes fixed on the little flames dancing along her fingers. Not burning him or the rod; not yet. Though he couldn't count on that long. The concentration to hold a Fire-shield and *talk* had to be agonizing. "You're breaking my hand. Relax, let me show you my badge...."

In the crowd she'd been wearing sunglasses. Somewhere in the scramble she'd lost them, and blue eyes were filmed with a gray opacity that wasn't normal at all. Allen swallowed hard. "You're *blind.*"

"Brilliant deduction. You *must* be an inspector." She let go, turning back to a steel chest the size of an apartment sink. "Port the hell back out of here. I'm not sure what kind of trigger it's got, but I'm betting on a timer. They wouldn't be trying to pin you here if they didn't think it was going to go. *Soon.*"

They weren't just trying to pin the Watch. Allen flinched as steam sizzled against one arc of the shield, jaw tightening as he saw their aim narrow, more and more Water-bolts striking one small point.

This, I can do something about.

He hooked the fingers of his free hand, drawing runes family training and the Watch had drummed into his head. With regular Water-bolts this would be tricky, but these were *venom*-bolts. Concentrated malice. Easy to grab... for a Master Spirit-worker. A Journeyman could only deflect them, throwing off deadly bolts by inches.

Enough to buy us time. Allen breathed a sigh of relief as more fire reinforced water-dimmed flames. "Ma'am-"

"Good aim." A thrust of her hand thickened the arc of fire nearest the Riparians, blotting angry faces back to a blur through flames. "Keep it up."

Keep it up? Allen swallowed a very un-Watch-like eep. "You're coming with me."

"The hell I am. Lava-Ward." She pointed straight down, steel scales shifting against the base of her thumb. "I can feel it."

She can feel it? He knew the kinds of protections layered over a major Ward, *no* Worker should be able to-

"Go!" She dropped back down beside the chest. "Or at least aim that thing someplace useful. For preference, I don't know, at the *bad guys?*"

"What do you think you're doing?"

Her finger traced white-hot lines on flat steel, metal melting away to either side in a sudden choking taste of hot iron and rivulets of molten orange. "What's it look like, Inspector?"

It looked like Lieutenant Aster ready to play with Fire in the most terrifying way. Only that Master Fire-worker couldn't melt steel *and* still snark. And the only people more skilled than Masters were.... "You're *blind!*"

"And we are all going to *die* when this goes off. Do I have to use little words? Bomb. Ward. Lava. *Dead people*," she growled. "Shut up and let me work."

He was Watch; she was a blind civilian. He ought to toss her over his shoulder and get the heck out of here.

But she was melting steel, holding a Fire-shield, and *still able to talk.*

This is no Master. This is a Flame.

A soul graced by the Sunlit Lord and the Lord's second created guardian, the Flame Upon the Deep. Or so the Hellesons' birth church claimed. Allen wasn't so sure. He'd known too many Stars in his family to believe anyone was filled with divine grace just because they were an Elemental.

But grace or no grace, no one grasped reached that power without tenacity, endless study, and plain hard work. If a Flame thought she could do this....

"Allen?" Callie's voice came through the shell bound near his ear. "I think these bastards *want* to die-"

"Callie, we've got a problem."

Most people linked metal with Earth, Shane knew, when they

linked it with Workers at all. Which wasn't wrong; it just wasn't the whole story. Metal worked just fine with Fire. You simply had to know how to ask.

Probably a dead-man's switch linked to the bolt. If I cut a hole here....

Hot metal stuck like molasses to her fingertips, flesh unburned by pure will. Shane lifted away the cut square, listening to the opening.

Tick. Tick. Tick....

Ship captain's watch. Between that and the water-bolts - probably a Riparian device.

Riparian trigger, anyway. Someone else Bound the Fire. But into what?

Reaching out with elemental sense, she *felt* inside the cut hole, adding just the slightest trace of heat. Quick-moving, easy-heating - air inside most of the box. Smooth solidity that picked up heat without moving - metal, probably the watch. And attached to that....

Something resonated with her power, bitter with the taste of volcanic steam. Not metal, not quite stone; cold, yet a sense of *movement* inside it, even now. The familiar slipperiness of volcanic glass - or as more reverent types called it, lava-hair.

Gotcha! Grinning fiercely, Shane reached for the hole-

Stopped, fingers just outside steel. Gritted her teeth.

Only have one shot at this. "Inspector! The lava-hair. Which side is closest to the watch?"

"Closest to-?"

"I have to pull the Fire *away* from the trigger!" She could feel heat warping silver and steel, almost taste how it radiated from glass... but they were so close to each other and *she couldn't see.*

Six months ago, Terry would have covered for her. That was his *job.* Off the field Strike Specialist Terry Felter had charmed and connived his way through anything the team needed; on the field he'd kept purely mundane lookout while the rest of the team killed the enemy and Shane shattered any elemental threat headed their way.

Terry was dead. She had to trust eyes she'd never seen. The wound in her soul yawned open, an endless cold abyss of fangs....

The man beside her sucked a breath between his teeth, as if that pain stabbed his own heart. His hand came down on her right wrist, callused fingers guiding it up and a little left. "The lava-hair's coiled around, but the braid of it goes into a shaft on the watch. Right in front of your fingers. Is that it?"

"Should be," Shane muttered. *"Get back."*

No fool, he yanked away, even as she plunged her hand into the hole. Hot fingers closed on an intricate, glass-slick knot-

Fire roared, threatening to break out of glassy strands, crisp flesh to ash and bone to cinders.

You will not.

Holding. Teetering on the edge. But holding.

A globe of chill drilled into shielding flames. More struck fast; the terrorists must have rigged their rods to full-auto, trading endurance for destructive power. Some bolts pulled aside enough to spread the blow, but the inspector didn't have the power to skew them all-

Heart full of Fire, Shane yanked out a hot thread of power and lashed it at her enemies. Screams, curses; a flex of water as someone tried to pour poison back down the fiery strand....

Another flick of fingers released flames to snap into the wall, sealing the shield.

A low whistle. "Didn't know even a Flame could do that."

He knew she was a Flame... well, if he couldn't figure that out just watching, the Watch had scrapped its recruiting standards. More important, the idiot inspector hadn't left yet. Damn it. He didn't have enough power to stay alive in this mess; why didn't he *get out?*

Sunlit, I hate civilians.

A passing thought, crisped and scattered by Fire. So *much* power within... this was a Master's year of work. More Fire than even a Flame should pull at once.

Not my city. Not my home, *you bastards.*

Shane breathed, fingers woven into glass that stretched like taffy. Fire sparked like dew drops at every twist and knot, flowing down glass, into skin.

Breathe. Be the flame. Breathe it in, and bank it. Nowhere safe to put it in here; breathe it in.

She couldn't take all of it, but that was all right; she had a construct of Fire just aching to be reinforced, as venom splashed against her shield. More threads of heat pulled free with a flowing wave of her hand, pulsing into concrete and steel.

Breathe....

Ah. There *was* one more place she could push Fire. Make that seven, all seething cores of poisoned Water.

Rising to her feet, Shane lifted hands full of flame.

"Hey, wait, you *can't see*, don't aim at-"

Stepped, and whirled, flinging flames free.

Seven bursts of flame, screaming from her fingers like fireworks on Founding Day. Seven flame-orange streaks struck the enemy, and every water-rod seared into steam.

Panting - the air *rippled* with heat - Allen tried to pick his jaw off the floor. She was blind. No one could see with eyes like that. And yet-

A Star could have done that. I think.

Elementals had that level of fine control. He'd seen fine-scale healing and teleportation at work. He just didn't know anyone who could do it while being *shot at*.

At least not anyone who'd admit it. "Who *are* you?"

The blonde waved a warning finger, sparks trailing in its wake. "Later," she said, as if from a great distance. "Busy."

I swear, my shoes are smoking. Allen dropped into a crouch anyway, peering into the hole she'd cut in solid steel. Inside pale fingers teased out tuft after tuft of flames, like carded ruby silk.

...Oh my Lord, I was hoping I'd been seeing things.

No, worse luck. A Pelean lava-hair knot; charged, and glowing what most would call a holy white-gold. Normally, you only saw a few strands; three bits of the golden glass could hold enough bound Fire to take down a small building. A braided knot like this....

Don't faint. You'd die of heatstroke before anyone could get to you. "Callie?"

"Bomb squad should be here in five," his fellow inspector reported breathlessly. "We've got three live ones; don't know if they'll stay that way. These guys got a nasty dose of their own poison." She paused. "Could use you out here, if things are under control."

"If they're not, I don't know what we can do about it," Allen muttered, eyeing their fiery shell of protection. Flames shifted scarlet through gold through blinding white, coruscating like sunset. The way fire flowed with the blonde's every move, no painstaking runes, no mnemonic chants... he'd never seen a Flame at work before. It was terrifying. "Have you ever seen anything like this?"

"Yeah. Once."

"Callie?"

"Just try to get out of there in one piece."

Yeah. Speaking of- Hell! "You said this was on a timer!" he swore at the blonde.

"Was." A graceful, floating step; counter-pointed by fingers flung out once, twice, thrice, sharp as knives. "Told you. Pulled Fire out of that thread first-"

The ticking stopped.

She nodded, sweat trickling down her face. "Guess it worked."

She guessed. She guessed? Allen found himself stifling a sudden, sinful, perfectly reasonable desire to throttle his would-be rescuer. "Are you *insane?*"

She didn't twitch. Just arched a pale brow, as if dodging infuriated inspectors was something that didn't even deserve prying her eyes open with coffee. "If you distract me, I might fry you. Does that count?"

Sadly enough, it probably wouldn't - not with this much elemental power flung around. The only crazy part was that she'd even tried to disarm the bomb in the first place... and how did a blind woman even know where to start?

Someone taught her when she wasn't blind, obviously. But she's so young....

"Allen!" Callie; loud, but hard to hear through the fire-crackle. "Bomb squad's here, but Lieutenant Aster doesn't want to make a hole if he doesn't have to. Can you get the shield down?"

"Give me a minute." Allen eyed the blonde; almost slapped his forehead, realizing how useless that was. "We've got someone here to disarm that thing. You can let go."

"No," she said; a careful, measured calm. "I can't."

"Listen, they're professionals-"

"I'm sure. Have to have somewhere to dump the Fire. How many people do you want to die here?" Both her hands were in motion now; knotting ruby power with an intricate flutter of fingers and sways he wasn't even going to try to watch. He'd seen elder Stars in Waycross bring power to heel with ecstatic dance. This was tighter, more intricate; a carved cameo to an Orthodox mosaic. Who in the *world* Worked like that?

Someone who's crazy... or knows exactly what they're doing.

Given his Spirit-calm lapped around her like a sauna stone, he had to bet on not crazy. "They're here," Allen stated, changing conversational gears to match her level, unyielding tone. "They're *not* going away. You make a hole, or they will."

"Tell them to be quick." A nod of her head, and an arc of flame behind him vanished. Aster and his people didn't wait, dashing across the line of soot on concrete in a heavy-geared run, before flames lashed up again.

"Hey!" Allen whirled on the blonde.

"Relax, Inspector." The lieutenant tromped over, boots heavy with rock-fiber and Wards against heat. "Whole dome's easier to hold than part of one. She's got the right idea, if we want to bleed this bastard dry before it crisps us." Confidence hanging on him like his armored coat, he walked over to the chest. "Let's see what we have here... *fuck*."

That, from a Master-level Fire-Worker. "You can handle it, right?" Allen said uneasily. Jerked a thumb at the blonde. "She's handling it."

...Which was absolutely no guarantee a Master could. Oh, they were *screwed*.

Aster shook himself, and gestured at one of his people. "Hansen. Get out the eater."

"Sir!" Hansen's eyes were wide enough to see all the whites. Given the man was *Bomb Squad*, this did not give Allen a happy feeling. "Do you think even the eater can-?"

"She's peeled off about half the Fire in there. If we can scoop off another third of what's bound-"

The blue-helmet on the squad snapped her fingers for luck, chanting to call water out of the tank on her back to hover around them in an icy mist. Hansen and his two fellow Fire-Workers started their own chants, scribing symbols in air with the measured strokes of people who practiced every day for this split second of terror.

"Ma'am," Aster said to the blonde, with a humble respect Allen had *never* heard from the man. "We're going to start pulling Fire off the device now."

"Go for... the threads farthest from the watch," the blonde said distantly, never still for a moment. "I'm... working backwards from there."

"Yes, ma'am." Crouching to glance into the chest again, Aster bit back another curse. "On three. One." He raised his hands, echoed by his men. "Two." Air turned to frost about them, a moment of winter in the midst of inferno. "Three-"

Allen hit the floor, as the crimson wisp Aster pulled free roared into a snapping orange column of fury, flashing frost back to raging summer's heat. The Bomb Squad chanted and scribed for their very lives, mist gathering, boiling almost to steam, and gathered back again by the Water-Worker's frantic efforts.

All the while the blonde danced with her thread of ruby flame. Sweating. Trembling; he could see it in her steps, her stiffened shoulders. But she didn't *stop*, even as she had to step farther and farther from the Squad's desperate battle-

Eyes wide, Allen dove for the cane on the floor.

Not fast enough I'm not going to be-

He almost was. But her heel was already coming down as he pulled polished ironwood away, and she stumbled.

Hissing like a snake, ruby blossomed into blue flame, hot and hungry-

She yelped as she went down; rolling, hands still *moving*, even as she came back up to her knees. Fingers slashed the air. Bleeding. Commanding.

Blue snapped back into a strand of ruby, tame as a kitten.

Allen numbly crossed the distance between them, in a cold sweat despite the snarling flames. They'd been dead. He'd been sure of it. Not even a Master could yank that much power to a dead halt once it'd broken free. It'd be like trying to stop a volcano mid-fury.

Which, granted, Calderans had *done*, to build Caldera City in the first place. But that had taken more than Masters.

How much Fire is in that bomb? Who made it? Why here?

"Ma'am, we can't take any more off!" Aster signaled Hansen. "We're going to drop it in the eater. Count of ten."

"I... hear you," she rasped.

"Good. Listen up, people! One-"

Allen barely heard the count, eyes fixed on the blonde as she pulled out strand after strand of crimson, even as Aster and the others carefully maneuvered the steel-and-pearl-charmed massive bag around the chest.

"-Nine, ten!"

Her hands clapped together. The bomb dropped, the eater's

Worked flap closing a heartbeat before-

The shockwave blew them all across scraping concrete.

Ears ringing, Allen staggered back to his feet. Aster and his crew were dusting themselves off, trading back-slaps of grim satisfaction. And the blonde-

She was huddled in a protective ball on the floor, steel shielding one wrist, flames flickering about her hands in time to deliberate breaths. In and out. In. And out.

"It's over." Allen held out a comforting hand, remembering that glancing Spirit-ache of *pain, alone, no one to trust.* "You were very brave."

She snorted, flames damping out as she shoved herself to her feet and pushed back the simple tail of her hair; whisper of pain gone, as if it'd never existed. "Please. Don't tell me that line actually works on people."

He stepped back, stung. "Fine. You don't want help up? Be my guest." He dropped the cane. No surprise, her head followed the clatter instead of his face-

As she took tentative steps, toes down gingerly before each foot was planted, Allen felt a rush of shame.

She couldn't see my hand. How could she know I was trying to help?

Still. That was no reason to be rude.

Aster was staring at the cane, white-faced. "You're *blind?*"

"Shout it to the world." Toes brushed wood; the blonde crouched, patiently running her fingertips over every inch of the floor until she grasped the smooth handle. "Has anyone seen my sunglasses?"

"I see them," Allen said after a glance. And winced. Charity; he had to remember that virtue, no matter how little the criminals he dealt with deserved it. Maybe he was no priest, but he could at least try to be a good man. "Wait there. I'll get them."

Aster threw him a troubled look, then turned back to the blonde. "Mind showing us some ID, ma'am?"

"I'm going to reach for it," she said neutrally, one bloodied hand bracing herself on her cane as she hooked a finger in the chain around her neck.

Allen wasn't surprised by the dogtags; born Worker or made, almost everyone with strong elemental powers served. He hadn't. A weak Spirit-Worker was no help, not on the kind of missions the Army had fought the past twenty years. And... there were other reasons.

The dog-tags weren't a surprise. The enameled ruby flame on gold with them....

He wasn't surprised. But it still turned the world silent.

"Flame Shane Redstone," the blonde said flatly. "Retired. And you are?"

We got so lucky.

Allen gripped the viewing rail on this midlevel of the city, letting solid steel take his weight as he breathed out the rest of the venom. The crime scene personnel Lieutenant Aster had called in had taken one look at the survivors and slapped detoxifying Earth poultices on every throat. Worked volcanic clays would draw out most of the poison, and break down the rest into something human lungs could get rid of, given time.

Which was why he was here, staring into the heat-shimmers dancing above the heart of the caldera, rather than heading straight back to the station. Aster had ordered everybody to take a quarter-hour to breathe before they even considered writing reports. Neurotoxins played merry havoc with trying to get your story straight.

And here I thought it was just the adrenaline. Allen let his eyes close a moment, exhausted; opened them wide, to take in the city Riparia had tried yet again to destroy.

The caldera's walls were almost a circle, with one longer arc to the northeast where skyships swooped in and out of the main docks and oddball Sunrise sects gathered on solar feast-days. Here on the midlevels the slopes were steep enough to make a foot-chase interesting, but not nearly as stark and high as the richer parts of town, where fancy pale granite mansions had their own Air-elevators up to the sunniest edges.

Not that it was dark here. Enough sun slanted down that the parks only needed to be lit at night; beams glinted off mica in gray and pink granite, gilding more common tuff where it'd been carved and mortared in place. Only a few warm shimmers drifted past the Worked railing; the bulk of Caldera's heat not diverted through Fire-pillars to the forges stuck to the red-black lake of lava far below. The blood of the volcano flowed freely there, laced with glowing orange veins and red-hot pools opened by bursts of superheated gas. Or, if you were lucky enough to be watching at just the right time, the flaming wings of a dragon.

Months in the city and I still haven't seen one. Do they really fly through lava like rays in water? That'd be something to tell the folks back home.

Assuming anyone back in Waycross ever spoke to him again. A good Orthodox boy putting his soul at risk not just by taking up arms for the militia, but joining the Watch? His father was never going to hear the end of it.

And some days, that suits me just fine. Allen peered down, imagining that lake of fire as most of his home congregation saw it: not the wellspring of Fire to be cautiously tamed, but the prelude to eternal damnation....

Oof. Dizzy.

Looking across is a lot easier than looking down. Allen pulled his gaze up toward green-touched levels again, determined. *Wonder why? It's as much of a drop either way... oh for the Sunlit's sake. Those idiots.*

A shimmer of sun off blue and orange-striped silks yanked Allen's gaze back down, as silken wings skimmed so close to magma the glider had to have singed his nose-hairs.

But the blurp and pop of lava missed, and the glider banked toward one of the Fire-pillar thermals, And there was a blue-and-green, and another blue-and-orange; this one with the orange as wide diagonal slashes that made an arrow of long wings.

They. Are. Insane. Allen sighed, tempted to thump his head on reassuring steel. *And going to get themselves arrested and thrown in the drunk tank, even if their parents own the most gilded mansion in Crown Point. Magma flyovers are illegal for a reason.*

Not his problem. Fortunately. He'd mustered the determination and tenacity to become a Caldera City Inspector, but there was no will in the world that could push him to join the Air Patrol.

Leave that to Air-Working maniacs who like *heights. I don't even want to think about trying to 'port out of lava.*

Familiar footfalls, and Callie joined him at the railing. "So, is this one of those Orthodox penance things, or are you a closet masochist?"

Allen eyed her casual slouch against smooth steel, and his own white knuckles, and deliberately stopped looking at the depths. "More a stubborn thing." Finger by finger, he made himself let go.

...And took two quick steps back, because stubborn could only go so far against, *that's the edge of a very long fall.*

"So." Allen cleared his throat. "How's your poultice working? I wouldn't want to run down one of the dock glider gangs, but I think I could make a report without splashing ink everywhere."

"Never going to let that go, are you?" Inspector Freeport's lips quirked, annoyed and vaguely amused. "Waycross. How was anybody supposed to know you could slam your way around a typewriter?"

For a moment, Allen was tempted to roll his eyes. *Because it's part of the Watch entry exam?*

But he let it pass. There were volumes full of stories about Orthodox towns, and not all of them were wrong. Getting his hands on a typewriter had been one of his first adventures in rebellion. Or as his family would say, the long step on a slippery slope.

Which made him want to grip the rail all over again, because if his family thought *typewriters* had been bad....

"Hey." Callie caught his gaze, flicked her brows up. "You okay? I know you've dealt with a couple crazies, but guys who want to die and take you with them? Not something we face off with every day." She let a few moments pass. "Need to talk about it?"

"I'm not sure," Allen mused, half to himself. Hesitated. "It's not as if I dealt the lethal blow to any of them."

"You backed up someone who did." Callie's shoulders were stiff; she took a breath to loosen them. "That can feel worse."

"She needed the help." Allen shuddered. "All that Fire... if you'd seen the lieutenant's *face*...."

"Saw enough," his partner admitted. "We were *that* close to the starry desert, huh?"

"Don't even joke about that," Allen muttered. One thing to put up with his family's letters of purgatory and damnation. Quite another to hear his fellow Watch speculating on their eternal destination.

I don't know if I'm doing the right thing. I'm doing a right thing. That has to be enough.

Right now, it wouldn't be; the thought of family was going poke sore spots in his soul now that life-threatening peril was past-

Family. "Why was she alone?"

"The Flame?" Callie stiffened against the railing. "Why shouldn't she be?"

"Because she's *blind*." Seriously, why was Callie even surprised he was asking? "I've seen blind people out in the countryside, they can deal with it. But this is Caldera. It's *noisy*." Noisy, crowded, and the steam-cabs flashed around corners at speeds that'd give a horse a heart attack. "All she'd have to do is walk into a street crossing at the wrong moment. Where's her family?"

Callie's nostrils flared... and then she leaned back on steel, giving him an up and down look. "You're not just worried about a young *lady* out without her father's blessing."

Okay, fair, it had taken him a while to stop being flustered by the fact most Calderan girls past the age of majority didn't think twice about walking the streets at night. But it wasn't night, and anybody could see Redstone's bracelet, and- never mind. "Right now I'd bet Aster thinks *we* were blessed. A Flame right when we needed one most."

"...Uh-huh." Callie nibbled her lip. "And I thought you believed in miracles."

"Absolutely," Allen nodded solemnly. He might argue with his family about many things, but never about faith. How to express that faith - that was the sticking point. "Only real miracles are like adventures. They get you in almost as much hot water as they get you out of. The Sunlit Lord never makes things *easy* for His faithful."

Callie clapped a hand across her face in disbelief. "You think surviving a bomb was easy."

"I think it needs an explanation." Allen let his gaze dip down toward lava, just for a moment. "Elementals don't appear full-grown out of a firestorm. She has to have kin, and they're probably fretting themselves to death with everything that could go wrong for a blind daughter. Let's get back to the station and look them up." *So I can yell at someone who deserves it.*

And he stopped, and took another deep breath, ashamed. Taking out his anger on a possibly innocent civilian who... actually might not have had much choice in the matter, now that he thought about it, Redstone was a literal force of nature. If she'd had any clue about the bomb, he could easily see her using that same ironwood cane on an unsuspecting relative's knees, and taking off to face down the firestorm.

Although on further thought, he doubted that was the case. The way she'd jumped from cover... if she'd known there was a bomb from the start, the sane thing to do would have been find an Air-call box and get the Watch. Bolting into the line of fire, even if she'd known exactly how to take down the closest threat - that was desperation. Controlled panic. Fear turned into steel nerves and *action*.

She didn't know.

Though if the Flame had known, and hadn't so much as stopped to call it in before running in to play with Fire, he was going to have *words* for her.

But if not... well. Getting mad at someone else, as an excuse not to think about the people he himself had... killed today. That would be sinful. And stupid.

Killed. Not executed. There's a difference. They were shooting at us. We were protecting ourselves, and our city. Legally.

His head knew the difference. Now if he could convince his heart.

Callie's gaze flicked over him, hat to traditional coat to plain dark shoes. "You're not going to like what you find."

"We're Watch. We're used to that," Allen quipped. His partner's face was neutral, honest; but he could sense the unease and distaste radiating from her Spirit. Why? "Do you know her family?"

"Doubt it." Callie turned on her heel, stalking back toward city streets. "Let's go get it over with."

Dusting off his black coat, Allen followed in her wake. Wondering. *She has a grudge against a woman she doesn't even know. Why?*

Elementals held Caldera together. Why did Callie Freeport want to tear this one apart?

Chapter Two

The Watch station was quiet, if you didn't count the rattle of typewriters, the chiming of message-shells, and the occasional strangled swear from one of the officers trying to file yet another report on glider-gangs buzzing local corporate offices and what sounded like three separate nations' diplomatic residences. Considering the noise Shane was used to in military patrol offices - this was quiet. Too quiet.

I guess they don't get Elementals in here often.

No one ever did. Command spread out active military Elementals, even teaching Elementals, whenever possible. And civilians were strongly encouraged not to bunch up without damn good reasons. Caldera's worst nightmare was a single lucky strike taking out her strongest Workers, leaving the tiny nation defenseless against its enemies.

Far from defenseless. We beat them all once. We could do it again.

But it was the Elementals their enemies feared. Storm. Wave. Mountain. Star. And most of all, Flame.

She was lucky to be alive. Everyone told her that. Alive, with most of her power intact or healing. She could still serve... if there was an emergency, and they needed something *big* blown up, with someone willing to risk death to be her eyes.

Funny. I don't feel that lucky.

"Coffee?"

Shane jumped, one hand clenching on the polished grain of her chair to restrain a *perfectly reasonable* flash of fire at whoever'd had the bad judgment to sneak up on her. "Who are you?"

A swift intake of breath. "Inspector Allen Helleson, ma'am." Polite, if wary. "We, ah, met inside your ring of fire."

Ah. Now the man's voice sounded halfway familiar. "Sphere," Shane corrected, trying not to grudge the words as she told venom-jittery nerves to *stand down* already. "A ring's harder to hold. And it leaves an open top. We didn't need to breathe any more poison."

"So the floor really was smoking," the inspector muttered. "We could have run out of air."

Huh. Shane kept her eyebrows from twitching. That was an *interesting* reaction to *oh, by the way, we were inside a globe of lethal Fire.* Usually there was sputtering, if not shrieking and gibbering. Sometimes to the point her team had had to knock more unreasonable rescued hostages out cold. Which always made the medics *so cranky.* Tch.

Without sight, shaking her head sometimes left her disoriented. She lifted a shoulder instead; let it fall. "Not with that timer. It would have gone off before we could pass out."

A chair shifted, but the warmth of his body came no closer. "You... don't sound like that bothers you."

"There are worse ways to die." She'd seen four of them. Bones pulled out through tanned skin, blood boiled inside living hearts, and what they'd done to Terry-

I'll kill them. I'll kill them all. I swear it.

Well. She had killed quite a few of them, before the world had gone forever dark.

"...Flame Redstone?" Quiet. Level. Like a man trying to gentle a junkyard dog.

And why should he treat me any differently? He's an inspector. He knows violence when it's breathing down his neck.

Shane took a breath, gripping ironwood as she pushed fury back into the darkness. "Coffee. Yes." *Manners. A little civility won't kill you.* "Thank you. But half it with water." That should cut the lingering venom headache and make her a little less likely to jump down some idiot's throat. "I just need to stay awake long enough for Army Intelligence and your Lieutenant Aster to stop shouting at each other."

Silence. Helleson shoved back his chair, and headed toward the warmth of the coffeepot.

Reaching out with elemental sense, Shane tried to follow him in her mind's eye. Sure, humans all had roughly the same level of heat, but there were differences. Clothing, mass, silhouette against air - she'd used them before, picking out Calderan and enemy uniforms to bring down very personalized firestorms. If only she could figure out how to do it without her eyes.

Earth-Workers can do it with vibrations. It takes training, and not everyone can, but - I've seen blind Earth-Workers on the lines. Not on strikes, not without help, but....

She had to try. Even if Medical said it was impossible. How could they know, if nobody tried?

"It's not going to work." Normally friendly, Dr. Marian Black's voice had echoed off the sterile walls of the medical ward, strained and angry. "If you were an Apprentice, even a Journeyman... but a Flame? Mountains don't move by themselves! Tsunamis don't *form* by themselves! You're *blind*, Shane! They're *not* letting you back in the field. Ever. Be glad I know you're still hurting. If I reported this - if anyone *ever* thought you were serious - they'd have you on the table to crack your chest so fast, you'd be missing a pearl before you could say *fire*."

Marian was a friend. She hadn't said anything. Shane hoped.

And... she'd lost Helleson in the crowd. Damn it. Too many desks, too many people; overlapping echoes stifling the shape of the room.

"What'd you do to him?"

"Excuse me?" Shane turned toward the voice; a woman's, vaguely familiar, with a light hint of lilac perfume, the Fire of a rod, and a shush of fabric that spoke of pants, not skirts. One of the inspectors who'd been with Helleson, maybe?

"My partner. Helleson. What'd you do to Allen?"

The rod was dormant, but someone was boiling. "Nothing." *Oh, what the hell.* "Besides tell him to get the hell out of there before he got us both killed."

A slap of shoes on tiles; one aggressive step closer. "*He* was the one keeping *you* from getting killed, sweetheart."

"And I thought I was the one who was blind," Shane muttered. Yes, he'd intercepted some shots, he'd helped - she'd take any help she could get taking a bomb apart. But she'd been fine-

No. No, you weren't. Without eyes, you'd never have grabbed the right strand to keep that thing from going up in your face.

It grated, like twisting a broken bone. But she had no right to lie to herself. Killing herself with a damn fool mistake would be just her hard luck. Killing Watch? Would be *inexcusable.*

Breathe out, calm down - no, calmer, that was steam. "Inspector-"

A hiss of breath, and the body-heat in front of her *moved.*

Heat-spike, adrenaline, hand near rod-!

Hostile and *civilians* meant *evade,* Shane shot out of her chair-

Pain cracked through her knee. More stabbed her lower back as she jerked away, dull points that hit nerves like a torturer's pushpins.

Desk edge, pencils on desk behind me, no clear exfiltration route-

Shane dropped, chair clattering to the tiles, making herself as small as she could. If she had to use a Fire-shield, she didn't want to set the whole room ablaze.

Rod's core there, *be ready to grab it!*

Normally she'd use the hubbub rising up from the onlookers and *run.* But running and a cane and a station she'd never been in before - she'd be lucky if she didn't knock herself out trying.

Nerves screaming, Shane waited for the heat of a thumb to touch the rod's trigger.

At which point the unknown inspector would get a very nasty

surprise. Rods were crafted to be as safe as human hands could handle. Their core of Fire was ringed with safeguards. Even the strongest Flames couldn't tamper with a Watch rod.

...The strongest *civilian* Flames. She was a striker.

"What on earth is going on here?"

"Inspector Helleson." Shane dared to lift her head, listening to the stunned silence. Whatever'd been about to go wrong, the woman probably wouldn't try to shoot her in front of Helleson. Probably. "Do you know the person who just drew on me?"

"Drew on-?" A heel stamped down, but moved no closer. "You pulled *Fire* on me, you-"

"Inspector Freeport." Helleson's voice was level, cautious as the quiet footsteps angling to get between them. "What exactly happened?"

"She was getting ready to breathe fire!"

Bracing herself with her cane to stand, Shane blinked. "I... what?" Because seriously, *what*. She was a *Strike Specialist*. Trained to be unfailingly lethal to Caldera's enemies, yes; but this was a Watch station. Which meant the *surrounded by civilians* flag was flying, and trained reflexes discarded lethal measures for off-duty tactics: *escape, evade, self-defense only.*

If someone laid a hand on her, all bets were off. But just a threat? She wouldn't kill civilians for just a *threat*. No striker would.

And nobody here knows that. Damn it.

A near-inaudible growl. "Don't play innocent, we all saw the steam-"

"Yes, I do that, when I'm *having a bad day*," Shane bit out. Hair brushed the side of her face, one strand pulling as it caught in the hinge of her glasses. Terrific. Another blink; another moment of useless sparks-to-black-to-sparks. "With all this *paper*? Steam is a lot safer than flaring body heat. Or, say, *this*." She didn't even snap her fingers. Just *lit*, keeping the flames tipping her nails cool as an alcohol fire. Just in case. "What's the problem?"

"Callie, I think you'd better back up." A shift in Helleson's voice; turning to look at her? "Ma'am. Please put that away."

"I don't like people pointing rods at me." Shane kneaded flames, hoping the crackle around her fingertips would drain away jittery nerves. *I want my coffee. I want my team. I want five minutes out of sight with a hairbrush so I'm fit for civil society. I want all these idiots to go away and leave me the hell alone!* "How do I know she's even a Watch officer?"

"Freeport," Helleson sighed, "your badge."

"Say *what?* She-"

"Just do it."

Swearing under her breath, the woman moved, cloth and leather rustling. Helleson stepped closer, and cleared his throat. "Right in front of your left hand."

Flames shifting to the back of her knuckles, Shane reached out to take the leather wallet, running fingers over the familiar phoenix-roosting-on-star of the Caldera City Watch. Traced numbers she couldn't see with her finger, wishing they made sense. "All right," she acknowledged. "How about yours?"

He took Freeport's ID, and handed her another. Stiffer, newer leather. Same symbol, different numbers. "Satisfied? I know you might feel like barbecuing idiots in self-defense, Redstone, but you're safe in this station."

Trying not to let breath or fingers shake, Shane handed it back, and dismissed the fire. "I wasn't a minute ago. Apparently your partner thinks I did something to you." Shoulders back, she let some of her annoyance flare. "As if I had the time. Has she ever cross-trained with your bomb squad? You can't exactly pull Fire out of a bomb - *without* setting it off - and dance the Seven Veils at the same time. I don't care what the light-plays say."

"You can if it's a setup," Freeport bit out. "A Fire-Worker, just in the right place to take a bomb out? How *convenient.*"

"Callie," Helleson groaned.

"What?" Air wafted, as if Freeport had waved it off to their unseen audience. "I'm not the one who believes in miracles."

Eh? Shane listened harder. Most Watch she'd met didn't believe in miracles, any more than the army did.

"Aster says it's not a miracle," Helleson stated. Level; as if he wasn't surprised, and definitely not offended. "Talk to him. As soon as he's free. Trust me."

Believes in miracles and expects everyone to know it. Shane glanced down to hide her curiosity; covered it by fumbling with her cane, dusting off hands sore from hitting the floor. *And he's Watch? Weird.*

Freeport made an angry noise, but walked away. "Windows, Allen. *Windows.*"

"Windows?" Shane asked, after the noise in the station had picked up to near-normal levels.

"Just - forget it. Here, your coffee... um...."

"Just put it down on the desk." Even diluted with water, it was warmer than air or human bodies; she found the mug's handle on the first try, and carefully sipped it.

Strong and bitter. Just like Aunt Jehanna's. Well, she'd expected as much.

Windows.

The Watch had its own superstitions. Not that different from the Army.

The eyes are the windows of the soul.

Hers had the blinds pulled, forever. Who could trust someone whose soul was hidden?

"She had a point," Helleson said neutrally, sitting down again in a squeak of wood on tile. "How *did* you get there?"

Shane shrugged. Freeport might have been rude as a knife between the ribs, but it was a reasonable question. Hell, it was the first thing Shane would ask, if she were shaking down witnesses. Not that she usually had, unless half her team were busy or, well, *busy*. In a way that had earned Terry a snow-pile of reprimands and a dozen husbands, fathers, and brothers after *very* specific portions of his tender hide.

Couldn't stay away from a skirt, but he got anyone talking. He was always the charmer....

Slam that memory back. *Not helping.*

Worse than not helping. Thinking of her team had brought up all her reflexive subtle Workings for going unnoticed in the field - or being chewed out back at HQ. And she was just too *tired* to take them down.

Tired my foot. I haven't even been up for three days. I just don't want to.

Heh. And why should she, anyway? At least the field Workings made her feel a little more in control. Trapped in a station she couldn't see, she'd take any edge she could get. A Watch inspector wouldn't notice. "I was out for a walk, and someone seemed suspicious."

"...Really."

Shane rolled her eyes, imploring the ceiling. "Oh, come on. What was he going to do if he saw me? Yell at a blind woman for following him?"

A shuffle of papers. "I was thinking of something a little more final," Helleson said dryly.

"So?"

"You *are* crazy."

"Realistic." Or a Strike Specialist. Same difference. "Either there was a good reason he had traces of weapons-grade bound Fire on him, or there wasn't. If there wasn't-" Shane cradled the mug in her hands, soaking in tame warmth. "This is Caldera City, Inspector. I *know* what's under the lava-Wards." *I helped build some of them.*

You couldn't just chain down a volcano and expect it to behave, after all. Wards had to be checked and rechecked, reinforced or loosened, every year. Sometimes every month, if the volcano was feeling particularly tetchy.

Pencil scratching notes, Helleson let out a slow, near-soundless whistle. "If it'd been me, I think I'd have called for backup. There were a lot of them."

"I started out following one." Shane set her jaw, and admitted the truth. "By the time I knew I should find a call-box, I realized I..." She waved a hand at her eyes. "Couldn't find one."

"Awkward," the inspector agreed. "But you kept following him."

"Couldn't afford to lose him. Worst case scenario, I'd be missing, dead, or kidnapped." Shane tapped the mug as she listed them off. "Any one of which would lead to the Foxes turning the city upside-down. Meaning any plan they had would have been seriously screwed."

He was silent. It might have been her imagination, but it felt like he was staring. Ah, right. Most people didn't refer to Army Intelligence so casually. Not unless they'd saved a few Fox-skins themselves.

Helleson blew out a breath. "...Just what did you *do* in the Army?"

"Who, me?" Shane almost grinned. "Hmm. Well, I used to do a lot of clerical work. Boring stuff."

Which was perfectly true, as far as it went. She'd been far too young to go on the front lines, those first years after she'd finished her training. So, paperwork. And a lot of incineration of classified materials.

There was an exasperated sputtering across from her. Which was *interesting*. The last time she'd heard coffee go down the wrong way like that was... oh. "So you have heart-training as well as jumps. I thought most of you Watch Spirit-Workers trained for one or the other, not both."

A *trained* Watch Spirit-Worker. Oh sure, she'd known they existed, but one good enough to notice the subtle slippery mesh of Spirit taught to strikers, meant to slide aside prying senses like a cammo-net for the soul? Damn.

A swift inhalation. "How did you-?"

"You tried to truth-read me," Shane said simply. She was *not* going to let him know she was impressed. Not until she'd had more time to think. "And that calm you spread in the warehouse? Nice work. Panicked screams are so *distracting*."

Almost as distracting as a wide-area Spirit-calm should have been, if she'd felt it lap over her. She'd been very, very busy and focused, and under combat conditions she had *reflexes* when someone tried to influence her.

But it hadn't. Whatever Helleson had done, had left her completely untouched. Lucky for him.

Or not lucky at all. Shane sipped her coffee. *Very, very skilled Work. Even more than pulling off a teleport in the middle of a firefight. Doesn't seem to have much power, but he knows how to use what he's got. So why is he an inspector, instead of a hospital healer?*

Who knew. But there had to be a reason. Meaning she'd better handle him with a bit more caution. Just in case.

I don't have to make it easy, though. "So did you like hearing the truth?"

His chair thumped. "You - you lied by omission!"

Aww. Honest indignation. Cute as a Search and Rescue puppy still stumbling over his own big paws. Though a little odd. If he was good enough to notice her slipping truth-reading, she'd think he was experienced enough to know anyone blocking it probably had malicious intent in mind. She didn't, but what cynical officer would believe that?

Terry would know how to convince him. Or Erastus. Anyone but me.

That kind of help wasn't coming. Shane buried the stab of pain in another hot sip, letting the mug hide any steam from her ragged breath. She'd have to play to Helleson's honesty, and see what happened. "Ooo. You *are* an inspector."

"...I think I hate you."

"I get that a lot." Smirking, Shane finished the dregs. Coffee was good for post "we're all going to die" jitters. Let people blame any lingering shakes on an innocent cupful. Hopefully Helleson would figure that out before he gave himself a bleeding ulcer.

"All right." And there was definite challenge in his voice. "*Why* is Army Intelligence yelling at Lieutenant Aster?"

Shane frowned. He couldn't really be that clueless. Could he? Then again... inspector. Not bomb squad. He honestly might not know. "You saw what was in the chest."

"A bomb, yeah."

"A *two-nation* bomb," she corrected. Trying not to let her voice bite; not everyone spent years studying how to set everything on fire. "Ask your lieutenant if you want details. I'm sure *he* knows."

"I'm asking you," he said tightly. "And how do you know what was in there? You're-" He cut himself off.

"Blind," Shane said, voice carefully level. Maybe if she pretended she didn't care long enough, she'd believe it. "There's nothing wrong with my other five senses."

"I don't understand."

Shane curled her fingers in toward her palm, sitting on a strong desire to flick his forehead. Only she'd probably miss, and she refused to look any more foolish than she already had. "When you reach out, does Worked steel feel the same as regular metal?"

A reluctant sigh. "Not exactly."

"Right. Lava-hair doesn't feel like a watch. And given who makes that specific kind of watch, and who's *supposed* to deal in lava-hair-" Shane cut herself off, and carefully did not shake her head. Picturing the whole bomb in her mind as she Worked its Fire free... even coffee couldn't fight all the lingering dizziness. "Ask your lieutenant. Once he loses."

"You're assuming-"

"Oh, I don't think so." Shane carefully set the coffee mug down on the paper-covered desk. "And neither do you." *Argument ought to hit the main point right about-*

A door crashed; metal against painted wood, with the fluttery rattle of a window-blind hitting glass. "Helleson! Get in here!"

Blandly, Shane waved him goodbye.

"...*Really* hate you," came the mutter under his breath. Shane didn't think she'd been meant to hear it. Probably.

But even through the station chatter, she picked out an all too familiar measured stride, uniform carrying the faintest scent of late-night sweet-mints. "Flame Redstone."

"Captain Stewart," she acknowledged. Picturing the dark-haired Intelligence officer's pinched mouth, the disapproving flare of nostrils.

An almost soundless tap, fingers against a uniformed thigh. "We'll speak in Interrogation room three."

"Oh, we will? Joy." Shane stood, rapping her cane on the ground, listening for the echoes. Noisy in here, but if she just took a minute to sort it out-

A near hiss. "That's *not* going to work, Flame."

"How do you know?" Step, and rap. Listen. And step.

"You're not an Earth-Worker." Brusquely, Stewart grabbed her shoulder, fingers pressing just above nerves. "Walk."

She could walk, or she could fry his face off.

Jaw set, Shane walked.

"She's what?" Allen exclaimed in disbelief.

"Keep your voice down. And was. She *was* Strike Specialist Flame Redstone." Shifting behind his desk, Captain Mason's gaze flicked to drawn office blinds, as if checking for listening Foxes. "Before her medical discharge. So far I can't get my hands on the details, even calling in favors. Outside of, she wasn't the person you called if we planned to *negotiate* with our enemies."

Allen inhaled at that, getting a whiff of what had to be the captain's Atlan tortillas from lunch. The nose-bite of hot peppers was unmistakable. Briefly he wondered where the captain had hidden them. For all the file cabinets hugging the walls and various Watch paperwork piled in and out of trays on Mason's desk, it was a very neat office. Barely any pens scattered in amongst the paper instead of in their little jar, and only one dart had strayed from the little target-board on one wall to impale a hapless lump that might have been a raisin, once.

Who knew nearly dying could make you hungry?

"Oh yeah, she's real up on negotiating," Callie fumed, barely standing at proper ease. "What are they thinking, letting someone like that walk around with power? They ought to crack her chest and-"

"She's a wounded veteran," Mason cut across her words. "And you will treat her with all due respect, Inspector Freeport."

Respect, nothing. Allen swallowed, keeping his hand from touching his own heart by an act of pure will. Removing pearls was lethal. Oh, it was a better chance of survival than a hanging, and some convicted murderers would take that sentence over death - but Redstone wasn't a criminal. What was his partner thinking?

"Respect?" Callie's hands fisted. "Sir, she's a catastrophe waiting to happen! Bad enough if she was just a Flame, but a striker? All she has to do is flip out and attack someone. She can't exactly see tinder catching on fire, can she?"

Mason eyed her, and deliberately shook his head. "Freeport. I know you're got problems with Fire-Workers-"

"This isn't just a problem for me, sir!"

"Quiet." Staring her down, Mason sighed, and turned to Allen. "Helleson. What have you got to say?"

Outside of, I really need to sit my partner down and ask what's going on? "Just thinking it explains a lot, sir," Allen said after a moment. Because this, at least, made the day almost sane. Strike Specialists *knew* bombs. They certainly set enough of them.

And it went a long way toward explaining the attitude. Much to his family's displeasure, he'd met a few people in that line of work. Normally, they were quiet, competent professionals. If they didn't want you to, you'd never know they were there.

Medical discharge....

Going from the best of the best, the swords and shields of Caldera, to a blind civilian. He still didn't like her. But... if he'd been blinded, never to chase a suspect again....

Don't think I'd be all sweetness and light, either. "They're taking the investigation, aren't they, sir?"

"Yes." Mason didn't bother hiding a grimace. "Since this is *apparently* now a matter of national security. Not that they're mentioning why, besides the fact it was a really big bomb."

"A two-nation bomb," Allen muttered.

"What?"

"That's what Flame Redstone called it," Allen amplified. "She said Lieutenant Aster would know what it meant."

Mason *hmph*ed, slightly less irritated. "If the good lieutenant ever gets permission to talk to us."

"They can't do that!" Callie slammed her hands down on the captain's desk. "This was our bust!"

"This would have been thousands of people's *funeral*, if that bomb had gone off, Freeport," the captain shot back. "They can, they will, and I for one am just as happy to let them have lead on this one. We don't need this kind of political headache. We've got *ordinary* criminals to catch. Or did people stop murdering each other while I wasn't looking?"

"...Understood, sir."

"Lead?" Allen asked.

Eyeing him, the captain smiled.

Oh, this is not going to be good....

"Again."

"What, for the fifth time?" Shane leaned back in her chair, casual as if she were back in her dark uniform with bolts shrieking over the next hill. Let Stewart sweat. Not that he would. Ever. Even if she turned up the heat in here... which she had, just a flicker of warmth added to air as he'd shoved her in here, so she had at least a *guess* at where all the obstacles were.

Wide flat wood under my hand, slightly warm, heat sinking down through metal at the floor - table, bolted down so a suspect can't throw it. More warm-not-charring wood, but thinner and no metal... Stewart's perched in one, must be a chair. Two more besides mine, I think? Better keep my feet clear of those. Wide panel that sucks in heat on one wall - that's got to be the one-way mirror, too much glass for anything else.

Shane hid a cough, and tried not to wrinkle her nose. Heat brought out not only the scent of wood and worn polish, but old sweat, ink, and the acrid scent of fear. Guilty or innocent, no suspect wanted to be in this room.

And which one does Stewart think I am? Shane almost bared her teeth. *Three guesses.*

A *thump* of fingers on the table. "You don't expect me to believe you knew it was a two-nation bomb, *blind*."

"I never expect you to believe anything," Shane said dryly. "Ticked like a Riparian captain's watch, resonated like Pelean lava-hair. All inside a nice, bland steel box that could have been made in half a dozen countries, possibly including this one. Why don't you ask an Earth-Worker to test the alloy and find out?"

Stewart snorted. "You know it was obliterated in the bomb-eater. Almost took out the eater in the process."

"There should have been a square of steel left over, about this big." Shane traced an outline in air. She didn't call up flames to draw it, no matter how tempting. Stewart was looking for reasons to toss her to the wolves; no need to put Fire-Working on the list any more than it was already. "I cut it out to look inside."

"Look?"

"Sense," she stated dryly. *Answer the question, not the anger. The anger is a trap.* "It's easier to feel the Fire in things without steel in the way."

"Cut?" was the next clipped inquiry.

Shane tried not to roll her eyes. "Like welding, in reverse. Did you find the metal, or does the Watch have it?"

A moment's silence. Shane felt sorry for Lieutenant Aster. Just a little.

He's not the one hung out to dry here. He can take a bit more yelling. Stewart wouldn't be able to do more than that to a Watch officer. The Army might have priority investigating the mess, but Aster was a civilian. Safe.

She wasn't. Discharged, yes - but a Flame was never really a civilian. Not with that much Fire at their fingertips.

"You say you were out for a *walk*." Accusing. As if she ought to be in a wheelchair, confined to safely padded walls. "Alone."

Breathe. Just breathe. "That's the point of rehab, Captain. To get us back on our feet, so if we can't go back to the field, we at least won't be a horrible burden on the rest of the nation. Yes. I can walk. By myself, even." Shane gestured at the table between them, where she knew he'd spread every item taken off her person. "Somewhere in there is a map. I'm still working out exactly how to read it, but I have a few streets down."

Which was downplaying just how well she could read the thin, carved wooden sheets. But Stewart had her files. He should know how many night missions she'd been on.

"And you *saw* someone suspicious?"

You used to be a little more subtle, Shane thought grumpily. *I'm blind, you bastard. Not stupid.* "I heard a foreign accent - Riparian, I think Southern docks - and I sensed traces of high-level bound Fire. It didn't seem like a good combination."

"So why not contact the authorities?"

"Oh, sands. How would that have gone? Excuse me, sir, I don't know exactly where I am, and I don't know what he looks like or where he's going - could you go fetch everyone with a Riparian accent?" Shane shook her head. "He walked like he was going somewhere. I intended to find out where that somewhere was, and then call it in." Aaaaand she was just going to leave out that bit about realizing she couldn't find the call-boxes. Stewart could find it in Helleson's report. If he bothered to read the inspector's report.

"Only you ended up in a firefight instead." Disgust rippled in Stewart's tone. "You needlessly endangered a valuable national resource-"

"Ask Lieutenant Aster how big a hole they would have blasted in the lava-Ward. I doubt *he'd* say it was needless." Shane planted her hands on the table. "I did my twenty, *Captain*. The last few months of it in a Spirit-burn ward, yes - but I did it. Last government finance report I read, that pays off even a Flame's training. How many years have *you* got left?"

The snarl was almost silent. Almost. "They were operatives, Redstone! You could have been taken!"

"Don't worry," Shane said flatly. "That's one thing that will never happen." She let herself smirk. "And if you think it could, you need to brush up on how Elementals are trained. None of us have been taken by enemy forces for three hundred years."

"None of them were *blind*."

Shane *tch*ed. "Now, see, that's what happens when you sleep through history, Captain. I can name you at least three Waves and seven Mountains who've been blinded in the past century. They managed to avoid being kidnapped. Even here, in the heart of Caldera City. In the middle of Caldera itself."

If I'm not safe here, I'm not safe anywhere.

She was a striker. *Safe* hadn't been an option for a long, long time.

A strangled huff. "You're determined not to take this seriously."

"I take bombs in my city very seriously. But if this was a kidnap attempt, it's the lamest I've ever seen," Shane said dryly. "This was terrorism, and sabotage, and it had nothing to do with me. Outside of the fact that I happened to be there."

"More of the Redstone luck?" Stewart stated, just as dry. "I know good men with nightmares because of you."

"Richter's Pass was a firestorm waiting to happen." Shane could still smell the creosote tar of dry mesquite-pine, taste the bitter dust of desert loess starved for lack of rain. "It was start a backfire, or hope we could hold enough cold spots that people wouldn't asphyxiate when the Peleans' Fire sucked all the air away."

His pen scratched the page, swift as a knife in the dark. "And Command thinks you're a *hero*."

"I could care less what Command thinks. It worked." *Most of us lived.* "Ask your men if they'd rather not have the nightmares. I hear you don't dream when you're dead."

"You're a reckless, glory-seeking fool," Stewart hissed, cold as ice. "And this is just another in a long line of examples." He leaned in closer; she could feel the heat of his breath, almost taste the mint lingering on his lips. "Only *this* time you're not useful enough for people to look the other way."

"Go ahead," Shane said, voice even. *Don't flinch. Don't even twitch.* "Make your report. I'm sure it will look *wonderful* when you emphasize the *glory-seeking Fire-Worker* as more of a problem than one nearly sabotaged lava-Ward."

Silence, taut as a bowstring.

Really, Stewart. I'd think you'd realize a staring contest isn't going to do you much good.

Shane kept her breathing light, measured. She'd have to contact General Bones, as soon as she got out of here. A civilian couldn't file a formal Army report - but she knew Stewart. If she didn't get some kind of word in, he'd be free to paint the picture as black as he liked.

I'm not losing my Fire. Not because of a careerist idiot.

Even Stewart wouldn't lightly cross Strike General Iris Bones. Bones would listen. Or at least take a message; they didn't keep Caldera's Black Flag flying stationary, not for long.

Get Lieutenant Aster's info, and pass it along, Shane decided. *She can get the Watch report - and if I know the Watch, it'll punch holes all through any slant Stewart puts on the facts.*

The chair across from her shoved back. Footsteps carried body heat toward the door.

"Leaving so soon?" Shane quipped.

"This isn't over." The door slammed.

"It never is," Shane muttered to empty air.

Ah, but look on the bright side. So to speak. She hadn't been charged. She hadn't even been requested to stay. And, though Stewart seemed to have conveniently forgotten it, she was, technically, a civilian.

Gathering up her personal items, Shane stuffed her pockets, rapped her cane on the ground....

Echoes. Walls, table, mirror window... okay.

Step by careful step, she headed for the door.

"She'll never buy it, Captain," Allen argued, one hand on piled case folders as if he could throw paperwork between himself and imminent doom. From the quietly gleeful look on his superior's face it was a lost cause, but he'd be flayed if he'd go down without a fight. "We don't assign Watch officers to protect witnesses when the perps are already in custody." Or dead. Of those that'd been taken alive, only two looked like they'd last through the night, and the doctors weren't even offering odds for the day beyond that. The venom they'd used was nasty. "We definitely don't assign inspectors."

"Ah. But we do sometimes assign inspectors to bring in a fresh eye for our Cold Case volunteers." Mason clasped his hands together, as if in pious prayer. "At least for a few days. To keep you on the payroll while your rod-use is reviewed. Freeport was wounded, so no one will dock hers; but if you want full pay this week, you'll assist Ms. Jehanna Sanders with her inquiries. Ex-Inspector Sergeant Sanders. Who, I hear, is helping her niece get back on her feet after a medical discharge."

"You're serious," Allen managed. "Sir, this is a *bad idea.*"

"I always wondered why Jehanna never went into specifics," Mason mused. "I suppose now I know. Why is it a bad idea, Helleson?"

"Because-" Allen cut himself off.

The captain raised an interrogatory brow. "Well?"

Because my family would kill me, Allen thought ruefully, slumping onto his files. *Bad enough I joined the Watch. Worse that I ran off to the flaming pits of iniquity of Caldera. Protecting a retired military assassin? One word of that gets back to Waycross, and they'll send one of the uncles out to* deal *with me.*

Strikers weren't assassins. But he couldn't argue definitions with a family heritage of faith that only believed in raising hands against the enemy in *immediate* self-defense. That was one of the reasons he'd left.

Which wasn't exactly something he could say to his superior officer. Even if Captain Mason could probably guess-

His sense of Spirit twitched; an odd ripple in the energy of life, right where his ears picked up a soft scuff of something moving. *What on earth?*

"Inspector?" Mason prompted.

Wordless, Allen pointed. Thank the Sunlit, the captain respected him enough to look.

She wasn't fast. Some of her steps were tentative, toes testing for objects underfoot before the heel went down. And the hand without the tapping cane hovered near a wall, reaching out to brush fading blue paint.

But given Interrogation was three flights down, Allen was stunned she was here at all.

That has to be one of the most bloody-minded, stubborn *women I've ever met.*

"Well, don't just stand there," the captain *tsk*ed. "Where are your manners? Offer to walk the lady home. Rosa should have your new case folders." He clapped Allen on the shoulder, and walked off.

"Young people these days...."

I feel like a monoceros being led off to slaughter. Bracing himself, Allen headed for the Fire-Worker. "Flame Redstone?"

"Inspector." She nodded, but didn't stop. "Is Captain Stewart still on the premises? I'm good for one more daring escape today, but there's no point in showing off if he's not here to turn pretty colors and froth at the mouth."

Erk. And, *gah.* If that flicker he felt of her spirit was true, Shane was perfectly serious. "You don't like him much, do you?"

Even blind, the way her eyebrows arched made him feel he'd been looked at askance. "Call it professional incompatibility."

Allen fell in beside her, matching step for careful step, glancing at passing Watch to head off any awkward questions. "How's that work?"

The Flame frowned, obviously picking her words. "The captain's job requires subtlety, and a certain... flexibility, in dealing with less than public information channels. My job- well, I can tell you that if I've done it right, they may not know who was there, but it's very obvious *someone* was. Which makes certain information sources who may have been cultivated for years suddenly dry up."

He'd dealt with informants himself; sometimes there was no other way to break a case. But good inspectors didn't run them for years. That way lay enmeshment in lives that tended toward the immoral, if not the criminal. It wasn't good for either soul. "I suppose that could annoy a man," Allen said neutrally. "But why don't *you* like him?" Before she could answer, he added, "By the way, if you're looking for the maintenance closet, just keep going. If you want out the front door, though, you need to back up a few feet and turn right."

Practical. Aim for practical. Pity is salt on the wound. Just give her the facts.

Her jaw worked silently, but not a hint of a curse passed her teeth. "Thank you," she said grudgingly. Standing still, she took a few deep breaths, and just as slowly let them out again. Glanced his way... well, more or less. "I'll make you a deal, Inspector. Guide me out of this building, and I'll tell you why I don't like Stewart."

"Seems a little steep." Allen kept his tone light, feeling his way through the situation. Her Spirit was so contained. Silent as shadow. *Never realized how much I read from people's eyes. It's almost like she's not* there. "But I'd consider it. If you throw in how you got-" He cut his words off, cursing himself for six kinds of a fool.

"Blinded?" the Flame said flatly. "Let's just say, today wasn't the worst day I've ever had." She shifted on her feet, shod toes feeling at the floor. "I thought most people knew about Geistan Spirit-blasts."

"Well, of course." Allen shuddered at the thought. He hadn't been able to believe the first reports, but after more and more injured veterans had come home, some specifically to his family's church in search of healing for the soul, if not for their magic.... He'd had to believe. It still made him sick. How could even the kingdom of Geist pervert that most sacred of elements into such an awful weapon, just to target Caldera's Workers? "But those only affect-" He stopped. Stared at her.

"Made Workers?" Her voice hadn't warmed. "I am."

"But- you're a *Flame*...."

"Just because you're not born to an element, doesn't mean you can't be good. If you work at it." Cane in her right hand, she offered her left arm, bent. "So. Which way is out?"

Numb, he took it, and started walking.

Turns, steps, a brief stop at a desk rustling with papers while Inspector Helleson picked up a satchel of paperwork, a few catcalls from habitual offenders who seemed to know the man - and vice-versa, given his pithy comments - and they were out.

Shane drew in a breath, tasting a waft of spiced beef, ketchup, mustard, and a competing sweetness of powdered sugar. *Hot dog stand left... mmm, beignets around here somewhere-*

"So why don't you like him?"

Ah, damn. But a deal was a deal. And Helleson had been careful not to grip her arm too tightly, even when they'd headed down the long stone steps away from the Watch station. "You may have noticed, the man doesn't exactly volunteer information."

A huff of breath. "I didn't really talk to him."

Shane grimaced. "Let me guess. He talked to the lieutenant, and maybe Aster's second, and whoever's in charge of your squad?"

"Captain Mason," came the clipped answer. "Pretty much. And you."

Well, yes; hard for even the most thickheaded Army Int superior to buy a smear job if you didn't even interview the victim you were smearing. "That's what I don't like about him. He's good at his job. It's an important job. But he assumes the people on top have the most information. Which works, if you're talking political shifts with the king-makers. But not if you need conditions on the ground at spot X. And if you get those wrong...." She drew in another taste of salt and sugar, trying not to think of Richter's Pass, Marion Cove, and a nasty little back-alley fight that had melted down a venom-factory that didn't exist. Officially. And then just didn't *exist*. "I grant you politics has a lot to do with why our enemies' forces end up the places they do. But once in a while, there *are* skilled generals on the other side, and if you're not prepared for that a lot of good people will wind up hamburger."

"Did that happen to you?"

Shane cast him a look, swearing silently at herself at the reflex. The only way she'd catch his eyes was by sheer luck. "If it had, you'd know I couldn't talk about it."

"Right."

And there was a *tautness* to that answer. Shane was no Spirit-Worker, but that slight hesitation, as if the man had shifted up onto the balls of his feet, ready to fight.... Not good. Not good at all.

Only one way to be sure. "No military in your family?" she asked levelly.

"No."

"Do you mind if I ask?" Shane kept her voice level, even though every instinct was suddenly alert, screaming *run!*

Oh yes, run. Into the middle of a crowd I can't see. No; if something goes wrong, I fry him. *Here and now. It'll do less damage.*

Though if it came to that, hopefully she could do the opposite of fry. Leach heat away in one sudden rush; leaving him chilled and in danger, but alive. Hypothermic was better than dead. And almost as good for making sure someone didn't shoot you.

No. Wait, Shane told herself firmly. *Inspector. The Watch wouldn't have let him in if he were mentally unstable. Or physically likely to keel over from service. Whatever his family's like,* he's *got to be fine.*

Not to mention that carefully controlled tension in his steps spoke of a man who *expected* her to take his family's lack of service badly. Interesting. Unsettling, but interesting.

A soft exhalation; as if the inspector recognized they were both backing away from violence. "My family's religious."

"So's mine," Shane shrugged. "Of the *kick bad guys' ass* variety. Vengeance may be the Lord's, but nothing says we can't hand out a little temporal justice while we're waiting."

"That's... a very strange reading of Scripture."

"Not in the city," Shane observed. Those born in Caldera City, even the most Orthodox, knew their ancestors had carved their home out of living lava itself, with all the world bent on their destruction. They knew what they'd won - and what it had cost. "But you're not local, are you?" Religious. Hah. *Now* those flicks of singing vowels made sense. Almost impossible sense; after all, *Watch.* But it was the only explanation that fit. "Satsuma? Waycross?"

"Waycross." His voice was suddenly wary. "How'd you know?"

"Your accent, plus no military kin? Anyone not a first son has to be a conscientious objector. Waycross." *I tend to remember the accents of people who call me a murderer. Just in case they go beyond spitting.* "I'll take a wild guess, and say your family's not too happy about your job."

"No. They're not. Yours?"

That was a challenge, pure and simple. "Most of those who matter are dead."

"...I'm sorry."

"Nothing to be sorry about." Shane shrugged. "Ironic, though. All the hairy situations I've been in, and *I* came back." She took her map out of her jacket pocket, feeling the carved relief of it, raised symbols meant to be read without light. Who'd have guessed she'd be using nighttime ops training for this?

Ah. They ought to be right about *here*. Meaning she needed to go-

"May I walk you home?"

Shane tensed, smoke threatening to curl up from between her hands. *Do not light the map on fire. Bad idea.* "That's not necessary, Inspector."

"Unfortunately, it is. My captain gave me some case information for Jehanna Sanders. I understand she's your aunt?"

For a moment, the whole world was red. Medical, and Stewart sneering at her for not having a *companion*, and now this? "I don't need a babysitter, *Inspector!*"

"No," Helleson said flatly. "But you're a practical woman. You have to be; you made your twenty alive. We've both been shot at, we've both almost been blown up, we don't know if those idiots had any other friends, and my captain's feeling just a little jittery about letting you vanish back into the streets. All right? We have to go the same way anyway. And he *didn't* give me directions."

As if an inspector couldn't find Jehanna's flat in about two seconds, if he wanted to. Her aunt wasn't trying to hide. "Fine." She tapped the map. "We're going south. And we were *not* almost blown up, Helleson. Believe me. I've cut it a lot closer than that." She tilted her head. "Your bomb squad's good. You'll have to tell me how to contact Lieutenant Aster, so I can tell him that." *Not that he'll probably want to hear it, not from a blind woman... stop that. You're a*

Flame. If he can't recognize an expert, that's his problem. "2155 Damascus Way, tenth floor, and I hope you're not allergic to ginger."

"No," came the surprised reply. "Why?"

"We're right over a botanica." Cane in hand, she tapped to the edge of the sidewalk, oriented herself with the street noise, and turned. "Coming?"

"Okay." It was half agreement, half a sigh, as he fell into step beside her. "I have to ask. *How* are you doing this?"

"Rehab," Shane said flatly, as they crossed the street. "And I was born here. I may not have been back for more than visits the past twenty, but-" She heard the first warning squeak of a cab's steam whistle, jumped forward onto the curb, and gave the idiot the appropriate finger. "I still remember how they drive."

"You don't look more than twenty-five." A catch of breath. "I know heavy Working loosens the grasp of time...."

Sounded like personal experience. Meaning he'd joined the Watch against the wishes of *generations* of Spirit-workers. That took the kind of iron will she could get to like. Too bad Stewart would push and pry and *insinuate* until the whole Watch station wanted her thrown to the wolves.

And there's nothing I can do about it. Stewart's an officer. I'm... discharged.

Alive, instead of dying with her team. Funny, how brass and regular soldiers seemed to think blind also meant deaf. The whispers had started flying the moment she'd woken up, and-

And none of that's Helleson's problem, Shane told herself forcefully, stepping carefully across a patch of cracked concrete. *He's earned an answer.* "I'm thirty-six. I joined early." She'd still needed a guardian's signature, but Jehanna had been willing enough to grant it. They'd all needed time, after-

It's over. They're dead, and Barbara's dead, and there wasn't anything you could do. About any of them.

"So do you like it here, or are you just in Caldera City because it ticks your family off?" Shane said nonchalantly, listening to the steely jingle of cheap jewelry as a street vendor hawked his wares.

"Do you not like me, or are you just not used to talking to things that *don't* go boom?"

Shane snickered, almost not minding when she stumbled on another sidewalk crack. "Good call. Nobody really wanted me around for people skills. How's your Lieutenant Aster on those, by the way?"

"Umm...."

"I didn't think so," Shane said wryly. "When you talk to things that go boom, Helleson, you end up very, very tired with people's little social games. Life is too short."

A deliberate breath. "Master Workers can get to two hundred."

"They can," Shane acknowledged. And Elementals could last longer. "Average lifespan in my specialty is somewhere less than fifty." How much less, she couldn't say. It was classified - and the people driven enough to make it as a Strike Specialist, Fire, didn't care about the odds.

One hundred ways to retire, as they say. And I found the hundred and first.

"Why would anyone do that?"

"Why are you Watch?" Shane turned it back on him. "Someone has to do it." *And I was good at it.*

Hard to say what she'd be good at now. Teaching wasn't her strong point; assuming the Army would *let* her teach, when her very existence would scare off potential students. And the field was definitely out. Unless there was a real emergency - and that kind of trouble, she wouldn't walk away from. Not if she couldn't see.

It wouldn't be so bad, to die for Caldera. But I'd rather live *for it. There's got to be something I can do....*

"Look out!"

...One of these days, Shane thought, arm wrapped around her ribs as she spat out sidewalk dust, she was going to find the person who'd invented the bicycle. And *hurt* them.

"Stupid tourist!" the rider huffed; upslope accent and a *shrrrip* of torn tight cloth. "Watch where you're going!"

"Look," Helleson tried to step in as the bicyclist brushed herself off and bystanders in the crowd paused and murmured. "She didn't see you-"

"Tourist?" Shane ran over his words, all too glad to have a legitimate target for this whole frustrating day. That'd *hurt*. Though the bicycle had undoubtedly gotten the worst of it; Shane had damped any obvious Fire-shield, but by this time she had melting impacting steel down to a reflex. "That's rich, from a Crown Pointer. At least when your hotshot gliders pull one trick too many, they take out roofs, not innocent bystanders. Why don't you head back uptown, where nobody actually deigns to *walk* on the sidewalks?"

A hiss of high-bred breath. "Ignorant little- do you know who I am?"

"Not a clue," Shane said dryly, dropping to one knee to feel around for her cane. No point wasting time arguing with someone whose nose was so far in the air they didn't recognize what kind of power had turned bicycle steel into so-called modern art. The rest of the crowd only paused to take a good goggle at warped metal, then sensibly picked up their pace and found an elsewhere to be.

A little pulse of heat, not even enough to take the chill off ice water... there was the seep of stone, and there was the quick shift of warm air, and there was the grainy absorption of polished wood. *Gotcha.*

There was a soft thwack, a leather wallet into an open palm. "Do you know who *I* am?" Helleson stated; cool, calm, and without an inch of give. "Bicycles are legally supposed to be on the road, ma'am. Not on the sidewalks, where they can run into *blind pedestrians.*"

"Oh." The gasp of guilt blazed back into rage. "Well, why isn't she using a *real* blind man's cane? Anybody could have that hunk of wood!"

"*She* is right here," Shane said flatly, "and *she* likes using this one.

And *she* had right of way on the sidewalk." Ignoring stinging palms with long practice, she went back to tapping her way down the walk.

And stopped. *Damn it. That didn't sound right.* "Helleson. Did I get turned around?"

"You did." Carefully neutral, he walked over to her, ignoring the bicyclist's renewed protests. "Want a hand?"

"Just tell me when to stop turning." Slowly, she pivoted.

"You're good."

Nodding once, Shane tapped off again.

"Hey! Who's going to pay for this?" came the aggrieved shout behind them.

"Ma'am, *you* hit *her*," Helleson called back. "That's your problem."

"Lousy Watch! I'll see about-"

A flux in the crowd around them, and the bicyclist was left behind. "Remind me why I took this job again?" Helleson muttered. "Why aren't you using a regular cane, anyway?"

"Too fragile," Shane said plainly. "One nightmare would melt the damn thing. And most people really shouldn't be walking over molten steel."

Which was the truth. Just not all of it. A traditional blind man's cane wasn't solid enough. Didn't make the loud taps she was trying to use, based on what she'd read of blind Earth-Worker navigation by vibrations. Wasn't massive enough to find easily, by reaching out with a little heat.

"Good reason." His voice was still level. "You didn't need to escalate that."

The hell I didn't need to- Shane stopped, right in the middle of the sidewalk, deliberately not reacting to a stray jostle before others in the crowd caught on and stepped around her. Took a deep breath, and let it out, feeling it waft to steam.

Helleson flinched; she heard the rustle of his traditional longcoat. But he didn't step back.

Watch, Shane reminded herself. *His job to protect civilians. Even from each other. To deescalate messes before someone gets killed. His captain wouldn't have put Helleson on your trail if he didn't know what he was doing.*

"You're right," Shane said at last. "That was stupid." Another slow breath; damp down the Fire inside before fury could fuel it farther. At least the roaring in her ears was quieter than the crowd, now. "In rehab, they started off telling me I'd be angry a lot. Then they'd find out I was a Fire-Worker." She grimaced. "It wasn't pretty."

"Because they were afraid?"

"That was part of it." She couldn't say this to Marian. Not to any of the people she'd worked with. Friendship was one thing; regulations, quite another. She wasn't about to put friends in the position of choosing between her and their oaths.

I'm not a hazard. I'm not worthless.

But until she could prove it - no.

Yet Helleson wasn't military. And he didn't like Stewart. It ought to be safe. To talk about the little things, at least.

The street sounds grew a little more familiar, air scented with blooming citrus and chocolate from the candy shop around the corner. Shane braced herself, and headed for the front door of her aunt's building. *Maybe she won't be home....*

Chapter Three

One of these days, Allen thought, still blinking at tangles of green climbing support pillars toward the skylights, *I'm going to get used to the fact that tenth floors can have gardens.* "This is your aunt's?"

"It's the whole floor's," Redstone corrected him. "Plus a couple of people downstairs who've bought in. But yes, my aunt takes care of a lot of it." She moved down the mulched path between raised beds of strawberries and a riot of salad greens with an easier gait than he'd seen on the sidewalk; probably relief at being out of the crush. "She's good at it."

There was something wistful in that; Spirit let him read longing and rueful acceptance. "You kill houseplants?"

"I confuse the poor things." Redstone let her fingers trail over a trellised melon vine, winding one in a tendril before she let go. "Plants don't really like severe temperature shifts. I can handle fish. Mostly. You?"

"I've only been in Caldera City seven months," Allen said plainly. "Not enough time to really settle in."

"You're telling me." It was half a laugh. "*The* city, Helleson. Locals call it the city. Nowhere else rates."

Good to remember, if he planned on staying. So far he wasn't sure. He'd wanted this job, and the city was everything he'd imagined - dreams and nightmares alike. He didn't yet know if the one was enough to balance the other. "So why are we taking the long way to your aunt's door?"

The Flame almost answered, then shook her head. "All right. We'll go straight."

Doesn't use the cane like a blind woman, either, Allen realized, watching her tap down the path. He hadn't noticed on the street, too busy watching the crowds to keep track of something near shoe level. But she wasn't sweeping with the cane. She *tapped* it, straight up and down; a quiet but distinct noise he could pick out through background ventilation, now that he was listening. "What exactly are you doing? That - tapping," he hastily added, realizing she didn't have a chance in hell of catching onto his waving hand.

"Echoes," she said shortly.

"I don't understand?"

A blonde nod. "Nobody panics when an Earth-Worker goes blind."

Right. Sure they didn't. He'd seen all kinds of Workers with less than perfect control of their magic, coming to his family for Spirit-Healing. Even if it was a Journeyman Earth-Worker who could barely turn a field without a plow, panic was a *given*. "Maybe in the Army they don't."

"...Right."

As if it hadn't occurred to her to think about reactions anywhere else. He felt a sudden, unexpected sliver of sympathy for Stewart. At least Intelligence had to consider normal civilian reactions as part of their planning.

"Doctors don't panic," Redstone amended. "Not if the patient's a high-level Earth-Worker. They can learn to get around almost as well as a sighted person. Using vibrations."

"That sounds like it would take Earth-sense," Allen ventured.

"It does," Redstone allowed. "And my elemental sense is only Fire. But sound is vibrations, too."

He stopped just before they would have stepped back onto the raised floor edging the garden. "You're trying to *hear* your way around? But-"

"Do you know what you get with a regular cane, Helleson?" She swept a hand across in front of her. "Five feet that way. Five feet this way. Beyond that, you don't know *anything*. With this-" She rapped her cane down on the polished floor. "I may not be much good yet, but if there's a hole in the floor, I can *hear* it." She took a breath, visibly grabbing hold of her temper again. "Come on. Least I can do is offer you a drink after today."

"I'm still on duty," Allen reminded her.

"Good. Then I won't be alone. Tea? Coffee? Juice?" She reached what he hoped was the right door, and knocked, shoulders relaxing when there was no answer. Got keys out of yet another pocket, and let them both in.

Stepping inside, he could see why Redstone had gone for tapping instead of conventional cane use. Sweep across the floor in here, you'd bring a lethal load of something down on your head. Casefiles. Gardening tools. Bookcases. Nothing disorganized, nothing out of place - just a *lot* of stuff. He whistled, hanging his black hat by the door. "Ms. Sanders has a wide range of interests."

"She says if she'd let the job be her life, it would have been. And then you wouldn't have a retired inspector to drop cold cases on, now would you?" Navigating by tap and fingers, Redstone worked her way into the kitchen and scrubbed off reddened hands. Took down two mugs from a cabinet, and opened the icebox.

Allen took water, and stared as she poured herself a glass of something dark red-purple. "You drink that? Straight?"

She sipped her cranberry juice, and gave him a raised brow. "This from the guy who drinks station coffee."

Well, yes - but you could add cream and sugar to that. Not that his family approved of either. "When do you think she'll be back?"

"Any minute," Redstone shrugged. "Maybe she got caught up in a good lead. Or saw something new at a greenhouse. Or-"

The front door almost crashed open. "Shane!"

"I'm *fine*."

"And I'm a monkey's uncle." But Jehanna Sanders closed her lips over whatever she might have said next, looking at Allen with the same wary eyes as her niece. But clear, blue as sapphires, under graying red hair instead of ghost-blonde.

Taller, Allen thought, and blinked. Flame Redstone wasn't exactly short; she just gave the impression of looming, like the captain in one of his *focused* moods. "Inspector Allen Helleson, ma'am. Captain Mason gave me some files for you?"

"The job never takes a holiday." But Ms. Sanders made no move to take the satchel, eyes on Redstone's scraped hands. "What happened?"

"Saboteurs, bomb, disarmed, yelled at," Redstone summed up. "If you're good with the inspector, I think I'll go treat these." Cane in one hand, mug in the other, she tapped her way over to what was probably a spare bedroom.

The door didn't - quite - slam behind her.

Ms. Sanders let out a tired breath. "I don't suppose you know any more details, Inspector Helleson? If she's decided someone's going to classify it I won't get another word out of her."

"A lot more details than I wanted," Allen admitted. Not one comment on the Orthodox coat? Then again - retired Watch. She'd probably heard about the new ugly duckling inspector the day he'd joined the station. "I was there. And Allen, ma'am. Or Helle. If that's all right."

"Jehanna." She shook his hand briskly. "*Ma'am* makes me look for Shane's grandmother. Sit down, if you have time to indulge a retired lady."

"More than I'd like," Allen shrugged, taking a chair across from her. "There was shooting. The rest of my squad inhaled some nasty venom. The docs are still checking up on them. I took less of a dose, so... I'm officially helping you out until the brass clears it up."

"Ah, the old make-work detail." Jehanna held up a hand when he would have protested. "Yes, I know, every case is important, every murder deserves to be solved. But we both know the recently dead get more time than these old bones. Though I can certainly use you while you're here." She watched him closely. "What happened?"

"It's an ongoing investigation."

"I know that," she agreed patiently. "What can you tell me?"

Stall. "If you don't mind my saying so, you seem a little more... calm, than Flame Redstone."

"Fire makes it hard to hold onto your temper." Jehanna sat straight, observing him. "Shane's spent years getting this calm. Add that to an involuntary medical discharge.... I imagine you've seen what happens to Watch who have to take disability."

"Is that why she's not allowed to drink?" Allen asked neutrally. Veteran or not, the thought of a blind, drunk Fire-Worker gave him cold chills.

"Not allowed to...?" Jehanna frowned at him; then winced, and glanced away. "Ah. I suppose I've been retired long enough, it's out of the casual gossip. Shane never drinks."

"Never?" At her look askance, Allen held up empty hands, apologetic. The Flame had made it clear her family wasn't Orthodox, but if even a retired inspector was a member of one of the abstemious sunrise sects, he was pretty sure Watch gossip would have carried the word to his ears. So where was the land mine, and how had he stepped on it? "After the day we had, a *reverend* would want to get drunk."

"Sometimes I wish she would," Jehanna mused. Closed her eyes, and shook her head. "I used to have two nieces. Then some bastard from upslope decided to unmoor his airship after a tear. He... didn't take up all the lines." She swallowed hard. "I hate funerals."

The way her jaw worked, there was a lot more pain to the story than that. "I'm sorry."

"At least Barbara never saw it coming."

Ouch. That chill in her voice.... "But Shane did?"

Jehanna blinked at him, taken aback. Started to speak, raising one hand - then closed her fingers like snuffing out a spark. "No. Shane was on duty. She didn't make it back until after... well. After."

Much too late, Allen got from that stiff set of shoulders. Land mine indeed; he'd walked into an old, old family argument.

"So... Shane doesn't drink," Jehanna went on. "And she'd probably never mention why. It's a good thing you're an inspector. Anything you really want to know about my niece, you'll have to investigate."

An opening if he'd ever heard one. "She must have a hard time taking communion... er." Augh, he could feel his ears burn. "Sorry. I'd never been to a Reform church before I came here." Seeing the holy feast split between bread for lay folk and wine for reverends had been a *shock*.

Jehanna snorted. "Don't worry about it. I don't think Shane's darkened a church door for years."

Even to speak with a reverend after her sister's death? That spoke of a soul not just wounded, but actively avoiding those who could heal the spirit. Why-?

Argh. You're a Helleson; think! Avoiding the faith means trauma, usually young trauma, and... oh. "How did she join up at sixteen? I thought you had to be legal age to have pearl surgery." Because even with the most skilled surgeons it was still *risky*. Two out of ten dying risky.

"There can be... extenuating circumstances." Jehanna looked aside. "You have Journeyman training in Spirit. Do you know about flail chest?"

Enough to shiver at the words. With the best modern Spirit-healing, keeping someone whose ribs had cracked in two places *breathing* was a dicey dance of emergency healing, worked Air respirators, and sheer tenacious nursing. "You mean...."

"Her chest was already cracked. It was her best chance." Jehanna's gaze fell to her hands.

Decades later, and she's still not sure she believes that, Allen judged. *Because... Sunlit Lord, the timing.*

If Jehanna had been the guardian who signed off on Shane's surgery, if remembering that was *worse* than her niece's funeral - then whatever had happened, had both killed Shane's parents and set her on the path to becoming a military Flame.

Untreated trauma spreads, Allen recalled from family lessons. *Whatever blame leaked over from the first trauma would have attached itself to Barbara's death. And it'd be worse because Shane* wasn't *here*.

Irrational, but humans didn't always listen to the truth of their Spirit. If he was going to work with this family, he'd have to step carefully.

"Please don't ask her about it." Jehanna's tone made it more than a request. "Look it up if you have to, but don't ask her. Not now. She... still thinks she might make it back into service. If this cane thing works out."

Allen tried not to let his brows arch in surprise. So far as he could tell, Redstone was bitterly aware that wasn't an option. She was just trying to get her feet under her before she started looking for something she *could* do. But he'd only known her a few frantic hours. Family would know better.

Mine didn't.

Exception that proved the rule, maybe. "Thank you for letting me know."

"Look in the archives twenty-four years back. You'll see why people don't talk about it." Jehanna's voice thawed as she leaned back. "So... *yelled at*. What have people been telling you, Helleson?"

So they were going to lay aside old wounds for fresh cases. Probably wise. "Not much. And when Army Intelligence shows up, and they're obviously *not* happy-" Allen shrugged. "You can see how it looks."

"Unfortunately." Jehanna grimaced. "I take it she had to do something unsettling."

Unsettling. Proof Jehanna was Shane's aunt right there. The understatement was obviously hereditary. "Depends. Do you call diving into a firefight, invoking a Fire-shield, and blithely taking apart a two-nation bomb in the middle of said firefight *unsettling?* Because I don't know about you, ma'am, but I'm thinking something a little less... polite." He let out a sharp breath. "What *is* a two-nation bomb, anyway?"

"Oh, *Shane*." Jehanna winced. "No wonder she's been missing all day, the interviews must have been hell.... It's just what it sounds like. A device made with Worked components from two or more nations. Since that means usually two or more *elements*, they're hard to disarm. Even for a team that knows what they're dealing with."

"She meant to tackle it alone," Allen said neutrally. "I'm guessing that wasn't well-advised." *Is she suicidal?*

"I'm sure it wasn't a good idea," Jehanna agreed, "but it wasn't as bad as Intelligence may have implied. I can't tell you what she did before the discharge, but I *can* tell you she has experience in... a number of devices." Her hand brushed through graying hair, as if adjusting the Air-Worked shell she would have worn years before. "Including some that don't officially exist."

The world seemed to tilt askew. He'd guessed Redstone knew bombs, he'd hoped she was as competent as she seemed, but something in the way her aunt said that prickled the hairs all down his neck. "What do you mean, *don't exist?*"

"I don't know. Officially," Jehanna said bluntly. "But from the little I have heard, the team Shane was on cleared obstacles that would grind most strikers into hamburger. However it needed to be done." She looked him up and down, as if even without Spirit she could see through cloth and flesh to his soul. "I have to admit I'm curious what Captain Mason is thinking. You could have just come to see me without walking Shane home." A flicker of teeth; not a smile. "Most people would grab any chance to keep their distance from a Flame."

And leave a blind woman to make her way home. Alone. After she'd survived a bomb. What did she take him for? "I don't scare that easily, ma'am."

Another considering look. "Some people might chalk that up to a lack of imagination."

"After this morning? I don't need to imagine anything." Forearm leaning on the table, Allen brushed a stray hint of ash off his sleeve. "If she'd been able to *see* those men, I suspect she'd have fried everything on them, and left us to collar perpetrators clad in nothing save the raiment they were born with."

Jehanna stifled a giggle. Glanced down at the cloth spread over polished wood. "Good thing none of you took enough venom to go down."

If any mote of his attention had strayed from her, it all snapped back now. "How did you know that?"

"Because if you had, she wouldn't have left one bloody scrap of *the raiment they were born with*." Jehanna met his gaze squarely. "Shane hates losing people."

"...Ah." And if that wasn't a warning to send ice down his spine, nothing would have been. "I'll be careful."

"Wise man." Jehanna gestured at the satchel, leather ruffling up the edge of the checkered tablecloth. "So why are you *really* here?"

The retired sergeant might be calmer than her niece, but her wits were just as sharp. "They cut us out of the investigation," Allen said bluntly. "*Our* investigation. This was *our* collar. Who says they only had one bomb? If they were working with anyone else - the captain's not going to sit on his hands and wait for Intelligence to miss another one. Neither am I."

"Good man," Jehanna nodded thoughtfully. "And my niece is your lead, hmm? The only one Intelligence won't wrap up and carry away."

That made his ears twitch. "Should they?"

Jehanna... hesitated, one hand clenching as if she wanted to check other equipment she wasn't wearing.

And she's wearing a rod. Inside her own apartment. "There was a mention of a kidnap risk," Allen ventured, smoothing down blue-and-white checks. "Back home, that couldn't happen." Though he had the family tales of those rare instances when enemies of the faith had tried. But in Waycross everyone knew everyone else, even if they weren't related, and a stranger would have a better chance grabbing the moon than getting close to a Star. "Here, there are so many strangers."

"And someone thought they might try for Shane?" Jehanna smirked, leaning back. "I pity the kidnappers."

So do I. "It's not impossible," Allen felt compelled to point out. "Anybody can be overwhelmed by enough bodies. Even if she *is* a Flame, she's...."

"Blind," Jehanna finished. "I know. I'm not saying it couldn't happen. But most of Shane's enemies would much rather see her dead. Safer. For them." Her lips pressed into a thin line.

Her Spirit whispered of years of pain and worry, never knowing if blood-kin would come home in one piece. Or at all. "So it was close."

Jehanna blew a frustrated breath through her teeth. "I imagine it was."

That rocked Allen back in his chair. "You don't know?"

"Apparently, it didn't officially happen." Jehanna leaned one shoulder against the back of her chair, as if braced to spring out of it. "Because if it did - though mind you, this is just my guess - either Caldera would have to admit they'd had a strike team somewhere we're not officially at war with...."

"Or?" Allen ventured.

Jehanna snorted. "Someone we're not officially at war with would have to admit they'd done something to Calderan forces that killed a strike team."

"Oh." Which didn't seem nearly strong enough for the shock icing through him. It was just hard, trying to reconcile the image of a woman who could get lost on a city sidewalk with - well.

"I have to say, I don't know how much of a lead she can give you." Jehanna's shoulders eased. "I know Shane. If she'd had any advance warning of what she was walking into, she *would* have called the Bomb Squad."

Okay, so maybe the Flame wasn't entirely insane. Just mostly. Allen spread empty hands. "She said she went for a walk, and sensed weapons-grade Fire."

Jehanna's fingers drummed the table, one thoughtful roll of sound. "Then I'm sure that's exactly what she did."

"I don't know *anybody* who can do that." Allen looked at her askance, noting how the retired officer had shifted so shadows fell over her features; an old, old, interrogation trick. "Unless Lieutenant Aster's got a trick up his sleeve I don't know about."

Jehanna sat up straight, one brow arched. "Fair enough," she said at last. "I've lived so long knowing what she can do, sometimes I forget. Even Masters have to be actively searching, to find those sorts of traces."

Right. That fit what he knew from his family about looking for subtle Spirit-damage, and what he'd learned in school about other elemental Masters- Wait. "A Flame doesn't?"

Jehanna shook her head. "No more than you or I, listening for the wrong footstep in a blind alley. A Master is strong. An Elemental is *practiced.*"

"Practiced? She doesn't even chant!" And that ate at him, Allen had to admit; an acid bite of the sin of envy when he thought of the years he'd spent trying to master his little bit of Spirit. And failing. Always failing.

"Not anymore, no. She's been Working a long time, Helleson." Jehanna looked past him, gaze lost in memory. "A very long time." She shook it off. "So what do you plan to do? Walk her through every street in the city, and hope she finds something?"

"I don't know," Allen said frankly. Caldera was bigger than he'd ever imagined, buildings of glass and steel reaching up to scrape the sky while volcanic granite and tuff armored factories plumbed the fiery depths. Walking it could take a lifetime. "But if she picked up their trail on the street, it seems like a good place to start. Not to mention, if we could determine how they located the Ward to try and breach it-"

"City maps," Shane's voice broke in.

Damn, but the woman could move quietly when she wasn't tapping. Allen turned to face her; no need to be rude just because she wouldn't see it. "The Wards aren't on public maps."

"Sometimes, you can tell a lot from what's *not* on a map." Shane stepped forward until her fingers brushed the edge of the table, flexing against polished wood. "Get all the water, sewer, and elemental-conduit lines marked down, and I bet you'd see some interesting patterns."

What, a bunch of straight lines-?

And he very much wanted to thump his head on his fist, because this *was not Waycross*. Caldera City had been built in the volcano's bowl, buildings stacked on top of buildings, for centuries now. All of which had to take into account the magic that kept the city intact in the first place. "Put them together, and you'd find where Wards could be." Which still wouldn't tell you exactly where they were... but burn the haystack down, it was a lot easier to sift for a needle.

"They could have." She shrugged. "Or they just found the right person to bribe. Or blackmail."

Spoken like one who knew it firsthand. "Is that what you've done?"

"What, map-compositing? Or espionage?" A wry half-smile flickered under blind eyes. "I couldn't say."

Right. "Like you can't say what happened to you," Allen challenged.

"Training accident."

It almost felt truthful. Just a little too studied a calm, shimmering over the surface of her Spirit. "With a Geistan Spirit-blast," Allen said dryly.

"Obviously."

Jehanna's knuckles paled on the arm of her chair. "Shane, no one who knows you is ever going to believe that."

"Oh, people are lining up to believe it." Hand sweeping inward until it met the edge of cloth, Redstone shifted it side to side, locating the table without jarring it. Felt her way into the second to last empty chair, and sat down. "I don't think I can help you, Inspector. If the Foxes really have taken lead on your investigation-"

"You're discharged, aren't you?" Allen broke in. "Just another citizen. Like the rest of us."

"Technically, yes." Her voice wasn't bitter. It just bit, like an icy gale. "Unless someone decides to call me in. That could happen, if they think you're trying to interfere. And then your captain would be in real trouble, not just annoyed."

"The *point* is, I want to be looking where they're *not* looking." Allen watched her face intently. "No one said you couldn't help. Did they?"

"As a concerned citizen?" Her wry tone matched the crook of her lips. "No. I doubt it even occurred to Stewart. I'm not in the chain of command, after all." One finger rubbed the head of her cane, the barest trace of a smirk twitching her lips. "And here I thought you hated me."

Jehanna shot him a disappointed look.

"How could you be so cruel!" Why would she think-? Oh. Drat. Allen tried not to sigh. *I should have expected this. No wonder Flame Redstone's so prickly.*

He'd had Spirit-healer training, before the best teachers in the family had thrown up their hands and his father had found the typewriter. Part of mending any traumatized soul was working with the family around them. And relatives tended to react to life-threatening injuries in one of two ways, or both at once: denial, and wrapping up the injured in so much swaddling they couldn't breathe.

Neither of which were wrong. They could help, at the right place and in the right time. But at some point the wounded needed to wrest their own lives back.

"I'm an inspector. I don't have to like someone to work with them." Allen threw the words down like a challenge. "You?"

Redstone smirked. "I've worked with Stewart."

As good as a yes.

"But if your captain sent you to help Jehanna with cold cases, you'd better put some time in on those, first. And get an early night. We're going to be up at... Aunt, do you have a tides chart?"

"Four forty-seven," Jehanna reported, crossing the room to flip through a stack of calendars. "For the nearest high tide down by Hazor."

"Ow. I *hate* Riparians." Shane shook her head once, absently-

Winced, and held very still a moment, before turning her face his way. "Meet me here at four AM. That should give us enough time to catch them stirring, if they have other agents near here."

"Riparian agents time movements to the tides?" Allen asked, puzzled. *Why didn't anyone tell me this?* "But the ones we caught weren't Water-Workers." Tides and the moon did make a difference to those who Worked Water. But why would non-Workers care?

Jehanna frowned, tucking calendars back into place. "Satsuma, Yoshae, or Waycross?"

"Waycross," Redstone stuck in.

"Ah."

"How do you two know that?" Allen demanded. Seriously, half the station didn't know or care where he was from, besides some Orthodox backwater, and these two had picked out the closest towns within minutes. How?

"Because if you didn't come from somewhere chock-full of Orthodox believers, young man, you'd have gotten regular history in school," Jehanna said plainly, coming back to the table to grab her mug again. "In other nations, Workers are born, not made."

Allen took a polite sip to match her, still not quite used to the mineral taste of Caldera water. "I know that." Caldera guarded pearl-making with their lives.

"Which means the families born with Working have power the average person can *never* touch," Shane pointed out.

Like the whole clan of Hellesons back home, right. Part of why he'd *left* was being fed up to the back teeth with the way perfectly competent people in Waycross would always run everything past his family-

Oh.

It was like staring down into the caldera all over again, with only the table to grab onto. Granted, made Workers weren't welcome in Waycross, but some of them had to be tolerated, and everyone knew they *existed*. Born Workers weren't the be-all and end-all of magic.

What is it like in lands where they are?

"I'd never thought of it that way," Allen admitted. In part because history back in Waycross tended to define other nations less in terms of the magic they had access to and more of the false idols they followed. He'd been trying to read up on more Reform-oriented history, but- Well, it hadn't been as important as learning the latest laws and evidence-gathering. He'd have to fix that. "I'm used to the Elders having pull, but.... You mean, in other nations, there's no one with power to balance them."

"Maybe a few military nobles and merchant princes," Redstone agreed. "Other than that? What the people with power do, *everyone* does."

"Riparians are Water-Workers, so they'd move to the tides. Makes sense." Allen mused. "But part of the bomb was Pelean."

"Which is why we'll stay out past dawn." She tilted her head, just a spark of challenge. "Unless you have a better idea?"

"...Not yet."

Dinner was quiet. Dipping a finger into the dishwater to warm it to steaming, Shane hoped the night would stay that way. Jehanna and Helleson had had a brisk, professional conversation about her aunt's various cases; some rapes, some murders, and at least one robbery turned homicide that'd been orphaned recently when the inspector who'd originally caught the case died.

That one had made Jehanna groan. Inspector Sorenson had apparently been a prolific and meticulous note-taker, but not always careful about organizing everything for other Watch officers to read.

And I can't exactly offer to help skim through and sort it, Shane reflected.

Commiserations had been made, Helleson had wished them a civil good night, and all Shane wanted now was a shower and bed before she had to get up in the darkness to meet a man she didn't even like.

I'm always getting up in the darkness, now.

Well, not quite. She knew when it was light. It just didn't do her any good.

"He's kind of cute."

So much for quiet. "I'll take your word for it," Shane shrugged, scrubbing away. Cooking still needed practice, but dishes she could do.

"Clueless, but cute." Jehanna rattled silverware into a drawer. "I'll have to ask Mason about him. He must have had a good reputation on his old force to get on our Watch when he doesn't know enough about Riparia." A huff. "Or maybe I need to talk to Mason. If they knew they were chasing Riparians, that whole squad should have been looking over the tide-tables."

"There are more ignorant people out there than you'd think," Shane grumbled. "Sometimes I think the Army does too good a job."

A familiar sigh. "You don't mean that."

"No, not really," Shane admitted; remembering bodies in the ashes, and the cries of those unlucky enough to survive. "But when people feel safe, they don't want to think about things that make them feel... not safe. They don't pay attention. Caldera's safe; who cares about what happens outside? Except that a lot of nations out there say they hate us. So if they hate us, we must have done something wrong, yes? Or so say those who haven't studied history. Who don't remember when the Slaves of Ba'al had armies, and what they meant to do before we stopped them."

"The Founding was centuries ago," Jehanna reminded her. "Most people are a lot more worried about who slept with whom last week. And who's going to get lucky tonight." A chuckle; the kind Shane remembered coming along with her aunt's knowing wink.

"Just don't leave his boxers where I can trip on them." Fishing around for the last fork, Shane rinsed it, and let out the dishwater.

Jehanna sputtered. "Young lady, you- I was talking about you! You're still young, you know. Go out! Dance! Have fun!"

"With an oh-four-hundred departure time? I don't *think* so." Clipping her oath-bracelet back on, Shane wrestled down a flare of irrational temper, biting her lip until more measured words surfaced. *Remember what Terry told you last leave, this isn't about you-*

Her teeth almost drew blood, remembering Terry with a girl on each arm, a fruity punch in his hand, and his head thrown back, laughing. No one knew how to have fun like Terry.

This isn't about you, Shane told herself, forcing those bright memories back. *This is about your aunt, and what she didn't do with her life, and wanting grand-nieces to bounce on her knee. You're just the convenient target since Barbara died.* "Aunt Jehanna, I appreciate what you're trying to do. Really. But I don't like dance clubs. Never have." Too noisy, too crowded, and most people who went there had more than *dancing* in mind for the night. Oaths were a lot easier to uphold when you didn't tempt other people into breaking them.

"You don't dance, you don't drink, I know you don't garden...." Jehanna let the words trail off. An old interrogator's trick, but a good one.

"You have to travel light, in my work." Shane shrugged, trying not to make it obvious she was feeling around for a hand towel. Where had Jehanna stashed the dry ones? "I did get out. I made the Fire-sculptures. That's a big thing, when you can't spare supply weight for decorations." And conveniently let her spend most party evenings away from the crowd, tweaking fiery displays to match the mood. No one had really wanted to deal with a fifteen-year-old Fire-Worker around tipsy soldiers. She'd seen more than enough by the time she was legal age to make the distaste mutual.

It wasn't that she didn't care about her fellow troops. She did. Even when they were drunken idiots. She just really, really preferred them sober.

"I should ask around," Jehanna said thoughtfully. "Someone might have a gig." A gentle poke in her shoulder. "It might even pay."

Shane rolled her eyes. Her pension wasn't enough to live lavishly, true, but it wasn't as if she were scraping to pay her half of the bills. "Not until I have a lot more time to practice." Which she'd meant to sneak down to one of the lava-fields for. If Helleson was serious, that would just have to wait.

"Oh, sure. You'll wade right into a bomb, but try to get you to a simple party-"

"Everyone in that warehouse would have died," Shane cut her aunt off, trying not to snarl. "The timer was ticking down. Bomb Squad couldn't get there in time, and the Watch who *might* have gotten past the Riparians had no *clue* what to do. There was no way I could make the situation *worse*." Fists clenched; she felt the lifting prickle, as droplets of water steamed off. "You think I'm afraid of a party? Of being where people can stare, and pity me? You're damn right I am. A Fire-Worker has to stay cool, calm, and collected *at all times*. Do you *know* what a Flame is trained to do when we're being attacked by something we *can't see?*"

"No." Finally, Jehanna's voice was serious. "You've never told me."

"And I hope I never will." Shaking out hot hands, Shane picked up her cane, and headed toward bed. "You've got enough nightmares."

"Shane." Jehanna took two loud steps; caught her shoulder. "It's *over*. You're out. Let it go. There's so much more you can do with your life-"

"I didn't *want* to do more with my life!" Almost, almost, Shane felt flame blossom around her hands. Almost. But not quite.

Calm. Control. You are a professional. Prove it.

"I'm blind, Jehanna." Shane's fingers twisted on the grip of her cane. "But I'm not dead yet."

"Riparia," Allen muttered under his breath, finger underlining words in the shelf-worn *History of the East* he'd borrowed from the local library before coming home. "Island archipelago nation... King Styrm the Sixth... noble families Water-Workers, with the notable exception of three families tied to the priesthood...." Damn. Why hadn't they covered this back in Waycross?

You know why. Before we were Calderans, we were the Chosen People. As far as everyone back home is concerned, we still should be. If we weren't "interfering with divine will" by making *Workers, instead of "accepting the gifts of Heaven".*

Allen really wasn't sure how he felt about that. On the one hand, he'd read about the steps necessary to make a person a Worker. And the mortality rate.

Breaking ribs to get at the heart. Surgery on the heart itself, while it's still beating. Forcing the body to accept an elemental pearl; an element that at least half the time, has no echo in that person's soul. I'm surprised anybody *lives through it.*

On the other hand - if you had the funds and the guts, almost anyone could try to become a Worker. Even just the guts, if you signed up for service and the military thought you were a good risk. As someone must have thought Shane Redstone was.

Which means we don't have noble families in Caldera. Rich ones, yes; families that have born Workers, of course. But they don't rule our people anymore.

Not like they did in Riparia. That Water-Working left a mark down to picking times for sabotage and murder....

Waycross had a lot of born-Spirit families. He should know; *Helleson* was a name with a very old history. A clan of those who'd stood against and destroyed the Slaves of Ba'al, so the People might live.

A clan that now had to make its living like everyone else, because Spirit-Workers *did not* rule Caldera.

Which, as far as Allen had been able to figure out, wasn't a bad thing. If old Orthodox beliefs had their way, there would *be* no made Workers. Which would mean no free use of the elements throughout the nation, and without that - well, people wouldn't be living half as well, that was for sure.

Though maybe the rest of the world wouldn't hate us so much....

That was his family's belief. The longer he was Watch, the less he agreed with it. Crazy as it seemed to the people he'd grown up with, some people really didn't need a reason to hate other people. Hell, some people didn't even need to hate another person to murder them.

"A criminal attacks you for only one reason," visiting instructor Darren had told Allen's self-defense class back at the academy, years ago. "Because *he thinks he can.*"

Right or wrong, if Caldera didn't have made Workers, there'd be a lot more people out there who thought they *could* attack it.

And... if that were the case, then maybe some of the free-floating anger that burned under Helleson family fights finally made sense.

We used to be the shield of the People. Those everyone relied on. Only for over a century the family's pulled the mother of all hissy-fits and kept us out of the armed forces, because if made Workers are so good then the ungrateful bastards can just rely on them instead....

No, that was his own anger roiling up. His family had better reasons than that. They'd just never chosen to explain to a youngster whose magic simply could not rise to their standards. It was a matter of faith. He didn't need to know more.

Yes. Yes I do. I believe. *But the Sunlit Lord gave us minds to learn and create for a reason.*

Even if some of what they'd created was truly horrible. What modern nations could bring to the battlefield in Worked destruction shattered the mind and soul.

But if we didn't have it - what would other nations do to us? We, who not only defy their powers, but refuse to acknowledge any other deity but the Lord?

...I wonder what Redstone would say?

Heh. And for once city customs dovetailed neatly with his own hometown's. So long as Shane held to that steel-bound oath, she wasn't a *Miss*. After months of trying to avoid giving unintentional offense by paying either too much or too *little* attention, one woman who wasn't on the hunt was a relief.

She's not a woman. She's a striker.

Silent Shadows was the next book in his pile; one of the few his quick search had yielded on Strike Specialist teams. Apparently Shane's reticence about her work was endemic to the job.

Skimming through the first few chapters - on operations decades back, which Caldera's government would finally admit had happened, even if all the details weren't released - he was starting to see why.

Gaah.

Contrary to popular belief, strike teams *did* have non-Workers on them. But not women. A female striker was a Worker, always. Master-level, at least.

They can't carry a hundred pounds of gear. Period. So if they're not going to be a drag on the team - they drop the weapons weight. Knives, hand-to-hand, and Working. That's all they've got.

Allen thought about how he'd seen Redstone in the station; crouched and blind, Spirit a coiled knot of restrained violence. And shivered. The last chapter he'd read had had a visceral description of what one anonymous Mountain had done to an entire Geistan battalion to make sure her team's mission succeeded, complete with speculations on exactly why the watershed in that area had run red for days....

And I thought Redstone had a temper problem. Hell. Maybe I'm not giving her enough credit.

For more reasons than one. The Flame was a freshly discharged veteran. Not that different from a Watch veteran who'd been medicaled out, and he'd known enough of those to wince at how hard they took it. Right now just figuring out what she ought to be doing on any given day was tricky enough, let alone doing it blind. On top of that, given what he'd gleaned from the texts, an Elemental like Shane was never the *leader* of a team.

She can tear apart a bomb, but she can't do that and *keep track of a half-dozen enemies at the same time. Elemental power takes too much concentration. She has to have someone else spot for her.*

Like a Watch sniper from one of the special response teams, relying on his partner to make sure no one coshed him from behind while he laid rod crosshairs on a hostage-taker. Take away that support, that extra pair of eyes, and they were... well. The ones he'd known were too well-trained to panic. But they were *twitchy.*

Explains half the temper right there. Add grief on top of that....

Not to mention the grinding frustration of being cast adrift when the Flame knew better than anyone how much she'd be needed - if she could only see. Elementals were rare; Elementals who could handle combat, rarer still. And if the book on Strike Specialists was accurate, even half a century ago, there'd been more missions than teams to go around.

The *kinds* of missions were eye-opening. He'd heard of Strike Specialists. Who hadn't? But knowing for certain that the Calderan government had ordered these things done? That was daunting.

Hostage rescue. Munitions sabotage. Area denial. Small-scale invasions, sometimes.

Allen was used to thinking of his country as a small but interesting place to live. A friendly place, when it was allowed to be; tourists and immigrants alike were heavily screened, but what nosy neighbor didn't do the same to any new family on the block?

Only this nosy neighbor carried a *very* big stick. And an inclination to crack skulls if the locals agreed someone was just flat-out trouble waiting to happen.

Given some of that trouble waiting to happen *hadn't* waited, but had dropped a bomb in his lap this morning... he didn't know *what* to think.

I want her to talk to me.

Not because of the investigation; at least, not just that. Whether Callie liked her or not - Redstone had thrown herself between his people and death.

That's the Watch's job.

Which was why he'd joined in the first place. Father, uncles, brothers, cousins; Allen had plenty of relatives looking after people's souls. He wanted to keep those he met alive long enough to save their own souls.

She didn't ask for anything. She didn't expect anything. She just - did it.

Why did that surprise him about Redstone, when it didn't about Lieutenant Aster?

He's not blind.

Redstone was; and as far as he could tell, she wasn't denying it. She *knew* she was crippled. She took steps to minimize it, she took plenty of steps to get around it - but she didn't shut out reality.

She just didn't let it *stop* her.

How does she do that? How does a person take a hit like that, and just keep going?

He wanted to know. Wanted it like the last glass of water in a burning desert. Because... because....

Sunlit, she'd hit the nail on the head. His family *hated* his being in Caldera City. Even more than they disapproved - oh, so *politely* disapproved - of him joining the Watch in the first place.

And he missed them. So much.

I want to know how Shane can live like that. How she can take bombs and idiots like Stewart and, my Lord, even Callie... and still laugh.

Shaking his head, Allen put the book down on his desk and headed to bed. It was going to be an early day tomorrow. And he still wasn't sure if he'd sleep. At all.

Not that it's going to bother Redstone, I'm sure. Bloody-minded, tough as iron....

In an endless dark-on-dark, Shane woke from dreams of crimson and terror. Lips sealed by long habit, muscles trembling to hold back the screams.

There's no burning. No scent of ashes. No blood.

No snore from the massive mountain that had been Ram Zabbai, after he'd woken her with one gentle touch to the foot before ending his watch. No liquid splashes as Paul Resen checked and rechecked information Terry had charmed out of who-knew-who this time and used his Water-Working to hid it all as ink-splotches in water. No sigh from Erastus as he added names to his list of husbands he'd have to head off at the pass - at least until Terry was out of the field and free to take his lumps. No careless flop of limbs from their team's own charmer, leaving worry for another day.

They're not here. They'll never be here again.

Shane let out a breath, high and thin as a mountain breeze. Turned into her pillow.

And slowly, cried herself back to sleep.

Chapter Four

Silence. Staring into the back of Shane's head as they walked. Or possibly, a little lower down. Most people would miss it, but Helleson had proved he was Watch. "Go ahead and ask," Shane sighed.

"Not sure I should." A rustle and sway, as if Helleson had shoved his hands into longcoat pockets. "After all, blades past a certain length-"

"Are allowed, with permits, to Knife-Masters." Shane shrugged, not surprised. Outside Strike Specialists, the fine points of the old Knife Arts discipline weren't well-known; and those who knew, didn't talk.

"I know that," came the wry reply. "I found the fine print in the back of the Watch handbook."

Really? Interesting. And oddly reassuring. Waycross or not, Helleson was at least trying to stay on top of the mountain of information Watch needed for the job-

Was that echo off?

Her foot came down on the edge of a sidewalk crack, knee dipping. Shane pulled back, pulsed a little heat into cold concrete, and used the wavery feel of that warmth to tip her foot forward enough not to stumble.

He saw that, Shane realized, hearing steps beside her slow. *He had to see it.*

Helleson picked up his pace again. "I've seen a few

demonstrations, but I didn't know Workers could be Knife-Masters."

He saw. But he's not asking. And was that wariness, or simply the man reevaluating what he'd thought he'd known? Either way, she'd have to pay attention; the sidewalks weren't going to be in better shape from here. "You need recommendations," Shane said frankly. "Your instructor has to attest you have both reason and skill to use them. And the calm head to know when *not* to use them. But the permit's actually easier to get once you get past Journeyman Fire-Worker. Hospitals would rather treat stabbings than burns, any day of the week." She tilted her head at him. "Have you had any training?"

"Watch basics," came the frank reply. "Keep people away from my rod, what to do if someone grabs it anyway. Besides die."

"You're ahead of me there," Shane admitted. "I haven't practiced those in years."

Not entirely true. She had practiced rod-disarms. But it was amazing what subtle heat in the right place could do to a close-in enemy. Do it right, and there was barely a whiff of cooked flesh. Just a body, heart charred to ashes.

Some military Fire-Workers couldn't eat red meat anymore. Shane had never had that problem... at least, as long as it wasn't organ meats.

"Why would you?" Helleson asked; with luck, blissfully ignorant. "Women in... your job, don't carry rods. Right?"

"If we did or didn't, it'd still be wise to know how to shoot and aim," Shane said dryly. "Given everyone else *would* be carrying them."

"Good point." Helleson hesitated. "How do you get into that, anyway?"

"It helps to be small and light," Shane chuckled. "Easier to carry you out if you're exhausted. Oathbound is a given; you're on a mixed team, there's enough that can go wrong under stress, every guy has to know you're off limits. Outside of that - ask your Lieutenant Aster what he looks for. He'll probably tell you he wants someone who can focus, and get the job done. Who *thinks* through problems, instead of just charging in with a battering ram. And... well, there is one more thing." She chewed her words over before she spoke. It wasn't sensitive information. Just - not usually spoken of. "Wyrd."

"Fate?" Helleson stepped slightly sideways, parting the warmth of a knot of chattering teens before they blocked her path. "We make our own fates."

"Yes, we do," Shane agreed. "Here in Caldera, more than anywhere. We make a different fate for all of us, by making Workers. Fate's twisted around us. Bent. Especially around *strong* made Workers."

"Wait a minute." Heat waving through air; hands, she'd guess, disavowing her words. "Are you saying...?"

"I'm saying," Shane said wryly, "that Command isn't going to be surprised by Stewart's report. Annoyed, maybe, but not surprised. I'm saying, Helleson, that your captain's idea of having you on my tail isn't as outlandish as you might think - and if he's been around a while, he knows that. Fire tends to find me."

Though nothing seemed to be finding her this morning, Fire or otherwise. Outside of a few half-heard catcalls from passing bands of construction workers heading out to be on-site before dawn, a stray pebble or two falling from old wrecks of homes and warehouses, and the soft *boom* overhead of a cargo airship's sails; probably taking advantage of dawn's still air to transport something fragile. Oh, and the odd snigger from teenage idiots too caught up in the swaggering present to look a few seconds into what could be a painful future.

Beside her, Helleson's gait stiffened. "I don't like this place."

"Shows you have sense." Shane kept her voice down. She didn't sense any immediate cause for concern, but the inspector might be picking up signs she couldn't see.

"This isn't bad real estate, why hasn't someone rebuilt here?" An indrawn breath. "At least people could have pulled out the rubble and planted it."

"Bad idea," Shane shuddered. "Don't 'port here, either. You might pick up dust someplace you really don't want it."

"What? Why-?" Helleson cut himself off; she felt the edges of his Spirit-sense sweep past, like a tickle of dawn. "My family talked about the Harvest bombing. They never said the bombs weren't... clean."

So even Waycross had heard of this place. Why was she surprised? "From what I heard, most of the toxins were short-lived. It's safe enough to room here, but I wouldn't trust anything out of the soil. Not until at least three Mountains verify it's safe more than two years running."

"Makes sense." His voice shifted, as if he were looking at something across the way. Evidently not all of the young things moving on the street lacked caution.

"Wait here a minute," Helleson said, gripping her shoulder lightly. And walked off.

Grrr... some inspector, leaving me here in the dark-

Shane had to shake her head, and smirk at herself. After all, she couldn't have it both ways. Either she let Helleson treat her like a helpless cripple who couldn't stand on the street alone, or she didn't.

Can't get mad at the man for treating me like I can take care of myself, now, can I?

Besides. She knew this wreck of a slum. Too well. She'd lived here, once.

Fire. Darkness. Crushing pain. A roar that blotted away the world....

Twenty-four years ago. When the Slaves of Ba'al had thought the cycles of the world were right to favor their cause, and slaughter their hated enemies.

Thousands dead. Hundreds more barely alive. Pain.

She'd told Helleson she'd joined early, and that was the truth. No need to mention that her life had been signed away years before that, because the damage from crushed ribs had been so extensive only elemental energy had given a child any chance at all.

Not his problem. Mine.

Besides. He'd figure it out if he looked up her family. The cluster of death dates, the street names marked where Workers had identified scraps of flesh....

Twenty-four years, and there's still rubble.

It hurt, but it didn't surprise her. Most who'd survived that horrible day had taken whatever family they had left and fled. The three of them - Jehanna, Barbara, herself - had been among the very few who'd stayed nearby. And then Barbara-

Enough. Shane made herself take a breath. *Can't see, remember? Don't get distracted. Be here and now.*

At least it was easier to follow the sense of Helleson now, in the cool before dawn. Concrete and steel were as cold as they'd get, body-heat standing out in a rush of warmth as he walked into the cooler shadow of an alley to meet-

Ah, hell.

"I told you to wait over there," Helleson said sharply as she tapped over to them.

"Kid's sick." Shane held out an empty hand toward that fever-warmth. "I can help."

"Don't look like a doctor." A young, surly voice; if it weren't for heat-sense, Shane was certain sex would have been indistinguishable.

"I'm not," Shane said flatly. Damn it, where was Terry when she needed him, he'd been almost as good at charming kids as women-

He's dead. Because you screwed up. Remember?

"You want to lose that arm, fine, don't see a doctor. But I can let you use it enough to climb, if you have to." She pointed above, where heat still clung to the metal rungs of a fire escape. "You were up there, weren't you?"

"Thought you said she was blind!" whipped at Helleson.

"Blind doesn't mean deaf, Tace," Helleson said practically. "Redstone, back off. *Can* you help?"

Must be his contact. Good. He can do the sweet-talking. "It's an infected cut, isn't it?" Because *of course* it was, there were reasons people didn't trust the soil here. Get even a little in a scratch, and you were in trouble.

The silence was enough answer. Shane waved at the escape. "Let's get off the street."

Helleson snagged ringing steel, and they all climbed a few floors up, Tace shivering when the kid thought no one would hear. The metal was cold, with ragged spots of rust that said maintenance sweeps were few and far between. Shane gripped carefully. The last thing she needed was torn-up fingers.

"All right," Helleson said bluntly, as they sheltered behind a brushy pot of vanilla mint, well away from the edge. "You're not a Spirit-Worker. What can you do?"

"Oh ye of little faith." Tucking her arm through her cane's carry-strap, Shane held out her hands. "I can't do this at a distance." Not blind, anyway. "Let me hold your arm."

"Yeah? And what are you gonna do?" Tace challenged.

"Kill some of the infection," Shane said frankly. "I've done it before." More times than she ever wanted to think about. "It's ugly, messy, and mostly just buys you a little more time for a medic. Helleson can help you resist the rest of it. Unless you want to lose that arm."

Shallow breaths. The shift of them sounded like a scared kid looking between her and a maybe-trustworthy inspector. Maybe.

"Redstone used to be Army," Helleson said wryly. "Manners are something you set on fire and feed to dragons."

Tace huffed. Not quite a snicker. Reluctantly, a threadbare sleeve was shoved back, a thin arm grudgingly held up in front of Shane's face.

"Thanks." Shane crouched, left hand holding a bony wrist, right hand tracing above fever-heated skin. There. She spread her fingers over the scabbed slash, taut with tainted matter. "This is going to sting a bit." *Focus. First, breach the scab, or the pressure's really going to hurt.* "It's going to be gruesome, too. You might not want to watch."

A snort. "Like you know gruesome."

"Probably not the same way you do," Shane said candidly. "I've never lived on the street for long. But the first time, most people find this just a bit squicky." Focusing Fire to a pinpoint at the end of her forefinger, she touched heat to the wound.

"Son of a-!"

Shane held on through the curses, the threats, and the stifled whimper. Under her finger part of the scab flashed into ash, crackling like foul bacon. Heat drew infection from the rest of the wound with a quiet squelch she wished she hadn't heard before.

"Oough."

"Don't pass out on me now, Helleson," Shane muttered. She couldn't blame him for being woozy; not when her own stomach was doing a threatening quiver. It didn't help that the water-gel consistency sizzling in her Fire brought back vivid memories of Paul's shoulder after they'd gotten him out of enemy hands; dribbling, nauseating yellow mixed with stagnant crimson blood. "First-aid kit?"

"What?"

"You're a Spirit-Worker. Don't tell me you don't have a first-aid kit." She'd use her own if they had to, strike kits were made so you could find everything in the dark, but that would be a pain to restock. She didn't have easy access to Army dispensaries anymore, and it'd be pure hell to fit in civilian supplies and still make sure everything went back into place so she could find it in an emergency.

"Ah. Right." Helleson swallowed, and dug into his coat. "Here, let me wipe that off...."

"Wait on that. This will be cleaner." A flicker of fingers, and all the infection Shane could get at hissed into white-hot steam, swirling clean into the wind with another push of her hand. "I think an alley cat like this could do with a good defleaing. How about you?" A practiced, flowing wave, and a flicker of flame sparked and vanished over the kid's frame, killing the myriad pests of the street in one hot pulse. "There. All done."

"Call *me* a-"

"Tace." Helleson stood resolutely between Shane and the street urchin. "I know you've got friends with ruder manners. She's trying to help."

"If he cleans and wraps that now, you'll be able to climb," Shane said evenly. "You should still see a doctor. I can't be sure I got all of the infection." *And if you've been on the street any length of time, I* know *you're not eating right. A healthy person could kick that bug's ass, with what I did. Someone not well to start with....*

"Tsh. Doctors," Tace grumbled.

"Kay's clinic," Helleson said practically. "You know she won't ask questions."

A young *hmph*. "Yeah, yeah, whatever-"

"You want to lose that arm, Tace?" Helleson mused. "I'm not skilled at healing and you know it. Some lifter you'll be, one-handed."

"Hey!"

Pickpocket, hmm? Why Helleson, I didn't know you had it in you.
"I saw nothing," Shane smiled.

"Very funny," the inspector sighed. Tape ripped, and Tace swore; the all too familiar sounds of wounds being bandaged until real help could get there. "So. Did you have something for me?"

"Heard there was a big rumble, over on Hundred-Third yesterday," Tace said warily.

"We were there," Helleson agreed.

"You and *her*."

"Do I look like an idiot?" Shane shrugged. "I hid, most of the time."

"...Yeah." It was meant to sound cocky, but there was a wariness in it Tace hadn't yet learned to cover. After all, if Helleson had seen her main knife, a lifter probably had, too. And possibly some of the others. "Maybe you're not as dumb as you look, Blondie."

"Oh. Ow." Shane clapped a hand to her chest, as if stabbed to the heart. "At least mine doesn't come out of a bottle." *Heh.*

"You can't even see it! How would *you* know?"

"Tace, even I can smell your dye job." Helleson's grin was audible. "I have to say, green looks good on you. Edgy."

"Yeah?" Shy hope there.

Oh Sunlit, a crush, Shane thought. *Kid, you need off the streets. Bad.* "So what about the rumble?"

"Well... word is, venom-bolts, right?" Tace rustled in the pockets of threadbare clothes, drew out something that whispered like paper in the wind.

"Shed snakeskin," Helleson informed Shane tautly. "I don't recognize the kind."

Shane held out a hand. "May I hold it?"

It was silk-slippery in her fingers, an empty shell only warmed by Tace's body heat. *Probably as thick as my thumb, alive,* Shane considered, feeling the belly scales. *Don't have the whole skin, but this was a slender snake. Meaning it probably wasn't counting on constricting its prey.*

And there were traces of Working on the scales. Faint, and not what her elemental sense was meant to detect. So much not Fire, she could tell exactly what had touched it. "Whatever kind of snake it was, it was Water-Worked. Probably to milk out venom."

"You're sure?" Helleson pounced.

"As sure as I can be without handing this to a Wave." She faced Tace's direction. "Good call."

"So what's it worth?" Tace said. The last word had a hitch in it, as if the urchin had tried to nonchalantly dig a thumb into a belt loop, slash or no slash.

Shane shrugged, and jabbed her own thumb Helleson's way. "He's the nosy one. I'm just along for luck."

"I don't think so," Tace shot back, defiant. "What's it worth to *you?*"

This is your informant, Helleson. But the inspector was no help at all; leaning against the railing, silent.

Faking it, Shane judged from the heat in tight knuckles. *No way does he want to be that close to the edge. But he doesn't really know me, and Tace knows he doesn't know. No way will a street brat take secondhand trust. Think, think, what would Terry do-? Probably say go with your strengths, Red. You can't do charming, so do honest.* "You've got a point," she said at last. "Given these guys nearly blew me up yesterday... I'd say, breakfast."

A hand thunked on railing steel. "You gotta be kidding me."

"Well, it's not like they're the first idiots to try it." Shane shrugged, with an air of nonchalance she'd bet Tace would be trying to copy for hours. "I mean, if they'd dropped me into a tank of flying electric eels, or tried to give me the Death of a Thousand and One Paper-Cuts- you know, something different. As it stands, though; bombs, venom-bolts... boring. So, breakfast."

Another rattle; a too-thin back jarring against the railing. "Lady, you are grade-A crazy," Tace said faintly.

Shane grinned, and felt metal thrum as Tace flinched from it. "I get that a lot."

Helleson cleared his throat. "I might think it was worth more than breakfast. If you can show us where you found it."

"You're not gonna like it," Tace warned.

"They almost blew me up. I already don't like it... oh." Helleson swallowed audibly. "Doesn't anybody in this city keep their feet on the ground?"

Tace snickered. "Get used to it, farm-boy."

"I hate to say it, but he has a point," Shane put in, before the inspector could object that he hadn't been raised anywhere *near* a farm. Which was her good deed for the day, sparing the man's soul the stain of what would have been a blatant lie: Orthodox families outside the city were never too far from a hayrack. All those verses about making the earth fruitful by the sweat of their brow, and so forth. And she knew from personal unpleasant experience, not all the jokes were city prejudice. "I'm still working on sidewalks. Roof-running is going to be a little problematic."

"Then stay here," Tace sniffed.

"She's coming," Helleson said flatly.

"You think I'm going on the *ground* down there? That's Iceblades' turf! You can keep your damn *breakfast*, Blondie-"

"Redstone," the Fire-Worker cut in. "Or Shane. *Blondie* will get your green hair turned to charcoal." She turned toward Helleson. "I trust you."

"What."

"I trust you," Shane repeated, trying to picture the stunned face that must have gone with that. "Tace will lead you; you'll lead me. I *have* run these roofs before. Not in a while, and not blind, but...." She stroked a line of heat down steel. "Unless you think you can't be my eyes, Helleson?"

"I think Tace is right," the inspector said after a beat. "You are crazy."

"No," Shane replied, wondering how many years it'd been since she'd been that innocent, blissfully unaware of exactly how crazy people could get. "I just have a lot more practice knowing where my limits are." She aimed a blind gaze Tace's way. "Let's go see if you've found one."

Clinging desperately to Redstone's left hand as the Flame dangled off a roof edge, Allen cursed himself for a stubborn idiot. *We should have gone on the ground, I* know *I could have talked Tace into it....*

The girl disguised as a boy was breathing hard behind him, caught between a street kid's instinct to run and a more humane impulse to help. He didn't think *help* would win in time-

Shane *yanked* on tuff bricks with her right hand, using the leverage to eel her body up just enough for feet to catch a moment's grip, and push her up and over.

Still pulling, he fell with her to the roof. And laid there, shaking a little.

"Nice save." The Flame barely seemed out of breath. "Guess I need to work on my jumps more."

Allen had to almost physically restrain himself from shaking her. "Do you *want* to die?"

"No. I want to live." She untangled herself from him, cautiously getting to her feet, cane still slung over her back. "And believe me, locked up where they sand all the corners off and keep telling you how *sorry* they are? Not much of a life. Especially when some of them are just sorry you're-" She cut herself off. "Tace. Is this the place?"

Sorry you're what? Allen wondered. *Still alive?*

It made sense, in a creepy sort of way. A dead hero would be a lot easier to deal with than a crippled Flame. But... no one really would... would they?

Which was a *stupid* place for early healer-training to rear its persistent head again; but an all too normal human displacement reaction to the fact that in the next few minutes, they might be facing lethal enemy agents. Alone.

Not alone. You called the captain before we started the roof craziness, there will be a team on standby. And Shane can handle any bombs... if they're not bigger than the last one.

Not likely, from what he knew. Still - they were going in alone. Captain Mason had agreed; hours counted, evidence was perishable, two people in civilian clothes would draw less curious eyes than a swarm of Watch, and any surviving contacts of the Riparian team *should* be long gone. Lord knew Allen would be, if a plan had gone that badly wrong.

You can never count on people to do the smart thing. Which is why Tace is going to make herself scarce, Allen told himself firmly, giving the street kid the eye he'd used on his swarm of younger relatives when they were out to do some damn fool thing that'd break their necks. "This is the right place, Tace?"

"Y-yeah," Tace managed, not coming closer. "This is it. Fly-By-Night."

"They rent rooms by the hour," Allen said, recognizing the name. Oops. Civilian clothes, nothing; he was going to stick out like a sore thumb. "For-"

"Believe me, I know what they're for," Redstone said wryly. "Always bring your own sleeping bag. You don't even want to *think* what's happened between those sheets."

No. No he did not, and now he was having dark suspicions about the muffled noises on Captain Mason's end of the line when he'd called in the address. He'd thought they were gruff coughs of concern. It hadn't occurred to him they might be *stifled laughter*.

"*You've* slept in *clocks?*" Tace's face screwed up in disbelief, tinged almost as green as her hair.

"You do a lot of things undercover you never would have dreamed of." The Flame shook out her hands, ran through a few finger-stretches Allen recognized as the prelude to Working in a hurry. "People see a guy and a girl, or even *three* guys and a girl, duck into a clock with a few beers and backpacks? They never think twice about what's going on. They already know."

"You worked the streets?" Tace sounded a little less wary. "Like Helle?"

"Helle, huh?" Redstone grinned at him. "Have to remember that one. No, not exactly. I'm not Watch. More of a headhunter."

Allen eyed the ex-Strike Specialist who'd just identified herself as a bounty hunter, and tried not to groan out loud. *Sane, my foot.... Focus. Case. Possible scene.* "You really think they've been using this place as a base?"

"Long term, probably not; it'd be too suspicious. A week or so? It's not cheap, but it has one major advantage. No one thinks it's strange if people are paid not to ask questions." Shane waved a hand, indicating the unseen horizon. "I'm turned around. Can you see the warehouse from here?"

Allen faced the boundary of the roof, frowning. No... no... that shadow was a glider, oddly early for the idiot crowd... ah, official

registry numbers on the right wing, that was actually someone
working for a living... there. "Got it." Though the view wasn't perfect,
partly obscured by a massive sign of Worked Water and Air, swirling
through a rainbow of ads for two restaurants and a strip joint. Or
maybe it was the other way around. He still wasn't used to how blatant
city ads could be.

"Two floors down, sign's not in the way," Tace said smugly.

Allen raised an eyebrow, and nodded. "Two floors down?"

"Better be more than just *breakfast*."

"Oh, I don't know; you look like you could use a good-"

"*Not* funny!"

"Hey!" Allen held out empty hands, voice as soothing as he dared
make it. Tace had no pearl, like the rest of her gang; one of the reasons
they kept slipping through the city's cracks without notice. But she
had a knack for sensing outside influence. Force Spirit-calm on her,
and she'd bolt. Make himself calm, and that perfectly justifiable
paranoia might ease off. "Get breakfast at Kay's. If you can pay for
the visit, she'll let you all grab a corner of the basement for the night.
That'll buy you some time to think, right? Where Rebar can't get to
you."

Tace bristled. "Who said-"

"Tace. I may have hay in my hair, but I'm not an *idiot*. This wasn't
Iceblades' turf last week." He eyed her bandaged arm. "From what
I've heard, Rebar's known for that dirty ice-hook."

"*Thought* I'd dealt with holes like that before." Redstone
grimaced. "There's a man who could use a lesson in proper manners."

"Yeah? And who's going to give it to him?" Tace glared defiance
at them both, hand almost reaching for the solid length of chain
bundled in her pocket. "Rebar's too slick to do stuff the Watch can pin
on him."

And Tace wasn't about to come in and give a statement, Allen
knew. Assuming she survived what Rebar's *boys* would do, she'd be
exposed as a girl. Which would leave her little band of street rats

defenseless against other gangs.

She won't leave the kids, and if I bring in the Fosterers, she'll never *forgive me. If the kids would even stay with Fosterers... well, Mikey would, I think, but one out of five?*

Which wouldn't stop his family from doing exactly that, if they were here. Give a person one chance at redemption, his father would say. If they didn't take it, they'd made their own hellfire bed.

There's got to be a better way.

He just hadn't found it. Yet.

"So is the roof door usually unlocked, or did you persuade it?" Redstone broke into his musings.

Another green-dyed bristle. "None of your business!"

"Yes, it is," Allen stated. "We need to know how they worked, not just what they were doing. In case they're linked to someone else. So? Open, or not?" He cleared his throat. "What were you doing inside a clock, anyway? Not that it's any of my business...."

"Scavenging, right?" Redstone grinned. "Someone I knew used to call it raven-picking."

"Who?" Tace challenged.

"I never asked what he went by before. He got out of the life. Now, he teaches people enough to keep them out of trouble. Well... some kinds of trouble." Redstone flexed her fingers again, making sure they were ready to burn. "Weren't for him, I'd be a lot more than blind."

Tace eyed her, sniffed, and shrugged. "Yeah," she allowed grudgingly. "You lift a guy, could be anybody, right? Guy up playing in a clock, though - he's not calling the Watch if he figures out he left his wallet."

"Or anything else," Redstone agreed.

Allen couldn't help it. He had to laugh.

"Hey!"

"Sorry, Tace." And he was, really. It was just... Sunlit Lord. His father would never see the humor in this. Vice was its own downfall, indeed. Theft and carnal sin were both wrong, who knew how much blood the Flame had on her hands - yet here and now, hunting would-be murderers, he wouldn't trade these two for a choir full of Helleson Spirit-Workers. They knew this dark territory of the soul. Even blind.

Tace was too young to understand that. He hoped. "I knew streetwalkers had light fingers," Allen said instead, "but I didn't realize they had *help*."

"I work for it!" Tace still looked affronted. "You got to get in and out before the landlord does. You gotta be *fast*."

"And it helps to have a bunch of friends along," Allen said, half to himself. *Like an unkindness of ravens.* "Did you find the skin?"

"Hell, yeah!" She moved off a few feet, ready to bolt.

"It doesn't matter who found it, as long as we can find the room," Redstone shrugged. "But if these are the people we're looking for, Helle's right; you should lay low. We've got some nasty Army types in town. The kind that like to pick people up, throw them in a cell on national security suspicions, and maybe forget to find the key. I don't know about you, but I could do without that kind of attention."

Says the woman who was part *of that kind of attention*, Allen thought wryly.

Then again, *was*. Shane wasn't now. And some of the things she'd said.... *No one panics when an Earth-Worker goes blind.*

Was someone panicking because of her?

That would be bad. For her, for my team... possibly for several city blocks....

He didn't think Shane would wreak wholesale havoc and destruction because someone else panicked. But she *would* defend herself. With the level of power he'd seen her use already, if someone high-level military panicked and didn't calm down, things could... escalate.

You have no reason to believe that could happen. None. You know military types. Someone up the command chain would have a clearer head, and anyone who overreacted would be stopped.

And seriously, what would be the point of panic? Callie's sour comments aside, you couldn't toss an innocent civilian onto an operating table and carve out their elemental pearl. Even with the best care, for most poor souls the doctors tried that on, it was a death sentence.

"I don't want to die."

And Captain Stewart... didn't like her. *Really* didn't like her.

Dawn was cold, but it was a snowflake next to the chill that went through him.

Paranoia. It's got to be, Allen told himself. *She was wounded, she's blind - and Strike Specialists are* paid *to be paranoid.*

So they were. And just how paranoid was she?

That is a terrifying and awful possibility that I will consider later, Allen told himself firmly. *It's possible. She doesn't* feel *out of her right mind. But she's very, very good at keeping her Spirit quiet.*

For right now Redstone was calm, controlled, and the person he needed backing him up in case there *was* another bomb. Allen took a deep breath, and focused on the hazard at hand. "So which room is it?"

"...Third on the left." Tace looked away, fingering the shimmer of skin. "An'... the roof was open."

"Pretty, isn't it?" Redstone said wistfully. "I always thought they were like gray silk. Useful, too."

Tace blinked at that. Allen raised an eyebrow. The Flame might not be good at normal people, but street kids lived in their own war zone. She'd definitely caught Tace's attention. "That's right," he noted. "Snakes are kin to Water and Earth. There are a lot of interesting ways someone can Work a skin."

"Yes, there are." Coins chimed between Redstone's fingers.

Allen glanced at the amount, and coughed. Silver, and worn, but not cheap coins. "Just where do you *go* for breakfast?"

"Nowhere this expensive, trust me," Redstone said wryly, still holding out the handful. "This isn't for breakfast-"

"You think you can *buy* me?" Tace snarled.

The Flame stiffened. Bristled; Allen would've sworn blonde strands frizzed like an aggrieved lion. "You. Think. I. Would-!"

He laid his hand against the outside of Redstone's arm, just above the bracelet; not gripping, just letting her feel he was there. Heat swelled against his fingers, a lava tide. He didn't move. "You, stay still. Tace-"

The grimy lifter was red and shaking. "I don't need to stick around for a *blind skank!*"

"No, you don't," Allen said bluntly. Controlled heat *rippled*, as Redstone twitched. "But she helped you out. So maybe you could be a little gracious, and let her try to explain what she meant. Since we both know she has *no manners.*"

Not his imagination. He felt the low growl, vibrating through his fingers.

But the Flame let a breath steam out, and nodded jerkily. "I don't *buy* anybody."

Allen kept his hand against Redstone's arm by an act of sheer will. Fury didn't boil through her Spirit; it was a razor edge, slicing and slicing as she kept her temper from leaking out into anything more than words.

Who tried to buy her? Or - who did she know who was bought?

Whoever it'd been, the outrage was real. Shane hadn't even *considered* using money as a lever for Tace. Which was... odd. Tace was a street kid. Most people didn't think they had morals; much less ones money couldn't buy.

"This is to cover expenses," Redstone went on. "For *equipment.* Because Helle wants you *in one piece.*"

Some of the red faded off Tace's cheeks.

Oh.

Oh, and Allen suppressed an urge to gulp. An Elemental was leaning on his judgment of Tace as someone who *couldn't* be bought.

Rented, maybe, Allen allowed. *But not bought.*

"There's a little place off Damascus and Greenbriar," the Flame went on. "*Skin and Water*. Ask Kaili what she recommends." She shrugged. "She might not have what you're looking for. But she's more up to date on the streets than I am."

Warily, Tace took the stack and made it vanish up a sleeve. "What makes you think I'll even go?"

"The way Helle's fidgeting over there, trying *not* to ask me how I know about it?" Redstone scraped up a wry smirk. "You know it's got to be interesting."

"Fine. How *do* you know about it?" Allen drew himself up, certain Shane would sense the aggressive shift of weight. What business did she have, pointing Tace to a shop that sold... well, they weren't exactly *illegal*, but there were some pretty nasty Worked items in the inventory. Tace was already on the wrong side of the law. She didn't need help going any deeper.

But Rebar got her with an ice hook.

And so far he *could not* convince Tace to bring this to the law. If he wanted the kid to stay alive - she needed help.

"Kaili offered me a job, once." The Flame's voice was matter-of-fact. "I had to turn it down."

"Uh-huh," Tace said warily. "You? Stay there." She beckoned Allen to a corner of the roof she probably thought was out of earshot. "What's her deal?"

"Still trying to figure that out myself," Allen admitted. For Tace as much as himself; there were things he couldn't do, as Watch, that an ordinary citizen might be able to pull off. If Tace could trust someone besides him, it might be a start on getting the hard-headed kid off the street. "But as far as I can tell, she doesn't play games. You might want to check it out."

"Yeah, but *why?*"

Why. Good question. Prickly, stubborn woman; yet the Flame seemed to have the same drive to hold out a helping hand that had drawn him to the Watch in the first place.

I know you're not as strong as I am. As trained as I am. As good as I am. But if you want to start making your life right, I'll pull you up.

Only now Redstone was the one who needed help. That had to bite.

"The people we're tracking tried to kill a bunch of Watch yesterday," Allen said, settling on something Tace would believe. "I think she'd like you as far away from any of their friends as possible."

Tace's lips curled in a snarl. "I can take care of myself!"

"What, and I can't?" Allen gave her a look askance. "I didn't stop shaking for an hour. I might have gotten a few gray hairs, I haven't looked. Yesterday? Was not fun." He shrugged, and headed for the roof door. "Shane?"

"Nice meeting you," the Flame called over her shoulder, tapping along beside him.

"Oh, *him* you're polite to," Allen muttered as they got through the roof door.

"That lifter might steal my wallet, but I doubt the kid would take anything I couldn't replace," Redstone shrugged. Cocked her head, listening, as if to make sure she heard the lock click. "And I don't think Tace would like knowing you've figured out it's really *Anastasia*."

Stupid, he berated himself, waiting a moment for his eyes to adjust to the stairwell shadows. "How did you know?"

"Defleaing. A low-intensity, quick Fire burst, over the whole body. Good as a pat-down."

"I never heard of anyone using it like that," Allen admitted, taken aback. Spirit-healers could sense a body at a distance, and Wind and Water-Workers could feel at anything inside their element - but a Fire-Worker could kill pests *and* sense the body under them? Without so much as singeing a hair on Tace's head?

Redstone gave a soft, exasperated *hmph* as he started down the stairs. "Don't be impressed. I had good teachers, and time to experiment between missions. Everyone thinks Fire's about raining chaos and destruction, and it's *not*."

"Oh, no?" Tell that to the fire and brimstone preachers in his family. They had scores of holy battle accounts that said otherwise.

"Well, it can be," she allowed, toes feeling the edge of each step as she followed him down. "But it's a lot more effective to hit most problems with a *small* solution. Save the flash and thunder for when you really need it."

"Minimal force," Allen quoted one of his academy instructors. "You can always escalate a situation. It's a lot harder to de-escalate it."

"Exactly," Redstone nodded. "What's better for Caldera? A ten mile swath of cinders cut through one of our neighbors? Or just one venom-bolt factory vanishing in flames in the dead of night?" Her cane tapped down to another landing. "Second down?"

"We're here," Allen agreed. Braced himself, and opened the stairwell door.

I am so glad I'm not on Vice.

He couldn't hold back a visceral shudder of disgust as a disheveled man brushed by them to head downstairs, belt still loose. Behind the clock's customer a heavily made-up redhead lounged in an apartment doorway, silky red dress half off bare shoulders, the look of satisfaction on a painted face as fake as patent-black lashes.

Ugh.

The body wanted what it wanted, Allen knew that - but to take that most sacred communion between man and woman, that which was blessed to form one flesh out of two, and reduce it down to fifteen minutes and a stack of coin? Pathetic.

The redhead watched him with hooded eyes, barely flicking to Redstone behind him. From the way she'd stiffened, he knew she knew he wasn't just here to hand out religious tracts and *tsk* at her... chosen trade.

And from that strategically placed choker, the oddly broad hands and wrists - she wasn't a *she* at all.

Good thing Uncle Micah isn't here, Allen thought wryly. *He'd have a stroke.*

Good thing most of the family wasn't anywhere near Caldera City. If they knew how many things he'd just, somehow, gotten *used* to these past months - well, after he'd finished spurting blood, Micah would be the first to haul him off for an exorcism.

Still watching, the redhead retreated, and shut the door.

Third on the left. Allen knocked, listened, and *sensed* inside. The whisper of the small lives of any dwelling; spiders, silverfish, a hastily-departing rat scampering above the ceiling, likely through the air ducts.

Nothing human. Good.

Tested the knob-

It creaked open halfway, jarring against something that *thunk*ed, in a way that dropped his stomach into his shoes.

"Don't go in there," Redstone said quietly.

"I don't see anything," Allen argued, scanning the mini-apartment. Room, bed; a closet of a toilet. No human Spirit within. Nothing out of place, besides whatever was behind the door. That noise... like the thunk back in Waycross one bitterly cold winter, when a beef carcass had been knocked loose from one of its hanging hooks by blizzard winds....

"I know. That's why you shouldn't go in there." The Flame pointed at the concealing panel. "It's big, meaty, and mostly frozen. I think we found the landlord."

Pulling the door toward him, Allen peeked.

Frost, caking the contorted body from head to toe. A grimace of agony twisted dead lips, and two dark circles stained a forearm otherwise ice-white.

Jumping back, Allen slammed the door.

"Animal Control?" Redstone asked.

"Animal Control," the inspector agreed fervently. Wait. If she agreed with him - she couldn't have seen what he'd just seen. "What the *hell*- you know what did that?"

"Water-Worked cobra, would be my guess." Redstone's shoulders deliberately loosened, breathing slow and deep. The tells of a trained fighter who very much wanted to be *anywhere else*. "People use them against Fire-Workers, sometimes. They're quiet, quick... and cold-blooded."

Meaning Redstone not only couldn't see it, she couldn't *sense* it, either. "Let's go down a floor to call it in," Allen suggested.

"Right behind you."

Chapter Five

"Here, cobra, cobra, cobra...."

Standing reluctantly beside her in the hall, Helleson sighed.

"Yes, I am constitutionally incapable of taking the threat of imminent death seriously," Shane said mischievously, one hand on the wall to sense any creaks from unnatural cold. Likely whoever had Worked the cobra had kept their effects confined to its venom; that would make the snake hardest to detect, and use the minimum of stored power. But you could never be too sure. They'd had enough funds or blackmail material to get their hands on a whole knot of charged lava-hair. They might have had just as much to get slivers of frozen quartz-water. "Relax, Inspector. You're going to get ulcers. It's just a snake."

"Just a snake," groaned one of the sweating snake-handlers. Not the phlegmatic calm she'd expect from Caldera's Animal Control... but from what she'd overheard, Animal Control had hastily co-opted these handlers from the Caldera Zoo, after enough bouncing through bureaucracy had convinced the Watch and anyone else who'd stuck their white-collared nose in that yes, Helleson *was* serious.

"A venomous, lethal snake," Shane allowed. "But it's not like it's looking for *us*." She paused, unable to resist. "I hope."

"Not. Helping," Helleson said faintly.

Apparently not. Drat. Teasing the man was one thing, but if she was going to work with him, he had to *think*. "Helle," Shane said deliberately. "It doesn't have a rod. It doesn't have a grudge. And unless somebody's seriously Worked its Spirit with a compulsion, all it wants to do is stay out of sight, eat rats, and keep warm." She almost hoped someone *had* compelled it. That would at least let a Spirit-Worker find the nasty thing.

And Terry would pout at you, Ram would sigh, Paul would roll his eyes... and Erastus would grumble to keep that behind *your teeth, Red. Realizing they're targets makes most people* twitchy.

"It is just a snake," Shane said instead. "You wouldn't be frightened if it were a hurricane, would you?" Then again Helleson might, Waycross was inland enough not to worry as much... but give him the benefit of the doubt, he had moved here. "You'd be fine. Because you'd know it might be coming, and you'd have prepared as well as you could." She waved a hand toward the people in front of them. "Which is exactly what we've done."

"...You really aren't worried, are you?"

"Cobra venom breaks down if you heat it," Shane said practically.

Which got her an indrawn breath. Why? Seriously, didn't people know- Oh. Right. Most people probably *didn't* know that. Given the control it took to fry venom without frying the person. Oops.

...And there was that odd *stillness* around Helleson again, as the inspector's breathing slowed to a normal rhythm.

What is that? The same thing he used with the bomb? It can't be an ordinary Spirit-calm. I'd feel that.

Yet it wasn't the ordinary biofeedback techniques she used to stay focused on explosives when all the rest of the world was going to hell. Ruling your own mind and body calmed *you*. It didn't do a damn for people who weren't your team.

So it has to be Spirit. A Spirit-Working I can't feel. What is it?

Whatever it was, it worked. She felt Helleson's heat dim; heard the shift of his weight as he stood straighter, drawing himself out of instinct's defensive crouch. And his calm steadied the others, quick breaths to either side of the corridor easing back down to where people could think.

How is he doing that?

"Last I checked, hospitals have specially Worked heat-shocks for snakebite," Helleson said wryly, voice even and steady. "Something about the control they need to not fry tissue around a wound."

Right, right, and she really *hated* feeling like an idiot. "Training," Shane stated, trying to ignore her face burning. "I can boil the venom right out of a vein. If I get bitten, I'll be sore, but I'll live. If anyone else is, as long as I get to them in a few minutes, *they'll* live. Whether we've got good healers on hand or not."

Maybe especially if they didn't. Not every healer trained to handle venoms that could sink icy fangs into unwary veins. Shane had. So she leaned a little more on the wall, blatantly nonchalant, and raised an eyebrow at the inspector. "You've got Spirit. Can't you handle snakebite?"

After all, Helleson was from *Waycross*. Everyone knew what Orthodox worship services in the heartland got up to. Hairy enough to make a Strike Specialist look at them cross-eyed.

"Healing and I don't seem to get along," Helleson admitted after a long moment. "The fire escape - that's about as good as I can do."

When he'd cleaned out Tace's wound after her own work, strengthening Spirit and flesh against disease. The very lowest grade of Spirit-healing; no more than most born Workers managed years before they were old enough to apprentice. *Sounds like a sore spot. Not surprising; he can truth-read, and short-jump, he's definitely got the* power *to do more. I wonder why he can't?*

Huh. I wonder if that's what made him up and move right to Caldera's own pit of Fire and iniquity. Orthodox types are really into the 'healing hands' as divine favor, and if he can't-

Well. That wasn't really her business. "There are things you can do short of healing the venom," Shane said matter-of-factly. "I know a variant on that cleansing that slows it down a lot. Would you like to look at some of my manuals, when this is over?" *Say yes. I really,*

really want you to say yes. You know a trick I don't! I've got to find
out what it is.

Helleson shifted on his feet, as if he were trying not to be obvious
about wanting to be anywhere but a snake-haunted hallway. Silly. No
one sane wanted to be here.

Then again, she'd rarely been accused of sanity.

He settled again, though a brightening of his warmth showed the
effort it took. "Why does a Fire-Worker have *Spirit* manuals?"

"Cross-training," Shane shrugged. Calmly. Stay calm, Terry'd
always said, act like you knew what you were doing, and odds were
you could walk civilians right past the blast zone before they ever
realized there'd been a danger. Not that the Watch were civilians, but
they weren't used to the variety of *weird* ways to die Strike Specialists
ran into every mission. "And if you've got stored charges in a rod -
there are ways you can improvise a Working the rod wasn't originally
designed to do. If you know what diagrams to scribe."

"Your aunt's right," he muttered. "You *are* scary-"

Someone screamed. Someone else yelled. A crack of a fire-bolt-

"Aw, no," Shane groaned, listening to the gurgles. "Helle. Is that
water?"

"Looks like," the inspector agreed, shifting to peer down the hall
as the yelping went on. "Gentlemen! Ladies! Pipes aren't snakes!"

"It *moved!*" somebody ahead protested.

Sensing the not-Fire tickle of water trickling into the hallway
carpet, muffling crucial echoes, Shane sighed.

"You know, it could have," Helleson said suddenly, as another
clamor of clattering, banging, and swearing started up. "If it wants to
be warm-"

"Hot water pipes," Shane said along with him. "Brilliant," she
added, grinning. "Watch the floor for me, would you? Just in case it
tries sneaking up on me."

"What are you going to do?"

"Convince it this place is too hot to handle." Eyes closed, she swept one hand outward-

Water was a channeled pattern of opposition, flowing through the plumbing, dampening the carpet near her feet. It didn't like her - but it didn't have to.

Fingers curling, Shane summoned heat.

Helleson strangled a curse. "You *do* realize, not everybody can see through steam?"

Oops. Working fast, she pushed and pulled on hot mist, currents whipping cooler, drier air in from the stairwell-

"There it is!"

Crash. Thud of bodies. At least one ominous *crack* of skulls.

When the silence swept in, a furious hissing.

"Careful!" Shane called ahead. "Some of them-"

A yelp, and a chuckling swear from one of the snake-handlers. "Spit, yeah, lady. Why did you think we're wearing goggles?"

Rrrgh. Nobody told me you were-!

Shane took a deep breath, and forced back the acid anger. Being blind was a fact. That sighted people were going to forget to mention what *everyone else could see*, was a fact. Facts had to be dealt with. No matter how much they burned.

"Is that why?" Helleson said faintly. "I hate snakes."

"Eh, they're not so bad," a gruff voice spoke up, hefting fabric bitter with the familiar antiseptic of a body bag. "I get more on my slab from lightning than snakebite, believe it or not." He huffed a laugh. "I thought all of you from Waycross were *used* to handling snakes."

Not going to laugh, Shane told herself. *Not going to.* Some of the best Strike Specialists she'd met were from Satsuma. Warriors against spiritual evil joined the army to face the darkness' physical allies in this world, and their churches liked to prove who ranked among the Elect with cranky gold-banded sea kraits. By that standard, Waycross' rattlesnakes were a bit tame.

"Some of us don't feel like asking the Lord to prove how upright and virtuous we are, Gare. Or aren't." Helleson hesitated. "Gareth, Flame Redstone. Redstone, Dr. Gareth Keller, coroner."

"Redstone? *You're* Jehanna's niece?" The coroner whistled. "Remind me not to clean her out at poker."

"Like you could," Shane said wryly. "I've heard about the showdown of aces."

"Who hasn't?" There was an amused lilt to the words. "Who do you think taught her?"

"Damn, you blew her secret." Shane forced lightness into her tone. "She was keeping you as a hole card to get me interested in the game, when I finally wouldn't be gambling with government money. So much for that plan."

"Hmm." Gareth sounded a little too thoughtful for her liking, even as the clang of steel and relieved swears told her the snake-trappers had just sealed their bagged catch into a lockbox. "Well. Is that my body in there?"

Familiar footsteps; Shane tried to fade behind Helleson. Her fingers brushed the inspector's shoulder as he sighed, closer than she'd intended to get. But he didn't move away.

"It most certainly is not," Captain Stewart said glacially. "This is part of an ongoing investigation... what are *you* doing here?"

"Sightseeing?" Shane said blandly, fingertips lingering on the heavy cloth of Helleson's longcoat. "It's not every day you see an indoor flood."

"An indoor-"

Weakened hot water pipes finally squealed and burst, billows of steam and water rushing down the hall.

Crooking her finger to swirl hot fog around her like a cloak, Shane retreated.

No fool, Helleson was right behind her.

Holding onto his temper with both hands, Allen stepped out of the Air-call box, and tried not to swear.

Heavy wood tapped up and down, raising faint echoes. "Earful from the captain, hmm?"

He eyed the Flame, letting the folding door swing back into place. "Not something you usually have a problem with."

"Oh, you'd be surprised." Redstone planted her cane; leaned on it with both hands, cocking her head to mark the chattering of an Earth-drill gnawing up asphalt down the road. "If you never get chewed out, you're a rules lawyer and dead last in the field. If you *always* get chewed out, you're a loose cannon headed for an early discharge, and maybe a stint of rock-breaking. You have to keep a fine balance. About one 'What the *hell* were you thinking?' for every ten 'good jobs'. Or something like that." A shrug. "So. Anything you want to tell me?"

"Stewart's got the body and the room," Allen reported, disgusted. There went any leads, damn it-

"Focus, Inspector," Redstone said soberly. "The object isn't who gets credit for the bust. You said you meant to look where they aren't. Well, they're looking there."

"Do you really expect Captain Stewart to do as good a job investigating as the Watch?" Allen demanded.

"No."

Allen narrowed his eyes. She couldn't see it, but he was starting to think she could *feel* the heat of someone's temper.

"And if this were just a murder, believe me, I'd be right behind you snarling at Command to get him the hell off the case," Redstone went on. "But it's not, and when it comes to tracking people, Stewart's not bad. He *will* have people who can find bombs. We're not going to have a repeat of yesterday."

Allen clenched a fist in his coat pocket, tempted to drive it right into the call box door. The sin of wrath was so very enticing. And still wrong. "That's not good enough!"

"It's not," Redstone acknowledged. "But right now, it's all I've got." She straightened, taking the map out of her pocket to feel along carved streets. "Any other ideas, Inspector? There's something I wanted to get to before lunch, if there's time."

He wished he did have another idea. *Any* other idea. "Thanks. For your time."

"It was interesting," she nodded, starting away.

And paused, fingers curling around her cane. "Look. If you do think of something else - call. Or stop by. I'll help if I can." Blind eyes were hidden by her glasses, but there was a weariness in her voice. "Like you and Tace showed me... I can't exactly dive into a mess like this on my own, anymore."

"You were good," Allen managed, still fuming at the captain's orders. Yes, he was supposed to be working on cold cases. Yes, the Army had priority on stopping suspected outbreaks of mass destruction. But *stay away from Stewart* was *not* what he wanted to hear right now. "You'll get better."

"Hmph. Don't let Medical hear you say that." Bowing politely, she headed into the crowd.

Don't let-? Allen wondered.

He was off the landlord's homicide. He should be working on one of Jehanna's cold cases. Marcus Wright would be a good one; better to re-interview witnesses and contacts soon, to keep as much continuity as possible with the deceased Inspector Sorenson's investigation. Not to mention he'd noticed that the murdered candle-maker had no wife or children listed, just a cousin for next-of-kin. Which might be normal for a lot of city-dwellers in their thirties but for an Orthodox man rang alarm bells all over. Meaning he might actually find something Sorenson had missed. It was late morning now; both the place Wright had worked and his congregation of worship ought to be open and stirring....

Stay away from Stewart.

Oh, hell. If Allen didn't have a lead to follow, he still had a mystery in front of him.

Decided, he slipped into the crowd.

Most people might think it was easier to tail a blind woman, but Allen wasn't that stupid. Flame Redstone had kept her head and kept people alive in situations a lot hairier than being stalked down Calderan streets. And he had no intention of winding up on the wrong side of a fireball. He hung back, as far as he could and keep her in sight.

We're not going back to the apartment.

The Flame forged her own stubborn path through the crowd, hopping onto and off a steam-fumed bus at one point to miss the worst street-crossings. All the time steadily making her way downtown, deeper into the caldera, toward-

The Forge. She's heading for the Forge.

Allen faded through the hard-bitten crowd. He'd seen it before, he'd been all over the city in Watch orientation, but it still struck him like a blow to the gut, the sheer numbers moving toward the massive lifts that sank down into Caldera's lowest working level. Back home no one would believe sane souls would go anywhere near the lava of a volcano, even if it was held at bay by an armory of Wards. Yet welders, forgers, smiths - anyone whose business thrived with focused heat, gravitated here.

Why is Shane here?

Allen slipped into a lift after Redstone, smiling neutrally at anyone who glanced his way. This was a rough crowd, but honest; more like the people he'd known, and sometimes arrested, back in Waycross. If they were coming onto work late in the morning, it wasn't because they were nursing a hangover; it was because they'd be on late into the night, or even to dawn. Natural Fire meant businesses could put on shifts around the clock without wasting fuel to do it.

He wasn't dressed to fit the crowd, and he knew it. Other Orthodox locals headed for work had left off the long coat and wide-brimmed hat in favor of summer's plain gray long-sleeves and light netted head cap. He stood out like a raven in a bunch of sooty pigeons.

Still, the rougher types knew Watch when they saw him, even if

they had to do a double-take at long coat and holstered rod. Some
frowned, some shrugged, but most left him alone.

Shane's not dressed to blend, either.

But she'd gotten *looks*, walking through the crowd. A few from
younger men, apprenticed to one sooty trade or another; more from
gray-touched men and women with the steady look of foremen, crew-
leaders, or even a shop steward or two. One of them was standing by
her in the lift now, glancing sharply at anyone who looked restless
enough to give a blind woman trouble.

That's not just being polite. "What's with the gentle-lady?" Allen
murmured to one of the older Orthodox gentlemen standing near him,
pitching his voice not to carry.

"No Fire in your veins?" came the dry reply. "That's a *Flame*, son.
I've seen her before, when the Wards needed patching. You mind your
manners. Weren't for folks like her, none of us would be here."

If she's patched the Wards, then she knows where they are.

An errant, paranoid thought. But he couldn't ignore it. Maybe it
wasn't a coincidence that Redstone had been in that warehouse. He
had no reason to think she could be a traitor, and yet-

Follow her.

Redstone didn't hurry. Just kept as steady a pace as she could
through the crowd, heading past factory after factory to pass out of
sight of most onlookers, stalking toward a small but well-maintained
guard shack, just inside the hazy dome of protective Water and Air
that shut out the orange hell of magma beyond.

Allen had to stop, and stare. He'd been all over the city, but he'd
never come down *here*. No one who didn't work in the Forge did,
outside of a few thrill-seekers who had to come face to face with the
fact that yes, Caldera City was still in an *active volcano*.

Sometimes I think we're all insane.

Red-black liquid rock lapped against the retaining wall of granite,
leaving glowing garnet spots of heat before Air-worked fans behind
wall and Wards blew the worst of it into shimmering air. Farther

below the light was brighter orange, as heat bled up from the core of the world. Over the surface of that molten sea twisted columns of pure Fire, feeding up into forges and factories to smelt ore, hammer steel, even run cloth-weaving looms. Find a way to manufacture with heat, and Caldera used their volcanoes to do it.

The earth burned, while Caldera held its fury back with rings of granite, Air, and Water. He'd seen it, and Allen still couldn't quite believe it.

The arrogance to challenge the gods. That's what other nations think of us.

Allen had to shrug at that. His nation had put their lives and souls on the line ages back, declaring there was only *one* Lord. After that, what was facing down a volcano?

Walking into plain view of the guard's window, Redstone bowed. Straightened again, and lifted out her dog-tags.

Now what is she up to? Allen kept back, even if curiosity itched at him to get closer. There had to be a gatehouse so people could pass through and work on the Wards closest to the magma, but anyone with sense knew it was some of the highest security in the city. There couldn't be that many people the guard would even talk to-

A sliding panel opened, and a uniformed security guard waved a rod over her Flame insignia. Waited, and nodded. The panel slid shut again, Air-white and Earth-gold shimmering from the guard shack down the chain-link fence a few feet inside the dome.

With a clunk, a man-sized gate opened.

Walking through steel, Redstone took a deep breath, and plunged into the mist.

...Erk?

He was not going to panic. Redstone was mostly sane. Not suicidal. A Flame.

She just walked into the heart of a volcano. Are you sure *she's sane?*

He was *not* going to panic. He was an inspector, he'd just seen something incredibly out of the ordinary, even the most paranoid security guard would at least let him live long enough to ask questions....

He hoped.

He walked into view of the guard's window, badge already in hand. *I'm reaching for my ID* might not go over well, so close to the Wards. "Inspector Helleson," he identified himself. "I just saw someone go through the Wards. Is anything wrong?"

The guard's gaze bounced between his badge, the little light-picture beside it, and Orthodox black. Each bounce seemed to push incredulous eyebrows higher.

One of these days, I'll get used to that.

The guard's hairy hand dipped down a moment, with a twitch like flipping pages. A muscular arm reached out, rod scanning his badge as thoroughly as he'd checked Redstone's tags. "Inspector," he nodded. "Sorry, sir. Can't let you through; you're not a Fire-Worker. But...."

Another flash of Earth-gold, outlining a door on the side of the shack Allen would have sworn wasn't there a second ago. There was the thunk of a lock disengaging.

"Come on in, Inspector." The door swung open. "It's going to be quite a show."

A *show?* When an annoying but probably innocent woman might be sinking into lava as they spoke-

Wait a minute. "Since when am I cleared for this?" Allen asked, still outside the doorway.

"Sorry, Inspector." The guard's grin might have fit neatly on a shark. "That's classified."

Somehow, that did not make Allen feel any better.

I'm not pursuing a suspect. The inspector walked in; the door locked behind him like the clank of shackles on doomed souls. *I'm not officially on a case. There's no way I should have permission to get this close to the volcano-Wards. Even inside a guardpost. So how am I here? Who put me on a list? And for all that's holy,* why?

A wide multi-part mirror gleamed inside, displaying dark and fiery images from Worked lenses set up along the mist-dome's periphery, and Allen almost forgot to breathe.

She's... dancing.

Lava was impossibly solid under Shane's feet, a raft of black in a sea of molten scarlet. Air shimmered everywhere but near her; a bubble of pure atmosphere held cool and breathable, by what act of will he didn't like to think. And in the midst of an inferno, she was dancing.

Not dancing. Movements.

Knife Master moves; Allen recognized the fluid force, even if he'd never seen half of them before. One knife, two, or bare-handed, she fought an imaginary foe. Letting herself stumble, if she tripped; catching it into rolls and sweeps that left gray bits of ash in blonde hair.

He had a foot of muscled height and a pair of working eyes over Redstone, and the hairs still prickled on the back of his neck. If there'd been a bad guy out in the flames with her, she'd have had him gutted and bled out in seconds.

Callie, you have no idea how lucky you are.

"Flame Redstone." The guard folded his arms, grinning with hometown pride. "What a firecracker."

"...She's done this before?" Allen said numbly. Because of course she had, no one could fight and pull off a protective Working like that without years of practice, but - in the middle of Caldera?

Then again, where better than a volcano?

"Every week she's in the city," the older man nodded. "A lot of Fire Masters come here. Good place for practice. Trying any of the flashy stuff in the cold part of town would get the whole Fire Department mad at you. Know what I mean?" He brightened. "Hang on, I think she's going to-"

One hand swept out, lashing Fire in its wake.

Allen wasn't sure when he'd sunk onto the guard's spare stool. Just that he was planted there, spellbound, as Shane danced... and Fire danced with her.

Topaz curtains of flame. Ruby shields. Thin silk-blue ribbons, precise as a whip. A roaring white blaze that *exploded* from her small frame, searing cooled lava into a molten sea....

Somewhere in there Allen realized his mouth was dry, his stomach was growling, and an hour and a half had vanished.

The guard cleared his throat. "You'll have to wait outside while she comes out. Regulations."

"Okay...."

Still stunned, Allen leaned against heavy steel some distance from the gate, fingers gripping chain link as he watched Flame Redstone walk back out, blonde hair dipping in a nod of polite thanks to the guard. Stood there, still trying to catch his breath, as she brushed off ashes and headed back toward the lift.

She's not a traitor.

Disconcerting. An inspector was supposed to base their conclusions on facts. All he had was the sudden, bone-deep comprehension of *what* he'd tangled with in that warehouse. Flame Redstone didn't need to keep anyone alive to keep a cover intact. Flame Redstone could have *incinerated* the place, Watch included, and walked out untouched.

"Something else, huh?" The guard called through his port, smirking. "Bet you don't see *that* in the Academy."

"No, you don't," Allen agreed. *There'd be a lot more paranoid Watch officers if they did.*

Paranoid, like Callie was paranoid? What *did* she know about Flames that he didn't?

Thanking the man absently, Allen walked off.

Shane could have killed them all.

But she hadn't. And he thought he knew why. Impressive as all that Fire had been, there had been no targets out there beyond the Wards. Or, if you looked at it from fire's perspective... nothing that *wasn't* a target.

No one innocent to burn.

Shane could have stayed safe and sound behind cover, fried *everything*, and dealt with the bomb at leisure. *If* she'd been willing to risk hitting his squad.

Instead, she'd jumped into the fight, sealed off the bomb, and left the Riparians to the Watch. Risking *her* life, rather than theirs.

The last time he'd felt like this had been a Watch funeral. Pride, grief - the awed humility that made him think the Sunlit Lord hadn't gone wrong creating humans after all.

It's not fair. It's not fair *that someone who - who can* give *like that, is crippled. Cast aside. Broken.*

Fair or not, it was life. And Shane wasn't broken. Angry, yes. Crippled, definitely. But-

"I'll help if I can."

Not, if it was convenient. Not, if you come up with a *good* lead.

I'll just have to find one. Allen's chin came up, determined. *Because she's coming with me-*

Reason gripped emotion by the throat.

Someone meant me to see that. Cleared *me to see that. Who?*

Captain Stewart? Intelligence might have the pull, but Stewart and Redstone loathed each other. He hadn't misread that, any more than he'd misread Stewart's determination to watch a very dangerous woman for any signs of instability.

So who?

Good question. Though if someone was manipulating what he saw, an even better question was *why?*

Which made it even more important to keep Shane in the loop. If she was too paranoid, the Watch needed to be right on top of her. If she wasn't... blind or not, Shane had seen more of Caldera City than he would in a decade. He *needed* what she knew. What she could sense.

And, he suspected, she needed to be needed.

Callie's not going to like this.

On the one hand, tough. The captain had made his assignments, and Inspector Freeport could snarl at the moon for all the good it would do. On the other - Callie was his partner. Whatever was eating her, he'd better track her down and get it into the open. *Before* the Wyrd Shane believed in bit them both in the nethers.

Not enough hours in the day....

A bell rang as Shane walked into *Skin and Water*, chiming through the conversation Kaili was having with a distinguished gentleman whose accent vibrated with Geist around the edges. Shane didn't even try to give the illusion of looking his way, preoccupied with making her way around a shelf that, last she remembered, had held certain less than sturdy Worked glass sculptures.

"Be right there," Kaili called, ringing her customer up. "Just - stand still, would you?"

"Ah." Shane dutifully stopped moving, an honest smile curving her lips for the first time today. She could picture the long black braids wrapped tightly around Kaili's head; feather-patterned silk sleeves with a minimum of loose drape, the better not to catch on stray merchandise. "Am I by something particularly fragile?"

"Several somethings," came the dry answer. "You break it, you bought it."

"Ouch."

The gentleman left, muttering under his breath. Shane arched an eyebrow, and waited until the door closed. "You might want to tell him that's not only physically impossible, but if you *could* do that with your grandfather's aunt, you'd be arrested for exceedingly deviant and wicked acts."

"Ten years in Caldera, and he still hasn't cracked a law book," Kaili sighed. "He'll be in for a nasty shock if he ever does slip over the line."

"Which you will, of course, charge him a finder's fee for, so he can get a proper lawyer," Shane smirked.

"Eww! Lawyers? Bite your tongue." A chuckle. "I'll let my cousin Van scoop that fee. Bounty hunting's never as profitable as it should be." Footsteps, and a warm hand was in front of her. "I heard."

No doubt she had. Kaili never *sold* information. But she gathered it. The better to know who might be seeking her wares next - and why.

"Was it bad?"

"Yes," Shane said bluntly. That, at least, no one could expect to leave classified. "Yes, it was." She lifted a shoulder, let it drop. "They've treated what they could. I haven't had a phantom pain for a month. Physically, I'm healthy." Outside of the obvious.

"Fair warning, I take it, to some of my other customers." Kaili's vicious grin rang through her voice. "Come on, I have a chair over here."

Shane let the shopkeeper guide her, keeping cane-taps to a minimum. She *could* reach out with Fire-sense - but carefully. Some of the Worked items were as fragile as glass, in their own way.

And just - barely - legal.

That was Kaili's specialty, after all; finding esoteric items for a reasonable price. Anything from that exotic tamarind an expatriate needed to make the perfect Riparian fish-flake stew, to tiny little Worked splinters of quartz and petrified wood an enterprising Strike Specialist could put to very good - and better yet, *untraceable* - use.

Shane had grown up in the same city as *Skin and Water*, yet Jehanna had never brought her here. Bones had. That Inspector Helleson knew where it was, was... interesting.

Could just mean he's good at his job, Shane reflected, easing into the solid wood chair. *You were still a kid when Bones gave you an address and told you to get five Worked bramble-berries.*

Thankfully the shopkeeper hadn't gouged a young recruit *too* much. Compared to the bargaining her team had done in the field later, Kaili had been downright gentle.

Which had been half Bones' point. Get a young Fire-Worker who was *going* to be out in hostile bazaars some experience haggling after the not-quite-legal, in a place it wouldn't get anyone killed.

Just my pride. Ouch.

A rustle of silk sat down near her. "So, what brings you to my humble workplace today?"

Active interest, in Kaili's calm voice. Shane inclined her head. "You might have a customer."

"Might?" A huff of a laugh. "Oh, tell me more."

"Tace. Young - I'd guess fourteen, maybe fifteen. Green hair; at least it was yesterday. A lifter." Fair warning, after all. "Apparently, Tace's crew was on what's now Iceblades' turf. There's been at least one violent incident already."

"And you think he needs an equalizer?" Kaili didn't sound surprised.

"A holdout would be better," Shane reflected, fingers tracing the fine carving that turned the arm of her chair into a lion. "I don't know what Tace has in mind, but I'm not interested in escalating a fight. Still, from what I overheard, they just need a little breathing space so they can move."

"Always tricky, finding a new territory to roam." Kaili rattled glass marbles in the little dish she kept on her work-desk. Innocent little translucent globes, if you didn't have the trained elemental sense to pick up their sealed-in Workings. "You're not usually around street rats in the city. What's going on?"

"Do you know an Inspector Helleson?"

"Know *of* him, certainly," Kaili allowed. "He's never been in. Rather strait-laced fellow, say the little birds. Surprising."

Shane arched a brow.

"Please, you've met plenty of Orthodox escapees in the Army. You know how they usually go."

Yes, she did. Once they broke loose from the iron discipline of their home congregations, they floundered, trying to find their own moral compass. Many did. Some... not so much. They could be the best soldiers, or some of the worst.

"Word has it he's still country Orthodox to the bone," Kaili reflected. "Just loosened up enough to use a typewriter. I know you're out now, but don't tell me you plan to thaw an ice prince?"

"I should get you together with my aunt. You could both go on dates *for* me." Shane tapped her bracelet. "I have good medical advice that it's inadvisable to change major personal habits unless absolutely necessary." One of the things she and Marian had actually agreed on. Even if she had been interested in ending her oath, which she was not, juggling attempted dating *and* learning to get around blind was way too much stress. "Anyway, why would he need thawing? He seems-" not *fine*, she'd never hear the end of that, "-reasonable enough to me. New in town, yes, but reasonable."

"Well, from what *I've* heard, his partner's just pining into her beer about how painfully aloof he is," Kaili said archly. "Poor girl's done everything but plant a flag and streak in front of his apartment."

"That explains a lot," Shane mused. "Apparently, she thought I was trying to woo him away from her."

"Well, now, that proves the girl has eyes-"

"In the middle of a firefight."

Kaili paused, mid-stir. Huffed a thoughtful, considered *huh*. "Do you know, I suddenly think the young man may be doing the sane thing after all."

"If he's even thought about it," Shane shrugged. Helleson *was* Orthodox. He probably wouldn't think Freeport was serious until her father sent a go-between. Not that Kaili would have any sympathy for anyone still clinging to that ironbound an upbringing. "He hasn't acted like a guy trying to get out of being chased. More like-" *A young lieutenant, still worried he'll screw up even though he's seen combat already. Like Erastus was, once....* "More like, he knows he's still new, and he's trying to find his footing."

"Hmm. Well, I bow to the expert." Kaili cleared her throat. A silken whisper; Shane pictured her interlacing her fingers. "So what really brings you here?"

"Riparians with a bomb."

"Ah." Amused. "I'd wondered why the rumors were so confused. So you were in that mess, were you? Unlucky for Inspector Helleson."

Yet another dark gloss on the legend of the Redstone luck. Only this time, she didn't have *it's classified* holding her back. "Not that unlucky," Shane pointed out. "His squad's still alive." She rested her hands on her cane. "I want them, Kaili. Whoever helped them, whoever provided them components, whoever so much as looked the other way when they snuck through Customs. I want them."

She didn't raise her voice. She didn't have to.

Not a whisper of a shift in Kaili's stance. "You are discharged."

"They tried to blow up *my* city. I don't care if I'm discharged. I want these people to have an up close and personal encounter with law enforcement. Watch or military; I don't give a damn, so long as it happens."

Kaili breathed out, silk rubbing wood; evidently judging exactly how furious her client was. "Or?"

Shane shrugged. "If I get close enough, I imagine some of them might come looking for me."

"It's always possible," Kaili allowed. As if one of her long-standing customers setting herself up as a target was just another Tuesday. For some, it probably was. "But what makes you think the Foxes haven't cleaned out the whole cell already?"

Heh. That, Shane had thought through. "First, the Foxes weren't first on the scene. The Watch was. I don't know how much Stewart knows, but he is definitely playing catch-up. Second," and Stewart would probably scream about this, but the Watch had had to call in *zoo handlers*, it would be out in the reptile gossip already. "Helleson and I found a Water-Worked cobra."

"Interesting."

I thought you might feel that way. Shane leaned back in her chair, letting Kaili mull that over. *Skin and Water* dealt in exotic skins; Kaili knew as well as anyone the permits needed to bring even an ordinary cobra into the country. And the kind of people who could get around them.

"You know it's easier to ship skins than live animals, particularly venomous ones," Kaili noted.

"There are always people who want interesting pets." Shane lifted one shoulder, let it fall. "Or specific Workings - you can tell them it doesn't matter if the skin was Worked while it was still alive or not, and they won't listen."

Kaili coughed discreetly. "Probably because for some Workings, it does."

"The gruesome ones," Shane muttered.

Kaili didn't deny it. "Well. If I were you, I'd ask your good inspector if the Watch knows anyone who fits the bill." The shopkeeper paused, long enough for Shane to count three heartbeats. "Though it might not be so easy. If someone were to ask, I would say this feels like politics. Yes... very nasty politics. And the sort of person who's usually mixed up in that, won't have been arrested for anything as down to earth as reptile-smuggling."

Politics, hell. Most people's first reaction to things going boom inside Caldera was scream and run from the crazies. Or, if armed, scream and jump *on* the crazies. After all, they had to be Caldera's own lunatics. It'd been decades since outsiders had set off bombs in the city.

Decades aren't long enough. She knows something.

But Shane only nodded, and waited. If Kaili wanted to talk, she'd talk. If she didn't - anything she might say would be hearsay. Nothing the law could act on.

"So!" Kaili said brightly. "What else can I interest you in today?"

"Lunch, huh?" Callie eyed Allen's offering from a Silver Coast-style pizzeria; calzones stuffed with cheese and three kinds of meat, a lemon water, and a hefty salad on the side. Eyed the paperwork still cluttering her desk, shuffled it under various paperweights, and rose with a game smile. "Sure. Let's do the balcony."

Allen hid a grimace and followed. *Heights. Why is everybody in this city obsessed with heights?* Granted, going up was one of the few ways you could get away from most people, but damn it, Callie knew he didn't like empty gulfs of space.

She just thought he had to get over it. Ugh.

"Guess you haven't been fried yet." Callie dragged a patio chair as close to the railing as possible and sat down, breathing in the heat-wavery breeze. As who wouldn't, tasting that clean, clear air Air-Workings drew down from storm-height, carrying away volcano fumes before they could leach into concrete and fragile lungs.

"No." Allen might have said more, but looking at her gray face... Callie had barely been brushed by venom, but that was enough for anyone. He settled for keeping his chair as close to the wall as possible.

Callie frowned. "You're *not* going to fall."

"I know that, and you know that, but convincing my screaming nerves is going to take a lot longer." Allen glanced down at the street much too far below, and tried not to shudder. "So how's it been going?"

"Oh, I've been worse. I can't breathe right, like a flu that won't let go of your lungs. The docs say that's going to last another week. But it could have been a lot worse." Callie gave him a determined smile, and broke off cheesy pieces to nibble. "You're the one I feel sorry for."

Allen eyed her, considering that. "Why?"

"Why?" Callie echoed in disbelief. "She's a *Flame*."

"Which definitely puts her on the list of scariest people I've ever met, but outside of that...." Allen shrugged. "What have you got against Fire-Workers?"

Callie's hand dropped limp to the table. "You're kidding, right?"

"Would I ask?" Allen frowned. "You don't have a problem with Lieutenant Aster. *Do you?*

"Yeah, well, he's just a Master." Callie said grimly. "She's a

Flame. Elementals are different."

"They're more powerful," Allen started.

"Yeah, sure, whatever. I'm not talking about power. They're *different*." Callie regarded her half-eaten lunch with a baleful glare. "I know, I know, you Orthodox types think they're blessed, they hung the moon and stars...."

"No, that was definitely the Sunlit Lord's work," Allen said wryly. "It's a little more complicated than most people think?"

That got a blink, and a slightly softer glare. "Complicated as in book verses and prayer breakfasts that need extra-strength coffee to keep your face off the table?"

"More that there's a difference between blessed and *gifted*," Allen said judiciously. It was an easy mistake to make; Sunlit knew enough people in his own home congregation had made it. "Elementals are humans gifted with great power. They're still as mortal and sinful as anyone else. But they deserve respect, and care, because they're more burdened than the rest of us with the ability to shape the power of the universe. And we want them to shape it to mend the world, not mar it."

"Still mortal," Callie muttered. Shuddered. "No, partner. Not the way you think. Mortal, sure, they die if they're killed... but they're not really human anymore. If they ever were."

"Why do you say that?" Allen asked neutrally.

"Because I've seen what they can do, all right?" Callie burst out. "My cousin dated a Flame. Bastard by the name of Charleson. He liked her; it wasn't mutual. When she broke it off, he *seared her to a crisp*." Her knuckles were white, tomato sauce dripping off her fingers. "We sat by Lisa's bed for days, hoping she wouldn't wake up. She didn't." She shot an angry glare at him. "*That's* what Fire does to a guy. Maybe a few Masters, like Aster, hang onto what makes 'em human. *Maybe*. The rest of 'em? They're *walking weapons*, Allen. It's all they're good for. It's all they love. And now they've got one roaming around the city that can't even *see?* They should have put her down like a dog."

Allen stared at his partner, horrified at the bone-deep venom eating into her Spirit. He'd known she was upset. He'd known she bristled just being near Shane. This? He'd never imagined this.

I've seen people kill for less.

Time to ease this illness. "That's horrible." Because it *was*, no one should suffer like that. But.... "Callie. Redstone's never met any of us before. She didn't have anything to do with your cousin." He paused. "She saved your life yesterday."

"So?" Callie shrugged it off. "If a snake bites the guy who was going to shoot you, it's still a snake. You don't pick it up and cuddle it. You kill it."

"Redstone's not Charleson," Allen argued. "Her sense of humor bites as bad as our coffee, but she seems - decent. Reasonable." He paused, and added, "Sane." *Like you're* not *acting, right now.*

"Just wait," Callie predicted, toying with a particularly bitter mid-rib of lettuce. "First time you tell her something she doesn't want to hear? I'll be picking my partner up from the morgue in a paper bag."

"Fine," Allen snapped. "If that's what you think, answer me this. Captain Stewart hates her guts, and the feeling is definitely mutual. Why is he still alive?"

"Flames are impulsive, murderous bastards, but they're not stupid," Callie snorted. "Kill an average civilian? Oh, that's just self-defense, sorry. Kill somebody with rank? Way to get a team of Waves assigned to freeze you solid, and shatter you into little pieces."

"*Impulsive* is the last thing that woman is." Allen leaned forward, worried. Callie was no serious Worker, not even a Journeyman; she just had a trace of Earth she put toward reading footprints better and sometimes tracking suspects to the last place their shoes had picked up dirt. If she didn't understand this much about high-level Working, they had a *problem*. "It takes patience and discipline to get that skilled. You don't throw that overboard just because you're having a bad day."

"That's what you think." Callie crossed her arms, hugging herself.

"Look. Partner. I know you're used to reading people. You're used to *knowing* when someone wants to cut out your heart and eat it. *You can't count on Spirit-reading.* Not with a military Flame."

He wanted to deny that. Everything he'd seen about Redstone said she was stable. Sane. Mostly, anyway.

But she slipped and slid around his Spirit-sense like a prickly ghost. And she was an Elemental. He knew, probably better than most Watch, what that meant for a person's control over their own Spirit. Not to mention, that very practical *stability* reminded Allen of too many people he knew back in Waycross, and things he hoped Callie never had the bad luck to see.

Waycross, after all, was a very peaceful town. Everyone knew that. How it stayed peaceful....

There were reasons he'd decided to join the Watch.

If Redstone decided I needed killing, I might not see it coming.

"If the Flame doesn't kill you, she'll get you killed. Do what the captain wants, but keep her as far away as you can." Callie reached out for her lunch again, swallowed, and gave him a tired smile. "Week or so, they'll clear you, and you can just disappear." A snicker, as she chewed. "It's not like she can come looking for you."

You'd be surprised. But Allen kept that thought to himself. Callie had made up her mind, and the past few months had taught him his partner wouldn't change it without overwhelming evidence. Not about people. Cases, she was flexible, or she'd never have made inspector in the first place. But people? She trusted you, or she didn't. No gray area.

Must be a comforting way to live.

And... that was why he'd liked Shane's company, Allen realized. The Flame hadn't given him any grief about looking out for Tace. Hadn't given the little pickpocket any serious grief, either, though he *knew* she knew exactly how Tace made her living.

It was funny. In an odd, dry as the Book's deserts way. Most people thought if you grew up in a priestly family, you saw everything as black and white. And for a lot of people, the ones who could call up faith like a fountain and believe their hands would heal... for them, that worked. But the *good* Spirit-Workers he'd known, the ones who'd made him believe life on the Watch wasn't a waste of his gift....

Scripture said any sin could be forgiven, if the sinner truly repented. *Any.*

If you were truly going to save souls, you had to take a little gray with you. Good and evil. Or *nobody* would be saved.

Callie slugged down more lemon water. "So how's the cold case work with Sanders going?"

"It's going," Allen acknowledged, thinking of boxes upon boxes of leads gone cold. The paper cuts might be more lethal than Worked venom. "I've got places to check out, interviews to follow up on. The usual."

"Not exactly the thrill of the hunt, huh?"

I don't know, Allen mused. *Would you think watching Fire dance was thrilling? Or just terrifying?* "Boring or not, I'd better get back to it-"

"Helleson!" a familiar voice barked.

"-After I fill in the captain," Allen finished, without missing a beat.

Close one, Callie mouthed, miming wiping sweat off her brow as the captain closed the balcony door again, mollified. "So. You want to grab dinner tonight?"

"I was up at four chasing leads, who knows where I'll be tonight-" He stopped at Callie's stormy look. "What?"

"Would you make up your damn *mind?*"

Okay, this was... odd. "About what?"

"You know what." Callie eyed him like a fish that needed filleting.

Allen counted to five, silently. There was apparently something he'd done, or not done, that had never been listed in the Academy handbook. Argh. "If I did, I wouldn't ask. What?"

"Hopeless." Callie crushed wrappers in her fingers, sashaying inside.

Utterly confused, Allen finished his water, tossing bits of crust to an ambitious blue jay. "Did any of that make sense to you?"

Tilting its head, it cawed at him.

"Same here."

Well. At least he could tell the captain what he'd found. And hadn't.

One more breath of peace, and Allen stepped inside-

And almost ran into a sympathetic-looking Rosa. "For you."

Surprised, he took the memo. Looked a little long, unlike the usual shell message.

Shane Redstone.

She called? he thought, startled. *Did she find something? What could she have found? She said she wasn't going to poke around anywhere dangerous-*

No, she'd said she wouldn't do that *alone*. Who knew who else Redstone might have dragged in?

Rosa coughed politely before he could unfold the paper. "*Velvet and Caramel?* Good chocolates. In case you were wondering what to do."

"I don't know; haven't asked Redstone if she likes chocolate... what?" Allen added at her startled look.

"It's not good for a guy to talk about other ladies that way, when someone he's *close* to is upset," the secretary said pointedly.

Allen blinked. And saw just a glimmer of red. Sunlit, was that what this was about? Of all the outrageous, forward-! Granted, people in the city were loose about propriety, but Callie hadn't even hinted that she wanted him to meet her parents. Which was good, because if she ever had, he would have had to walk right into the captain's office to be reassigned. An upright officer of the Watch had to avoid even the *appearance* of impropriety. "Redstone is oathbound. She's no lady." Thank the Lord; one woman he did not have to worry about *hunting* him. "And Freeport's my *partner*, Rosa. You know the regulations just like I do. Who's saying we're anything else?"

Rosa's brows bounced up. "Guess I'll have to put some people straight, then."

Allen grinned at her, relieved. Rosa could take the gossip-mongers with one hand tied behind her back. "You're the one who deserves chocolates."

"Pish. Almonds *and* nougat. Remember that." With a wink, she headed back to her desk.

Shaking his head, Allen unfolded the note. Stared at it. Read it again.

Someone political who might have an interest in exotic pets? Not exactly going to narrow things down.

But fires, it was a place to start. And he knew just who to go to. Records was a cramped but necessary part of every Watch organization, and archivist Nick Glass was more than happy to see people with unusual information requests. Especially if said people brought snacks.

And heck, he had to go out anyway. Whatever Callie's problem might be, he didn't know; he *hoped* it wasn't what he thought. But Rosa *definitely* deserved chocolate.

"Get as much sunlight as you can," Marian had advised Shane before she'd left rehab.

Shane had tried not to grimace. "Marian, I can't-"

"I know you can't see it," Marian had said with strained patience. "But your mind still gets some information from your eyes, enough for your body to know the sun's there. Spend too much time in the dark, you'll get depressed - and if you ever want to live independently, you can't let yourself get sucked down. Understand me?"

"I hear and obey, oh wise oracle of medicine," Shane had said dryly. "But don't expect miracles. I can't stay out all day. I burn."

"No kidding," the doctor had finally laughed. "You should have been a redhead...."

It definitely would have made things easier, yes, Shane thought now, leaning back against a boulder in Icerock Park. Centuries ago, a Wave's glacier had tried to quench Caldera's volcano the hard way. It hadn't worked, but melting ice had carried all kinds of erratics over the rim of the crater, leaving incongruous bits of granite and limestone scattered over and through volcanic soil. *People expect a redhead to be Fire. Blonde, they think Air. Or Spirit.*

Which the Black Flag had used to the Army's advantage in the past. Shane had been assigned to teams that *needed* to be underestimated, whatever the mission was; to places that saw her and thickened Earth and Spirit defenses, never dreaming of the volcanic force that cut through them like butter.

She wondered if Helleson had really thought about that. He'd probably sent to death people with far less slaughter to their name.

You did what you had to do. You saved *lives, you know that. Our missions broke up a dozen offenses before they could get started - ended countless skirmishes before they could become a war. There are people alive today, here* and *in half a dozen other nations, who wouldn't be if you hadn't stopped a lot of enemies dead in their tracks.*

Shane knew that. It was cold comfort. She was a Flame, she was needed....

And here she was, lounging in the sun like a lazy recruit, useless. *Stop that. You were wounded. You need rest.*

But for what? Oh, she could still Work Fire - still summon and control forces that turned lesser men white. But without sight....

Deliberately, Shane closed her eyes, and listened. Birdsong. People walking by, dragging out lunch just a little longer in the greenery. Kids chattering, creaking metal of swings. The distant honk of steam-buses and warning beeps of construction cranes. A rustling of leaves near her; maybe a brown thrasher, maybe a squirrel....

Fire-sense reached out, tracing four legs, fluffy tail, and fur. Squirrel.

It's a start.

Fragile tinder, soaked with enough moisture to make it tricky to light; fallen leaves. Rock behind her, open air around her, clover-covered ground under her feet. Not far off, the gravel of a path warmed in the sun, hotter than the soil underneath it.

So far, so good. What about the people?

Easier, and harder. They were warmer than air, alight with the low, controlled burn that fueled every living thing, in the higher pitch that said *warm-blooded*. Human was fairly easy to pick out; two arms, two legs, one head. Small versus large, likewise. Female versus male... well, some she felt sure of, others could have been anyone's guess.

Would I know Marian, if she walked up to me?

Probably not. Medium-sized female human, she might get. A specific person? She'd need more clues.

So how can I get them?

One calming breath, and Shane thumped her cane on the ground. Echoes, not as helpful out in open air as they were inside walls-

Wait a minute.

Another thump. She *listened*, focusing intently on fire-sense.

Not her imagination. It was small, it was slight - but the vibration of sound through earth *changed* its feel in fire-sense, compressing and expanding its resistance to heat.

There's a difference. A real one.

Hope leapt up; Shane banked it, carefully turning her attention from wild speculations of the future to this one *now*.

Again.

A subtle, defined ripple, like waves in a still pond. A ripple that *bounced*, as water did, off objects lighter or more solid.

If it acts like water.... Standing up from her borrowed rock, Shane listened for the chuckle of one of the park's many streams, and headed for the pond that had been marked on her map.

Quiet quacking of ducks, under the many conversations of fellow park visitors. The wet, marshy smell of cattails and duckweed, and a dozen other plants she couldn't name. Most of all, the loose fluidity of water, sucking up heat-sense like a black sponge, only flashing warmer where something interrupted the surface; leaves, birds, the minute flecks of mosquitoes hatching out.

Shane slapped the sting of a bite, grumbling under her breath. *At least I'm up to date on all my Healing. Hate to catch a bug just being out for a walk.*

Walking to the pond's edge, water's cool inches from her feet, Shane thumped her cane down again.

It does *ripple.*

Even in water, the heat-wave moved; black lightening to dark gray, compressing to ebony that would drink up heat. Air, water, earth - all of them shifted, and she could almost *see* it.

Knuckles white on her cane, Shane grinned fiercely. *This is it. This is what I've been looking for.*

It wasn't sight. It wouldn't let her pick out an enemy uniform-

I don't care. I don't care, *damn it - it's something! Targets* later. *If I can just walk, just* move, *and not run into people, or manholes, or rivers... it's* something!

"Whoa! Miss, you're going to fall in-"

Hands on her shoulders. She *moved.*

Don't kill him, probably just a civilian-

Shane shoved the unknown clear, halting the move before it did injury, squishing sideways along the marshy shore. Turned, once she had enough distance, glaring through her glasses. "I don't need help. And I *don't* like to be touched."

"Okay, okay! Man, touchy...."

Shane felt the heat of the stranger's body retreat, and swallowed, calming her frantic heart. *I didn't see him. I didn't sense him.*

Hadn't heard him, either, far too focused on the sense of Fire rippling out in front of her. This was going to take some work.

I need to find someplace quieter to practice.

Sane. Sensible. Yet something in her rebelled against the thought of retreat, snarling like a wounded lion at bay.

You know what happens to a lion that charges a full hunt.

Oh yes, Shane knew. But it didn't make her *feel* better.

One step at a time, the Flame told herself bluntly. *Figure it out indoors first. Get to where you can move around Jehanna's apartment without tripping over a rug.* Then *add distractions. They don't teach you to shoot a rod on the battlefield. You start on the range.*

Right. Exactly. What she *should* do. Angry or not.

Breathe in. Breathe out. Move.

Straightening, Shane tapped her way back to the path. Checked her direction from the sun's heat in the sky, let herself have one growl of pure aggravation, and headed home. No matter what she wanted. Because this wasn't a mission, and it wasn't going back to normal life. This was survival.

And one of the first rules of survival was, *avoid unnecessary risks.*

The goal is combat readiness. The first step, is figuring out how to move. Without *getting killed.*

And if she had to stop every block to check the map again... well. At least she had a map to read.

I miss getting shot at.

If that wasn't a sad commentary on the day, she didn't know what was-

The bump was subtle. Casual. Even most Calderan pedestrians wouldn't have noticed. Blatant as a red flag for someone who'd moved through Aeolian bazaars.

Shane took a very great satisfaction in thumping the idiot over the head, and plucking her decoy wallet back. "Moron."

"Have you been saved?"

"No, I invested," Allen said wryly, politely pushing past the stunned gray suit handing out literature. "Have you told your children, begotten of your flesh and spirit as the First Son was of the Father, of their grim destiny to help mend this fallen world of Man?"

Younger eyes went wide. "Ah... I'm not married yet...."

"No? For shame! Quit this sordid street and go unto the houses of godly women, there to seek a father's blessing," Allen scolded the alarmed young man. "How can you minister to those mired in sin and veniality, if your own house is not in order?"

"Er - I think - what...?"

Snickering under his breath, Allen skipped up the steps of the church. *When in doubt, confuse them.* "Father Jacobsson?"

"Inspector Helleson." The elderly minister regarded him with a distinctly jaundiced air. "I don't suppose you had anything to do with why poor young Samuel out there just dropped his collection bowl?"

"He could use a few more theology classes," Allen said frankly. "Rhetoric wouldn't hurt either."

Father Jacobsson scowled. "Your father would never use his training to confuse a malleable young man."

That's what you think. "My father also wouldn't leave a *malleable* young man to debate every heretic on the street," Allen said bluntly. "You don't take trash iron into a fight for lives and souls, Father. You take the finest steel." *Sometimes I really hate you, Dad.*

Coming to Caldera City, he'd been sure he wouldn't meet anyone who knew his family. So far, he'd been right. No one knew them *personally.* What he hadn't counted on was the reputation the Hellesons had among the Orthodox ministry.

Which, in a way, is even worse *than them knowing Dad.*

Worse, because every Orthodox clergyman he'd met so far thought he knew what the most reverend Fathers Helleson, all of them, would preach. Most of the time, they were right. *Most* of the time.

"But this isn't about whether or not I show up for church on holy days, or who I scare into showing up more often," Allen went on. "This is about Marcus Wright."

"Ah, yes. That poor soul." Father Jacobsson sighed, heading up the aisle to one of the front pews. Brushing off a speck of dust, he seated himself on worn purple cushions. "Three years this Leafturn... tell me, Inspector. What are the odds that the perpetrator of this grave crime will be caught?"

Allen met his gaze. "Do you want me to be honest?"

"That bad, is it?" The reverend frowned. "Well. The Lord's justice will be done; in the next life, if not in this one."

Allen shook his head, thinking of far too many unnamed graves. And one that had a name, back in Waycross, even if everyone else in fifty miles seemed bound and determined to forget it.

What Holwood was doing was wrong. What my father and Uncle Micah did to stop him... wasn't right either.

And the law in Waycross wasn't interested in stirring up that hornet's nest. Everything had been handled. Why start trouble?

Because it wasn't just. And one day, I'll find a way to prove it.
"Don't give up on this world just yet. You never know when reexamining the facts will lead a new direction." Allen took out his notes. "Marcus had been at evening service earlier that day?"

"Yes, he was," Father Jacobsson obliged. "I know I've told this to Inspector Sorenson, when he first investigated the death."

"You did, but given that Inspector Sorenson unexpectedly passed away two weeks ago, I'd like to reaffirm some of the details in his notes," Allen said matter-of-factly. All true. But there was another reason.

"The death"? Not "the murder"?

Like it or not, he was a Helleson. He knew all about the careful use of words.

Reaching out with Spirit-sense, Allen searched for truth. "While he was here, did he have any arguments with anyone?"

Father Jacobsson choked. "In a *church?*"

"It happens," Allen allowed. "Among true believers, more often than any of us might like to think. Scripture *is* open to interpretation, and when we hold strong beliefs, discussing them can lead to a certain amount of ill feelings. The holiest of us can fall to pride in defending our personal faith. So - were there any? Even a disagreement no one thought was truly serious, that people would have laughed about it tomorrow," he added. *Give him an out.*

"No, nothing like that." Father Jacobsson folded his hands together. "He was a fine, upstanding, charitable member of our congregation. No one ever had any complaints."

Truth-and-lie. Which, if Allen was any good at reading his element, meant that if nobody'd had complaints, they'd sure as fires had *reason* to have them. But what? "A good man, then."

"Far better than most will ever know," the reverend said piously.

He knows something.

That wasn't from Spirit-sense. The sense of his element was only giving *believed-true, believed-lie,* and shades in between, plus subtle hues of how strongly Jacobsson felt about each partial truth. No; this was hard-earned experience from years as an investigator, teasing out what people didn't know they knew.

As his Academy instructors taught, there *was* a good reason to poke into cold cases now and again. Most of the time a murder went cold because those who knew weren't talking. But silence ate at a person. Not a Spirit-reft soul; they could murder all the years of their life, if no one sensed them, and die with a smirk on their face. But an ordinary, decent person, with any kind of a conscience left? Yeah. It ate at them.

That, and most people just weren't, by nature, half as tight-lipped as a particular Strike Specialist. Conversation, the web of society, was part of their sense of self. They *had* to talk about who they knew, what they'd done, what they'd seen. *Had* to. *Especially* if it was supposed to be a secret.

Jacobsson knows something. It's getting to him. But is he ready to talk?

Time to back off. Ease up the pressure. Circle around, so the man didn't see it coming. "I'm sorry I had to ask," Allen said humbly, sitting down beside the Father at a respectful distance. "It's just- Well, how should I put this? Forty-eight, in good health, a steady job as a candle-maker and carver, but no listing of children having been notified? No wife? Just a cousin, for next of kin?"

For a good Orthodox man, that was very odd. And Father Jacobsson knew it. And while the good Father might not have seen fit to point out that discrepancy to Inspector Sorenson, he knew a Helleson would never let it lie.

"Marcus was a widower." Father Jacobsson's shoulders eased. "He married, perhaps a bit too young - but they were very much in love. They lost their first child, and were advised to wait before trying to conceive again... I hope you understand why I wouldn't have mention-ed this to Sorenson? Not to speak ill of the dead, but-" The reverend's eyes flicked toward the rod under Allen's coat, as if he still couldn't believe it was there. "The man's belief was not, perhaps, as strong as it should have been, for one bound to uphold the laws of our nation."

Translation, Inspector Sorenson was Reform instead of Orthodox, bordering on out-and-out agnostic. Allen remembered the Watch wake; not much religion, but plenty of shared grief for a good man. Wasn't that what faith was supposed to be about? "So they asked your blessing on avoiding conception while she healed... I know this is indelicate, Father. I just want to be perfectly certain of the facts, so no one needs to stir up more grief for the family."

"Good of you to think of them," Father Jacobsson said, sarcasm lurking under the words like a puma in the high brush. "I gave it, of course; the church is far better served by a family well and whole, than a grieving widower with only one baby - even if such tragedies show the kindness of the faith, as our people draw together. But in the end, it didn't matter. She was killed only a few months later. An *accident*." He stopped, and visibly composed himself. "They called it an accident, at least."

"What happened?" Allen asked carefully.

"What happened? The steel mills! All those Fire and Water-Workers with no element gifted in their souls...." Father Jacobsson shook his head. "There was barely anything left for a proper burial."

None of this had been in the files. Allen's nerves prickled. "So Marcus might have carried a grudge against the industry?"

Jacobsson bristled. *"He* might have-? The man was *murdered,* Inspector!"

"Love and hate," Allen shrugged. "If it's not sex, drugs, or something illegal - and you *said* Marcus was a good man - that's the kind of thing that gets otherwise harmless people killed."

"It was a *mugging."*

"It's a cold case." Allen leaned forward. "Even if it was a mugging, investigating it like one hasn't worked. So we look into other options. No matter how unlikely." He waited a breath. "Did he hold a grudge?"

Father Jacobsson's brows knotted, as if he'd like to smack the back of Allen's knuckles with a blackboard pointer. "He was a good man. He sorrowed, and he mourned his wife, but he bore malice toward no man. He dedicated himself to purity, charity, and good works."

A sense of *gray,* on that last. *Something Jacobsson doesn't think is good? Something he* does, *but he knows I wouldn't?* "Odd target for a mugger, then," Allen observed, sitting up. As if that oddness were just a matter of intellectual interest; rare meat to a mind that prided itself on analyzing the sinner's heart. "A charitable soul."

"Who knows how evil men choose their victims?" A gracious wave of a hand. "But then, that is your job. Is it not, Inspector?"

"We do what we can." *And you never answered my question.* "Do you remember who he spoke with, before he left that night?"

Sighing, Jacobsson fished in his memory for names, places, snippets of conversations. All of which tallied with Sorenson's original notes, so far as Allen could tell. Which was interesting all by itself.

Eyewitness memory changes over time. Unless he wrote it down after it happened, and re-read it to keep the memory fixed - there's no way he should give the exact *same story. But he made sure he would.*

He's leaving someone out.

Yet there didn't seem to be any tension in the reverend's story. No hesitation before certain names, none of the myriad little clues an average, unpracticed liar should have given, before mentioning someone who might yet be able to contradict his story.

Marcus Wright did *talk to someone else. Someone no one in the congregation knew was there. No one but Father Jacobsson, and Marcus....*

And the killer?

"I'll have to interview them," Allen let his pencil scratch, as if making a perfunctory note. Lifted his gaze to the reverend's. "Of course, it'd be a lot simpler if you'd just give me the name of whoever wasn't, officially, here that night."

It took Father Jacobsson a few seconds to catch all the implications. He reddened. "How dare you accuse me of uttering falsehood in the house of the Lord!"

"The Lord's house, technically, is over there," Allen jabbed a thumb toward the screened altar and its undying light. "That's a useful rhetorical trick, accusing me of something I didn't actually say. By such small distinctions is many a *good* Orthodox man's conscience soothed." He let his gaze harden. "You've read his sermons and theological treatises. But you should really talk to my father sometime. There's a good reason he wants me as far away from doubting souls as possible."

A reason with a properly carved gravestone marked *Holwood.* Proper grave, proper coroner's report, proper Watch investigation into a death unattended by a physician that *properly* marked the cause of death as self-inflicted wounds.

Physically self-inflicted, Allen believed. Whose will had been behind the hands... everything he'd been taught about Spirit said it should be impossible to force someone to take their own life. *Should be.*

All he had was the memory of grim looks as the clan elders held discussions a young boy would never get to hear. And the fact that there was not one record of the spirits twisted by Holwood's Working; some of which had been properly healed with only a few days' treatment at Helleson hands, others whom had needed looking after for years.

No records. But everyone *knew*.

"Do *you* doubt, Father? I think you do. Or you wouldn't leave clues for me to find." Allen let his voice gain an acid edge. "Don't worry. Your congregation's not about to disown you. I don't think your unnamed person was a prostitute. All you're probably involved in is *murder*."

Blood drained from Father Jacobsson's face, left him shaken and pale. "I would never be involved in anything that would lead to the death of innocents!"

"Another small distinction," Allen observed, with the same prickling anticipation he felt before he clicked on the handcuffs. "Define *innocent*."

The reverend's fists worked, as if they wanted to clench. "Why, you-"

"You don't think *Marcus* was innocent."

Blood rushed to pale cheekbones again. "You insufferable, heretical-"

"You *don't* think Marcus was innocent," Allen cut across the reverend's words. "If you did, you'd be bound in good conscience, as a *believer*, to help us bring his murderers to justice." He paused. "But you aren't. And you haven't. Which means you don't believe Marcus was innocent - despite being a *good, charitable* man - and you don't think he was murdered." He stood, advancing on the man; one calculated step. "You think there was *reason* for him to die."

"There are reasons for many men to die." Father Jacobsson straightened his shoulders. "I have given you the names of everyone who was here that night. On that, I would stake my immortal soul."

Pushing wasn't going to get him any farther. Not today.

Let him have a night to sleep on it. "Thank you for your cooperation, Father," Allen said formally. "Associating with well-intentioned citizens like yourself is exactly why I joined the Watch."

Closed his notes, and headed for the door.

"I'll pray for your father," Jacobsson said darkly. "He undoubtedly needs it, given that his son may be spending a *very long time* in the purifying desert of stars." *If you're that lucky*, his tone implied.

"You do that," Allen said dryly. Stopped, just inside the great doors. "Oh, and Father? I recently had a valuable lesson from one of our soldiers on how a man can tell all the truth... and lie, just the same." He smiled tightly. "Have a good night."

And I hope you have nightmares.

Chapter Six

Footsteps; firm and steady, but hesitating at the door. "What on earth are you doing?" Jehanna wondered.

"Listening," Shane said frankly, tracing subtle ripples as heat changed with vibration. "And sensing."

"Hmm." Jehanna stood on the threshold of the living room; standard to the apartment for formal entertaining, though as far as Shane knew no one in their building actually used it for that. A couple down the hall had looms set up in theirs. Some people painted, some sculpted, some had hobbies not fit for much thinking about. All considered the extra space worth every coin.

Jehanna's was for practicing kata. Shane had rolled up the soft mats for falling on and set them against the wall, standing in the center with her cane. Listening.

"Well," her aunt said at last, "you wouldn't be at this if you didn't think it would lead somewhere."

Shane tapped, and listened. "Part of heat is vibration."

"Is that right." Jehanna was silent for a long moment, obviously considering that from every angle. "You think you can do it. Sense, like an Earth-Worker."

"I think I can *try*." Shane held down hope with an iron grip. Inside four walls wasn't the whole world. One step at a time. "It's going to take a while. And Fire isn't Earth. They may never want me on active duty again if I *can't see*." She drew a breath. "But it's something. I know where the floor is. Where the walls are. Where *you* are."

"Do you." Heat *moved.*

Blind-fighting. Don't even try to look-

Shane stepped sideways, yanked Jehanna's reaching hand out into an arm bar, and spun her down to the floor. Hard.

"Point made," Jehanna huffed, breathless.

"I wouldn't want to try it on the street," Shane admitted. "Not without a lot more practice."

"Agreed." Jehanna got to her feet, dusting herself off. "I'm sorry I doubted you."

"I doubted me, too." Lying in bed between rounds of healing, the pain in eyes and heart too great to sleep without dangerous drugs... oh, she'd doubted. Long and often. A black pit of despair gaped open to swallow her if, if only-

I will not die. I will not yield. I will live, and so confound my enemies.

And one of these days, I'm going to find out who built that Spirit-blast, and I am going to kick *his* ass.

"So," Jehanna drew it out, feet shifting into a ready stance, "I was considering having company for supper tonight."

Great. Just great. Shane tried not to wince. "Oh? Who?"

A long breath. "Inspector Val Donovan."

Shane cast about for the name in memory. "Inspector Sorenson's partner?" There'd been a wake recently. She'd stayed home. The Watch didn't need outsiders leeching on while they mourned their own. That, she understood. "You have ulterior motives."

"I'm hoping she can shed some light on her partner's more obscure notes on the Wright murder," Jehanna admitted. "It's not just what you write down-"

"It's what you think about it when you write it," Shane nodded. Oof. Not as bad as shaking her head, but a nod on top of impromptu sparring wasn't fun. "Should I dress up?"

"Have you *ever* dressed up?"

"Out of uniform?" Shane smiled ruefully. "Not much."

"She's not that formal," Jehanna said after a moment. "Though it wouldn't hurt if you could find something a little less dusty."

Which was a polite way of saying Flame Redstone had been dragged over rooftops and through ashes, and probably looked every minute of it. "Noted," Shane chuckled. "Just let me clean up in here."

Jehanna exhaled. "You don't have to."

"I *know* I don't have to. That's the point." *Careful. Jehanna's not the one you're mad at. Sit on that temper, Flame.* "I *can* do it. So I will. Everything I can manage. I'm not *sick*, Aunt." Shane took a breath, let it sigh out. "Just blind."

Just. Evening Star, what a "just".

"Hmm."

Hands already on one mat, Shane let an eyebrow climb. "Have I told you you're scary when you're plotting?"

Jehanna chuckled. "And you aren't?"

"I've had less years to get into bad habits." Shane said dryly. "People keep making the mistake of thinking I'm salvageable." Braced on the curl of the rolled mat, she pushed, heavy fabric *shushing* across the floor. "So what's on what passes for your mind?"

"Well... we *could* just stick to having a girl's night in...."

"Or?" Shane asked, dreading the answer.

"I *could* invite that nice young inspector over for dinner, so you can terrify him some more. Who knows?" Jehanna's chuckle could have scared the flame off a firespout. "He may have found something."

Shane hid a groan. *Well, this is going to be awkward....*

Oh yes, Allen thought ruefully, seating himself at the Sanders' kitchen table after the ladies were properly settled. *This will be mortifying to the soul.*

Though not as bad as a formal Helleson holiday dinner. He hoped. After all, the table was smaller, meaning less of the icily polite arguments that boiled down to, *stop hogging the chili sauce, asshole.* And there were fewer people, which hopefully meant fewer egos to clash, crash, and burn. Best of all, no one here was actually related to him.

Still. It hadn't started well.

And by started, Allen meant *started*, from the moment he'd arrived at the door - a bit after Val Donovan, thanks be to the Sunlit Lord - and paid the proper grace to the lady of the household and the unmarried relative in her charge. Which had drawn a stifled chuckle from Jehanna, a blind glare from Shane - and a very dark look from Donovan.

Is it my flaw if I was raised to be polite?

Apparently so. Trying to pull out a chair for Inspector Donovan had been another bad idea. He wouldn't dream of doing so for the head of the household, of course, and he had enough self-preservation not to even try for Redstone; she'd probably memorized half the place to get around, and it would be cruel to tamper with that. But Donovan was a fellow guest-

And... truly not happy with him, as her look darkened further.

He'd stuck to a silent grace before the meal, trying to salvage *something*-

"For that which we are about to receive, may we be truly thankful," the Flame intoned formally. "And Sunlit? Let it not be slugs again."

Which brought Allen out of his contemplation with a quiet *Amen*, just in time to catch a flash of morbid fascination on Donovan's face. "Slugs?" the older inspector asked warily.

"Sorry," Shane said after a moment. "Old habit." A wry smile tugged chapped lips. "You can find some pretty out-there drill sergeants."

Which, Allen recognized, was yet another answer that wasn't really an answer at all.

I'd lay good odds she has *lived on slugs. And not because of boot camp.*

The way she'd handled Tace, the way she handled herself....

If she had white hair, I'd swear she was Angharad reborn; off to talk to dragons for the very first time, when everyone swore she'd be fried to a crisp.

Yet that heroine of old had striven onward; following what everyone claimed was divine guidance to find a way to save the Chosen People, though she had no Spirit-gift at all.

In her burned hands she'd brought back the first elemental pearls... save one. That, she'd carried in her heart.

The first made Fire-Worker. The Slaves of Ba'al never saw it coming.

Though Allen was sure Redstone would never call herself a legendary hero. Even if he did think she had the guts to talk to dragons.

But she was *strong*. Strong, and proud, and enduring as ancient oak.

Yet Donovan's eyes on her, as the Flame carefully maneuvered fork and cup, were only full of pity.

Jehanna glanced at her guest, and cleared her throat. "How are you holding up?"

"I'm... holding." Val looked away from Shane. "Some days better than others. Mostly just - numb." She shook her head. "Leslie doesn't want to see me."

"That happens," Jehanna murmured.

Leslie, Allen recalled. *That'd be Leslie Sorenson. The inspector's wife... widow, now.*

"Michael's... dealing with it. With me."

"That happens, too," Jehanna nodded. "Partnership isn't marriage, but it needs to be mourned. Men seem to accept that when it's them, but-" She shrugged, and smiled at Allen. "No offense. It's just something I've noticed over the years."

So that'd be Michael Donovan. Val's husband. "Not sure I can help you there, ma'am," he said politely. "It's just different."

"I think it has to do with who you leave behind," Shane mused, handle of her fork catching a glint from the overhead Spirit-lamps. "You go off on adventures, and those you love are supposed to wait, hold the line, and hail your return. Not get tangled up in adventures of their own, with their own pain."

Val actually jumped.

What, did you forget she was there? Allen leaned back in his chair, dryly amused. *She's blind, not deaf.* "Sounds better than a lot of explanations I've heard."

"I wouldn't call Watch work a silly *adventure*," Val said darkly.

"Nothing silly about adventures." Shane carefully set her water down, a barely perceptible thump on the tablecloth. "You're usually wet, cold, hungry, bored, and terrified. Often, all at once."

Val's mouth worked, as if she wanted to snarl denial of the Flame's right to claim any such knowledge of the savageries of life. But her gaze fell on the chain around Redstone's throat, and she pressed her lips together.

Allen bit back a grimace. *Don't know how you can act like that around* any *wounded veteran, much less a Flame-*

That thought stopped in its tracks, as Allen almost choked on the chicken.

The captain didn't know Jehanna's niece was a Flame, until she landed in our investigation. Jehanna didn't talk *about it.*

Does anybody *on the Watch know she's even a Fire-Worker? Besides my squad?*

Well, his and Lieutenant Aster's. But his squad had been ordered not to mention it, and he'd bet Aster had gotten the same. And Val Donovan was a Journeyman-level Air-Worker, not someone who'd sense the Fire sitting beside her. Val had no *idea* what she was looking at.

"I think the kids have it the hardest." Val picked up another shred of meat. "They want to go play with the rest of the family, and they don't understand why 'Auntie Leslie' doesn't want them around anymore."

"I could talk to her," Jehanna offered. "Or - have you asked Michael's sister? Anna, isn't it? It might come better from her."

"I didn't think of that. Thanks." And if that thanks was forced, no one at the table was going to complain; not with the pain in Val's voice. "It's just - it happened so *fast*. I walked around the corner for a minute, and-" She shook her head, voice flattening back into grief. "I never knew Saul was allergic to dark-twist wasps. I guess... he didn't know either."

Behind her mug, Allen caught Shane's sudden frown; there and gone, in an instant.

Why?

"You couldn't have known," Jehanna reassured the grieving inspector, voice firm as her hand propping Donovan's shoulder. "Most people never know about lethal allergies unless they've been stung before, and if there's not a good Spirit-Working doctor around...."

Allen listened to the rest with half an ear, surreptitiously watching Shane. Whose face held only sympathetic concern, now; nodding along with some of her aunt's words, otherwise silent.

"I heard you picked up one of Saul's cold ones," Val said at last, grief worn to numbness. "Any thoughts?"

"I'm not sure." Allen frowned at the remnants of his dinner. "What did Inspector Sorenson think of Father Jacobsson?"

"Stuck-up Orthodox prick." Val stabbed her fork down, screeching across the plate. "Talked a good line about charitable men and the sanctity of his congregation. Nothing that helped tell us why a guy who gave all his extra to the poorbox wound up on the wrong end of a knife." She eyed him, an acid fury in her gaze. "Did he like you any better, or did he rain fire and desert down on your head for dealing with the real, impure world?"

"Neither. Though if it makes you feel any better, he hates me even more than you," Allen said with forced lightness. "You're practically a pagan. I have strayed from the true path. A lot harder to forgive." He cast back in memory for what he knew. And didn't. *How much should I say?* "There's something he's not talking about. I just don't know enough to figure out how to pin him."

"Get out." Val laid her fork down, staring. "You've got a lead?"

Allen waved a hand; *so-so.* "I used some old-school rhetoric on him, and he twitched. He's hiding *something.* But I don't know if it has anything to do with the murder."

Val snorted, staring into the depths of her glass; she and Jehanna had both taken a bit of wine to accompany the chicken-noodle mix. Though Jehanna had only refilled her own with water. "Of course he's hiding something. Prim and proper and pure; that's what they'd *like* you to believe. Underneath the incense, they're as rotten as the rest of us...."

There was a lot more snarling in that vein, with Jehanna murmuring soothing words as she levered the bereaved inspector up and to the door. Left her there a moment, to whisper in Redstone's ear. Smiled at him, and then headed for her own coat.

The door closed. Allen breathed a sigh of relief-

"She'll walk Donovan home," the Flame said bluntly. "She wants to hear anything you found when she gets back." Her jaw clenched. "*I* want to hear it *now.*"

"Ongoing investigation," Allen said bluntly. "Not one you're involved in."

"Who the hell am I going to talk to?" Redstone bit out. "*Talk.* And talk *fast*, before I light your hair on fire for letting my aunt leave here with a possible assassination victim."

Allen stilled, sensing the cold certainty of that threat. *She's never threatened to burn me before.*

Then again.... "Say what?" Allen exclaimed in disbelief. "Sorenson died of natural causes-"

"Sorenson died of *anaphylactic shock*," the Flame said coldly. "Or so the Watch thinks. It's probably true; we have *good* coroners." Her fingers clenched and unclenched. "What do you know about dark-twist wasps?"

"They're not from around here?" Allen answered dryly. Caldera City had plants, animals, and who-knew-what from around the world. Watch orientation included an inch-thick book; *Sticks, Stings, Scratches, or Bites: Toxic Exotics on the Job*. Excellent color prints, very helpful in identification. Terrifying, but excellent. "They're from marshes, they cache caterpillars in some kind of poisonous plant. Any that got here probably came in a greenhouse shipment. And apparently, some people have a lethally bad reaction to them."

"They're from the Deltain Marsh," Redstone said flatly. "In *Riparia*."

He looked at her cross-eyed. "You're a professional paranoid, aren't you?"

"Dark-twists start as a parasitic sprout on a tree that's already been weakened by a marsh's rising water table," the Flame informed him. "They tap into the inner bark, feed on it, grow down to the ground, and eventually engulf the whole tree. But while they're doing that, they cheat. They sprout modified leaves, like little cups. The cups catch water, insects come for a tempting drink - and they never get out."

Parts of which Allen remembered, now that she'd brought it up. Though definitely not in that detail. What had Shane done, eaten the handbook? "They drown."

"They have help," Shane said dryly. "That water's laced with a neurotoxin from the leaves. And the reason I know all this is, in the field, you can improvise a pretty fair toxin from it. Perfect for lacing a water-bolt."

Allen swallowed. Water-bolts were lethal enough. What kind of vicious person added anything more? "They had a cobra for that."

"And almost all of them, hit with their own bolts, *died*." The Flame gripped her cane. "If it'd just been cobra venom, our doctors should have been able to save them. Your partner's still sick, and they barely grazed her. Is anybody checking what's really in her system?"

If they weren't, he'd make sure they did. "That's still a hell of a leap," Allen argued. "Sorenson would have had to be allergic, *and* in the wrong place at the wrong time when one of the bugs they brought in got loose and cranky-"

Fingers tapped dense wood. "You're assuming it was an accident."

"Well, you can't exactly make someone have anaphylactic shock *on purpose*," Allen shot back.

Shane was silent.

Allen stared into that stillness of spirit, feeling as if he teetered above an abyss of mortal evil. *You can't make someone allergic enough to die. You can't make a body betray itself.*

...You can't make someone kill themselves, either. Or so they say.
"Sunlit Lord, tell me you're kidding."

Shane blew out a breath. "Ever hear of the Thanes of the Needletooth Mountains?"

"Legendary Geistan cult of untraceable Spirit-Worker assassins." Allen tried to shrug. Not easy, given the shivers climbing his spine. "Supposedly some splinter sect of Ba'al. Everyone knows they're not real. Geist would have slaughtered half a dozen nations if they were."

"They're real," Shane said soberly.

They're real. Like, *the sky is blue.* Or, *fire is hot.* The gray-clad assassins of a dozen light-plays... were real.

If this is a nightmare, I'd like to wake up now.

"They don't have half the powers stories say. They can't turn invisible, they're stopped just as hard by Spirit-Wards as anyone else trying to short-jump through a wall, and they're not immune to Working. But they *are* real." Shane paused. "I've seen deaths like that before. The *perfect accident.* Unless you know the poor bastard next to you *loved* peanuts. Or shellfish. Or even, long back on a mission no one should know about, got stung by one of those exotic little wasps. All without so much as a rash."

"The bomb was Riparian and Pelean," Allen said. Not denying what she'd said, but - Sunlit. What was it like, living in a head that jumped to such dark conclusions?

What was it like, living in Waycross, knowing what you knew?

"I know it was." Shane stared blindly toward the hall, obviously itching to follow her aunt for a rescue - if she hadn't known damn well she'd probably end up needing rescue herself. "I just don't *like* it."

Neither do I. Put that together with his surety that Father Jacobsson was hiding something- Allen blew out a breath of pure frustration. Then, slowly, grinned. "Flame Redstone," he said formally, "how long has it been since you've attended services?"

She actually blinked at him. "Say what?"

Chapter Seven

"Couldn't you have left that at home?" Allen hissed under his breath.

"What, and let your reverend miss an excuse to be *really* angry?" Shane murmured back, smiling. As if the familiar weight of steel at the nape of her neck was nothing more than a bit of lace. *Besides, if you think I'm going anywhere near a potential assassination risk unarmed, you're the one who's insane.*

She had Fire, of course. She always had Fire. But a knife didn't jump out of her hands to cut up potentially innocent victims.

...Well, not unless she had some really creative Earth-Workers and a lot of prep time, first.

"Oh, this was a bad idea-" Allen cut himself off, as the congregation quieted and the priest read out the opening verses to the glory of clear skies.

Shane sat through it, relieved to be concealed in this back corner. Kept her head modestly down, hair covered with a simple brimmed hat; just another woman not currently confessed and fit to receive waiting through the formal call-and-response, the sermon, the passing of wine and bread. It wasn't that she didn't believe, though she'd had plenty of dark nights. Or that she thought ill of those whose belief *was* steady as the proverbial mountain, and bright as starlight. It was just, most of the time, her religious needs were covered by one simple prayer.

Sunlit Lord, let me not screw this up. And Evening Star, Handmaid of Mercy - if I do screw up, let me be the only one who pays for it.

She hadn't screwed up. That was the hell of it. She'd done it *right*.

But what she'd had to disarm would have needed a Flame, a Star, *and* a Wave to draw its fangs, and get everyone out alive.

I didn't have them.

Eyes closed, head bowed, she wished she dared weep.

Be strong. Helleson's counting on you. Even if he doesn't know it. He was raised Orthodox; this can't be easy for him.

And hey, at least they had good hymns.

Letting the music wash over her, Shane reached out with Firesense, combing lightly through the church. Not searching for anything in particular. Just searching.

Helleson thinks that Jacobsson's hiding something. And anyone who hides one thing, is going to hide more.

Wood. People. Thick stone, pierced with the high arches of stained glass windows, each depicting a scene from scripture. Shane felt the solidity of lead, the sun-spawned heat of colored glass, and noted with bemusement that she could pick out differences in the pieces.

I'll have to get someone to be eyes for me and go over them. See how much heat is due to color, and how much is just size.

Solid floor, but what felt like hollows beneath it. Which was only to be expected. They probably had several layers of basements. Storage, teaching rooms for the kids, crypts. Lots of crypts.

Give me a clean cremation any day. I don't want anyone poking around in my bones.

Not something everyone agreed with. Meaning you always *tried* to get bodies home.

If someone dies trying to get my body back, I'm going to be really *ticked off.*

A preference she'd made clear whenever the teams' talk turned to that darkness. Which wasn't often. Strike Specialists learned to acknowledge what could go wrong, and focus on making sure everything went right.

All the more ironic, that she'd come back.

The collection plate rattled around; the last farewell to sunset was sung. Shane surreptitiously stretched stiff legs. *Can't believe there are people who voluntarily do this every week. Helleson, you owe me. Big time.*

Now would come the real test, as the congregation filtered out and the inspector slipped out of the pew to snag his prey. Shane hid a smirk, and stood.

"Oh, my... do you need help, dearie?"

"No, thank you, ma'am," Shane said politely, cane in hand. *At the end of my pew, and - to the left? She was sitting further up, then.* "If it's too easy, it's not worth doing."

"Tch! I wish my Clara had your fortitude." A wheeze in the breath, as though the lady was just getting over summer sniffles. "Why, do you know, she broke her leg six months ago, and she still won't walk on it?"

"Some people's bones are different," Shane said frankly, not moving. She'd known a few people in the Army who could be up and around in a third of the time doctors advised; others who needed twice as much and more to heal. And they weren't malingering - though if they didn't transfer to a non-combat specialty, they were persuaded to leave for civilian life. "Have you seen another doctor? Sometimes a break can be more complicated than it looks."

A *tch*. "Now, now; the Sunlit Lord will provide-"

"The Sunlit tends to provide for the side with the heavy artillery," Shane said wryly. "Trust me on that one."

"...Oh." A hesitation. "Where were you wounded?"

Shane drew herself up straight, cane planted firm on stone. "Training accident, ma'am."

"Yes, one of those." An unexpected dry twist to the elderly voice. "My Peter was lost that way. Peter Wayland."

That name, Shane did know. "I've studied his-" *operations* "-

writings, ma'am. He was a good man."

"Oh, he was a rake, and an incorrigible flirt," the lady chuckled. Soft cloth *shush*ed, as if she straightened a knitted shawl. "But when he was home, he was all mine. And weren't the other young wives jealous, oh yes!" She laughed softly. "That was a long time ago."

"If he were here, ma'am, I'm sure he'd say you've only grown more elegant with time, Mrs. Wayland." Shane inclined her head.

"You're a Worker, then." The widow sounded pleased. "You're too polite to go with that face, otherwise."

"Yes, ma'am," Shane admitted with a smile. "Fire-Worker Redstone, late of your service."

"Oh, *my*." A swift breath. "Oh, how *awful* for you."

"I'm still here, ma'am." Familiar footsteps were heading her way, a heavier stride behind them. Shane kept herself from tensing; Helleson had to have a plan. "Don't worry; if you know your husband, you know we don't give up that easily-"

"What is *that creature* doing here?" Father Jacobsson's voice thundered.

The church went eerily silent.

"Father," Mrs. Wayland *hmph*ed, "that's no way to talk to one of our own."

"One who violates the will of Heaven could *never* be one of ours." Disgust heated Jacobsson's face; the same fury Shane had met in Waycross, and a dozen other places she never meant to visit again. "How *could* you bring that here?"

"Oh, I think he wanted to make your head explode," Shane said cheerfully. "How's that working?"

"You're a made Worker?" Mrs. Wayland stepped back, as if drawing her skirts aside. "But - you were in the *service*."

"She was," Helleson said bluntly. "And serves even now, Ma'am."

"Ba'al favors his children," Jacobsson snarled. "Fitting, that divine wrath has already struck you down - don't *touch* me, you heathen!"

"Don't, Inspector," Shane agreed, forcing down a red haze of *burn*,

burn the enemy, burn this place to the ground. "Don't give the hidebound bastard the satisfaction."

"You're right." Helleson's voice was very, very cold. "After all, it's *so* much more satisfying just to ask the right question." Power swept out from him; a moonlit goose-prickle down her nerves, a shiver of starry wind. "What's the name of the *heretic* that was here, the night Marcus Wright died?"

Silence.

"That's enough for me," the inspector said grimly. "Leave the hymnal, Father. We're going downtown."

Chapter Eight

"I can't believe you arrested a priest."

Seated on one of the two worn chairs behind Earth-Worked one-way glass, Allen gave Callie a wan smile. "Believe me, I'm not looking forward to the fallout. But he's got information on the homicide. That he's been sitting on. For *three years*."

"That's what gets to me." Callie leaned against the wall farthest from the door, watching the priest sit and pray. "Sorenson was good. How the *hell* did he miss Jacobsson holding out on him? Don't tell me it's just because you can truth-read."

"Something I'd like to know," Captain Mason muttered, stalking through the door. He carefully shut it, without so much as a thump.

"Sir," Allen nodded. "Simple. Terrifyingly simple. But if Redstone hadn't tweaked me the other day... Sorenson probably asked Father Jacobsson who was there that night." He grimaced. "Only to the good Father, heretics *aren't* a who. They're a *what*. They're *not people*."

"And that won't show up as a lie, even on a truth-read," the captain said thoughtfully. "Redstone?"

"Led me in circles without ever lying," Allen grinned. "She wasn't even being malicious. Just cranky. Which got me thinking about what else someone might be able to hide just by not thinking it was important enough for someone else to know. So I had to make Jacobsson care about what he knew. I thought if anybody would make a good Orthodox Father show his true colors, a heretic Flame would."

He sobered. "What I don't get is why, Captain. Marcus was a member of his congregation, innocent or not. Why lie? Especially if the person you're lying for is *just* a heretic."

"Good question," Mason nodded. "Going to wring it out of him, or are you going to make him sweat first?"

"Well, sir-"

Thump. "This damn well better be the right door," Shane's voice filtered through heavy wood. "Helleson. We need to talk."

Captain Mason opened the door before her cane could hit it again. "This isn't a good time, Flame Redstone."

"I know, but this won't take long-"

"Didn't the captain leave you upstairs?" Callie glared.

"He did," Shane said dryly. "Strain your public manners, Freeport, and give me a minute. Just one." She waved a hand Allen's direction. "How did Jacobsson know what I was?"

A Flame that wasn't an Orthodox believer? Allen frowned. That would have been obvious with just a few words. But- "We didn't get a chance to talk." And it hadn't been her *religion* that had set Jacobsson off.

A heathen made Worker. How in the desert did he know that?

"But the reverend jumped you two anyway? Well, obviously, he...." Callie trailed off, suddenly thoughtful. *"Huh."*

"Even if he has a strong Spirit-gift, which I doubt, you can't tell a made Worker from a born one. Not past Journeyman level. It *doesn't work.* The only way you can tell, on your own," Shane thumped her chest, "is to look for the scar."

"So somebody told him," Callie objected. But some of the heat had drained from her voice, washed out by speculation.

"Who?" Shane pounced. "I can count every person in this city who should know I'm a military Flame on two hands. You three. Aster's squad. Jehanna. Captain Stewart. Mrs. Wayland only knew I was a Fire-Worker, and Jacobsson didn't have time to talk to her before he started railing about heretics."

"People heading down to the lava knew you were a Flame," Allen objected. "Not to mention, the squad room saw you light up."

"I thought you left too easily... yes. Fire calls to Fire. Forge specialists would know I was a Flame, since I wasn't using gear to hide it. But not a *made* Flame." Gripping her cane, she spread an open hand. "How did *he* know?"

Good question.

"Sorry, Watch business, *you* understand," Shane muttered under her breath, stalking away from the station with a baleful glare that, from the feathery thunder of wings, made even the pigeons flee in terror. "Oh, you'll be sorry, Helleson, just wait...."

Blocks away and several creative curses later, she found an outdoor café, and gratefully sank into a seat. Put her head down on her arms, and finally let herself cry.

I thought I could be useful again.

Well. She had been. And now she wasn't. Again.

What do I do?

It was all she'd ever wanted, since she'd woken up at twelve with broken ribs - broken *everything* - no parents, a heart full of Fire, and only one living sister left.

Mom. Dad. David. Jennie....

All gone, along with so many other families. Only she and Barbara had survived that bomb.

"Workers are more resilient than the pearl-less," Shane had overheard one of the doctors arguing with Jehanna, after the world had swum back into focus. "It was her best chance."

"She could have died!"

"She was already dying, Inspector. She'll be regrowing bits and pieces of bone for over a year. One of the ribs stabbed so close to-" A sigh, and a rustle of papers. "Here. Sign this."

"But- this is-"

"She's *young*, Inspector Saunders. Much younger than our usual candidate. She'll adapt very well to the elemental force. If she applies herself, she stands an excellent chance of making Master." An exasperated growl. "Or can you afford the charges yourself? Unless they're paying you a lot more than me, I doubt it...."

She'd fallen asleep again, lost in the haze of drugs and Healing. But even at twelve, Shane had known enough to put the pieces together. A made Worker who couldn't pay went into the military. Always.

And that was all right. It was. Because there, she could find the kind of people who'd torn her family apart. Find them, and stop them.

And I did. I stopped so many. I was good *at it.*

She was good, and she was driven, and she was never home. It was easier that way. Jehanna had her hands full raising a child she'd never counted on, and Barbara - Barbara couldn't forgive her older sister for being alive, when their parents were dead. Alive, and a Worker.

"Give her time," Jehanna had always said. "She was young, she doesn't understand. Just give her time."

Shane had. Until the night eight years ago when suddenly there wasn't any more time.

I was out. On a mission. Didn't get the message 'til two weeks later.

Jehanna hadn't forgiven her for missing the funeral.

I was doing my job.

And now she couldn't. What else was left?

"Miss? Are you alright?"

"Life," Shane managed, wiping her eyes. Male, about six foot, heavy-set; heat-pattern muted by something not a skirt - an apron. Of course. "Just life."

"Sorry." A hesitation. "Are you going to order?"

I've been pounded flat and scraped dry. You think I want food? But yelling at an innocent waiter wouldn't solve anything. "I don't suppose you have hot chocolate?"

Fire burned a lot out of you, even if you weren't throwing fireballs every day. *When in doubt, treat yourself for shock.*

Shock meant thinking was numb and dulled. She had to take everything she thought she knew, and go over it again.

So. Apparently Helleson didn't need her, now that he had a new lead on a murder, instead of fumbling around hoping to run into more bombs or bombers. Who might not even exist, anyway.

I'm not going to count on that.

Sipping her chocolate, Shane considered fragments of suspicion. Water-Worked cobra, imported. Dark-twist wasp, sign of a dark-twist tree, also imported. And Kaili's feeling that this was political.

Money. That's what Helleson will chase.

Which was always a good angle. And yet... if Sorenson's death *was* related to his case, and Father Jacobsson *was* protecting a suspect....

Money doesn't drive that man. Hate and contempt - those, he'd lie for.

And kill for?

Hard to say. Shane ran her finger along the smooth ear of her mug. *He seems more the "go away unclean world" type than the old warrior-priests. But push him hard enough... well, push anybody hard enough, and who knows?*

How did he know what I was?

That was the gut-knotting question. If he knew, he'd been told; and given anyone Shane called ally wouldn't have mentioned she was a *made* Flame....

Then it was an enemy.

Given the vast majority of her personal enemies simply weren't *here* - Stewart being the exception, but he had more regard for his security clearance than to drop details like that without a life-or-death reason - then it was an *impersonal* enemy.

An enemy of Caldera.

Helleson would have gotten that far. He was an inspector, and definitely not stupid. Hence his razor focus on getting Jacobsson to crack like an egg, and *talk*.

But you didn't listen, damn it, Inspector. I tried to tell you why *he might know what I am. "Somebody told him," and you were off running - and damn it, that's not the bottom of the quicksand, you idiot!*

Telling a man like Jacobsson what she was, was a recipe for trouble, pure and simple. Meaning that was what the enemy *wanted*; an intelligent, well-respected man in the community, on the lookout for someone he impersonally detested. And willing to make a ruckus about it.

Someone wants to know where I am.

Sunlit curse it, someone *knows I didn't die.*

The letter she'd sent Bones wasn't going to get there fast enough.

Bones needs to know what I know. And... damn it, I need help. Before whatever they're planning blows up in my face. Or someone else's.

There was one sure way to get it. Shane stood, counted out a generous tip, and signaled the waiter.

"Ma'am?"

"I need a minute of your time," Shane said frankly, "and an address book."

It wasn't a long walk from the Watch station. Not surprising; a lot of near-adult delinquents got a choice between heading here, or spending a long time behind steel bars. Some of them even worked out all right.

Shane tapped her way into the leather and rod-smoke air of an Army recruiting office, listening to voices murmur as the officer on duty went over paperwork with a new recruit, his mother a hesitant but brave note in the background. "Be right with you," the officer called out.

Gruff, older male. A steady tone that made Shane relax without half thinking about it. Here was someone she could trust to watch her back, if everything went south. "Don't worry. I'm not going anywhere."

A chair scraped back; footsteps and body heat approached. "Redstone?"

I know that voice. An older, graying man in her mind's eye, still tough as Worked leather. "Sergeant Trillian?"

A pause. "Master Sergeant now, ma'am."

Meaning he'd added the cane, and the glasses, and knew why she couldn't read his new insignia. "Congratulations, Master Sergeant," Shane said soberly. Waved a hand toward the puzzled recruit and mother. "Keep going. What I need's a little complicated."

A wry grin lurked in that otherwise sober voice. "It always is."

In short order the master sergeant had papers signed and the pair ushered out the door, enlistment date firmly in hand. Let out a breath, watching them go; shut the door, and stepped carefully over her way.

"Knee still a problem?" Shane asked sympathetically.

"Least I still got one," Trillian said soberly. "Did I ever buy you a round for hauling my ass out of that mess?"

"You bought one for my team." Shane tried to smile. Couldn't, quite.

A quiet rumble of a sigh. "They're gone."

It wasn't a question. Yet it still needed an answer. "I can't talk about it," Shane said frankly. "But they went out the way they wanted to." She paused. "Except Terry. He always wanted to get knifed by a jealous husband."

"There's always one," Trillian agreed ruefully. "But you made it."

"I'm told the Sunlit Lord's saving me for hanging," Shane said wryly. Lifted a free hand, let it fall. "Theoretically, what would you get if you fit together a Geistan Spirit-blast with Pelean lava-hair and Caelian moon-crystals? With a few other assorted trinkets, just for fun."

"Hell of a lot of death," the master sergeant said soberly. "Though in theory, if you could rip out the Fire part, you *might* be able to duck the rest of it. Mostly."

"Mostly," Shane nodded. "Of course, it's just a theory."

"Of course." The master sergeant breathed a moment, probably studying her. "What do you need?"

"Help writing a light-letter for the Black Flag," Shane said bluntly. "It's Army business. Though she may not know that until *after* she gets it."

"Right this way."

Good, something was finally going right- Wait a *minute*. "You know I'm discharged."

"And you're on the list," Trillian stated, just as blunt. "Nobody wants to waste a striker's instincts, Flame." He huffed. "You think there's trouble? I guarantee, someone in Command wants to hear about it."

Months out, and she still hadn't lost the knack of writing up a brief report, Shane reflected, as Trillian laid inked paper down on the sending stone and pressed a Spirit-worked crystal over it. Half the nation away, a similar stone would be moving across blank paper, calling ink into place to match the bright and shadow its sister stone "saw".

Someday, they say, everyone will have light-letters; not just the military and high government muckety-mucks. Shane shook her head, dizziness or no. *That'll be a strange day, indeed.*

"It's sent."

"Thank you," Shane nodded.

"Heck of a story."

"A lot of gossamer and a few facts," Shane admitted. "I've just- This feels bad, Master Sergeant. Really bad."

"Don't know how much I can help, Flame," Trillian said gruffly. "I know how to take ground and get kids past the shakes enough to sign up. It's people like you who poke the bent leaves and triangulate a munitions dump nobody knew about." He cleared his throat. "But if you let me in on the guy who broke your heart, I can give him a hint that's not a good idea."

What-? Oh, for sunlight's sake. Shane lifted her left wrist, shook scaled steel. Seriously, Trillian was Army. If anybody should understand, *on a team with four guys, cannot be seen as available*, he should.

Only she wasn't now. And it hurt.

"Sure, sure; you make an oath, you keep it," the master sergeant grumped. "You're still young, Flame. You don't have to jump into someone's pants for them to skewer you in the heart."

The man did have a point. Still. "Nobody broke my heart." Shane pasted on a rueful smile. "Helleson's an inspector. Give him a choice between a solid lead on a murder, and chasing fragments that might not lead anywhere - I shouldn't have expected anything else."

"Helleson, huh?" Knuckles cracked.

"It's not what you think." Shane waved off the threat of imminent violence. *Really, really not what you think.* "Look, here's what's been happening the past few days...."

So she talked. And talked. Somewhere in the middle of that, Trillian got her a cup of coffee. Hot, dark, and salty; that was the problem with Watch coffee. No salt.

"No offense," the master sergeant said after she'd finally wound down, "but did you ever think of slowing it down a little?"

"There isn't time." Hands clasped on her cane, Shane blew out a breath. "Even if whoever they are didn't expect that bomb to be stopped - they have to know we're shaking the city upside-down for possible co-conspirators. Either that was all they had, and anyone associated is long gone, or-" She couldn't finish.

"Or whatever they've got is going to be bigger. And it's going to be soon."

"Yes."

"You're the expert." The master sergeant picked up a thicker rustle of papers; a city map, if Shane judged that quiet mutter about streets right. "Still. This may be your hometown, but you haven't lived here in years. *And* it's No Man's Land for you, if you're guessing right. You think it's a good idea to go prowling the city without a guide?"

He took a breath. "Would you do that in Riparia, Flame Redstone? Even *with* your eyes?"

"Not if I didn't have to," Shane admitted. "And I thought I had one." She shrugged. "Guess it was fun while it lasted... it's *hard*, Master Sergeant. If you can't look someone in the eye, if you can't see what they're looking at - they start talking without you, and you're lost. And not long after that, they forget you're even there."

A gruff chuckle, and papers slapped down on a desk. "I pity the civilian who forgets *you're* there, Flame Redstone."

"Yeah, well, I can't light them *all* on fire." Shane grimaced. "They didn't cover this in rehab. I should file a complaint. Plenty on how to walk, cross streets, and get directions. Nothing on how to talk the Watch into paying attention to you during an investigation."

"Obvious flaw in the system." Trillian shifted weight off his knee. "So how are you going to handle it? I'm going to guess you don't want to ask your aunt."

"I don't," Shane acknowledged. "She's got her own life. And... there are things she hasn't forgiven me for." She shrugged. "Somehow, *I was on a stakeout* excuses someone not being there in a crisis, and *I was on a mission under information blackout* doesn't."

"Not good," Trillian agreed. "And you don't have a guide dog because?"

"Ever see what a guide dog does when flames go off around it?" Shane said levelly. "Some reactions, you can't train out of an animal."

The yelps were all too sharp in her memory. As were the hissed whispers from the dog's trainer, telling the rehab staff that he'd train dogs for any other Worker, but he'd *heard* about this one.

Flames aren't supposed to come back blind. They're supposed to annihilate the enemy - or not come back.

At least the dog had been honest. Besides, she had a hard enough time handling her nightmares with just another human being in the apartment. A living thing that might jump on her unexpected and unannounced - the picture in her mind was all too gruesome. Granted, she didn't like dogs - too loud, too pack-oriented, too determined to be always *with* their person - but she didn't hate them *that* much.

"Too bad I can't lend you a handy private."

"Misappropriation of military resources and personnel," Shane stated, tongue in cheek. "Wouldn't be the first time that ended up in my file... but somehow, I suspect this time it would stick."

"Bean-counters back in command can be so unreasonable about pesky little things like that," Trillian *hmph*ed, just as wry. "Well. How about-"

A chime; Shane straightened, as the master sergeant stomped across the room. "Regular business?" she asked, heart racing despite herself.

"Not exactly." The grin was back in Trillian's voice, with the sharp edge of a man all too used to being shot at *again*. "Well. You lit a fire under somebody, all right." He crossed over to the front door, locking it.

"Master Sergeant?"

"Eyes Only," he chuckled. "Or ears, I guess. Just listen to this, Flame."

She listened. Took note. And occasionally, swore.

"...And remember, this is the year of the Azure Dragon, Riparia's got some kind of freak early winter going, and the *apparent* idiot on this list recently arranged to import a white tiger," Trillian finished. Scratched his head. "The hell?"

"Damn," Shane breathed. *Worse than I thought. Much worse.*

"Not good," Trillian guessed. "Anything you can talk about?"

If it'd been that classified, she wouldn't have gotten a light-letter back. Stewart would have; and he'd be here, and very cranky. "You could look it up in an encyclopedia," Shane snorted. "It's the destructive elemental cycle. The azure dragon is Air, winter is Water, the white tiger is Metal. Metal destroys air, air destroys earth, earth destroys water, water destroys fire. Caldera is Fire... and Caldera City is its center. Earth."

The master sergeant swallowed. "Fifth element's Spirit, not metal."

"Not in the teachings of Ba'al, whose cycle that is," Shane said flatly. Which was likely the other reason Stewart hadn't gotten this message. *Apparent idiot.* Used to describe a diplomat. From the Black Flag, that was a dangerously loaded phrase.

Trillian didn't say anything, but she could almost *feel* his raised eyebrow. "You know, a lot of people think all that talk about a 'resurgence in militant Ba'al-worship' is just military paranoia crossing with Orthodox desert-hell speeches."

Shane gave him a crooked smile. "You one of those people, Master Sergeant?"

"After what you dragged my squad out of, Flame? Hell no."

Shane nodded, recalling a very bad day in Aeolian territory. Or rather, what had *been* Aeolian territory. Caldera had annexed it the hard way, after the latest Aeolian king's third refusal to do anything about so-called 'rebels' raining tornadoes and other nasty Air-Workings down on Calderan towns.

Never let your enemies keep the high ground.

Unfortunately, by this time Caldera's enemies knew they'd take the heights. So when Calderan troops invaded to stop the damn tornadoes once and for all... it'd been a nasty ambush. Even if Command *had* figured out it was coming, and set up countermeasures. Like her team.

Forget Water against Fire. As far as Shane was concerned, Air against Fire was the nastiest elemental clash possible. Water plus Fire equaled steam, which was bad. Air plus Fire equaled *firestorms.*

Especially if you had a Fire-Worker hiding somewhere near the battlefield, ready to twist the blaze to his own lethal purposes.

They say Ba'al is a living fire....

Shane didn't *remember* half the things she'd done when that mess went FUBAR. There'd been screaming and *pulling* and twisting the firestorm away from the men and women it tried to devour, interspersed with flashes of knife-work and ducking and once, being yanked down bodily by Terry when she'd been too lost in the Fire to keep track of merely human enemies.

Aeolians didn't have Fire-Workers. They *definitely* didn't have Flames - even if that Flame had been so rough-trained, only the added interference of Air and infantry kept her from killing him in the first minute.

But kill him, she had - after an hour-long struggle that left the battlefield a blasted plain, good for nothing but careful tending to grow pine trees for decades to come.

Which suited Shane just fine. Caldera could always use another paper-pulp plantation. Better that, on the border with Aeolia, than a vulnerable town. Though the politicians hadn't been happy.

Then again, the smarter politicians hadn't been so much upset at the firestorm as what had been found after the fire. When Shane had led her team to her opponent's fallen body, so they could make *sure* he was dead.

Dead he'd been; no one survived having the top of their skull blown off from a superheated brain. But it was the rest of the body that set the hawk among the chickens.

Missing ring fingers. Both of them.

The sign of a Slave of Ba'al who would never covenant marriage, or be bound to it; for he had been gifted with their twisted god's own Fire, and had a holy obligation to pass it along to as many of the flock's children as possible.

One of these days, someone has to tell those poor women about inbreeding.

Not that women held captive in Ba'al's faith could do much about it if they knew. Woman was to man as man was to Ba'al, ran that unyielding creed; a soul cursed enough to be born female was fit only to be locked in a house, serving men, and bearing children. Fire-Gifted children, if she valued her life.

At least she's not considered an adulteress if it's a Fire-Worker who rapes her.

Which didn't mean an unlucky victim would survive. Many husbands killed their "treacherous" wives. Though they let the child be born, first. If it was a Fire-Worker, the mother *might* just be handed over to the temple harem.

There weren't many things Shane hated. Fire was too dangerous in the hands of someone consumed by emotion. But the fact that the Slaves of Ba'al *still* targeted her people, still slaughtered and tortured and plotted their agonizing deaths, when all Caldera wanted was to be *left alone....*

It surged like acid through her veins, made her lips draw back in an unconscious snarl. Oh yes. She hated that.

"Flame?"

"That fourth paragraph," Shane stated. "What was the first line, exactly?"

A fingernail scraped paper. "*Use your worst judgment.* That can't be right-" Trillian cut himself off.

As well he might. The master sergeant had been around long enough to know a code phrase when he heard one.

We need an opening. Make one, even if you have to get messy.

Shane mouthed one of Erastus' favorite curses under her breath. That wasn't an order. Even the Black Flag couldn't order someone medicaled out to risk their neck....

But the timing. That was one bomb. There will be more.

Shane breathed out sharply, dousing the flames flickering around her fingers. "I have to go."

"Not alone." And that, from a master sergeant, *was* an order.

"I won't be," Shane assured him; thinking of old tactical briefings, the realities of life in politics, and a few interesting bits overheard near the Watch station coffeepot. "I need some blueprints, or someone who can get them. Any friendly contacts you have with glider gangs; you must have had plenty of recruits who left on good terms, right?"

"The gangs that just like to buzz places for the skill points, instead of breaking things? I know a few," the master sergeant said thoughtfully. "But you don't know 'em. And you need somebody you *know*, Flame."

"You're right." Shane took a breath. "Do you know where to find a place called Kay's clinic?"

"You want me to what?" Tace said distrustfully.

"Help me get in somewhere I shouldn't," Shane said simply. She had to keep it simple; the walls here were different from either her apartment or the station, and echoes kept throwing off her grasp of what the room might look like. Thankfully, the other urchin children in Kay's basement were mostly silent; warm, too-thin bodies waiting for their leader to say yea or nay.

"Yeah, right. And this is legal since when?"

"It isn't."

Silence. Horrified or respectful, Shane couldn't tell. She gripped her cane, and waited. Terry had been better at this, but - this was far from the first time she'd dealt with local contacts on an op. It was always better to be honest, unless that would get someone killed.

A snarl. "You were with *Helle*."

"But I'm not an inspector," Shane shrugged. "I'm not any kind of law enforcement at all. I never have been."

A snort. "So what, you want the street kid 'cause nobody'll care if he gets dinged?"

"No." Shane kept her voice level, and very calm. Odds were Tace had been used that way before. Or worse. "I want you, Tace, because you seem to have a sense of self-preservation. Meaning if I get in over my head, you'll run."

A sharp, in-drawn breath-

"Which is *not* calling you a coward, you young idiot," Shane snapped out, before Tace could unleash a blistering denial. "If something goes wrong, I can incinerate every bastard who tries to lay a hand on me. Anything that touches me. Anyone with a weapon around me. The whole damn building, if that's what it takes to stop another bomb. I *can't* do that if you might be a target. So if I get in trouble, *I want you to run.*"

"Shit, Tace," one of the kids' voices rang in the sudden hush. "I think she's serious."

"I don't intend to encounter our targets," Shane said bluntly. "I want to get in, poke around, and get out. If something does go wrong, and it's not knives drawn, just go. I can handle any legal trouble."

"You're not thinking legal trouble," Tace said sourly.

"No. I'm not. I think," Shane let honesty ring in her voice, "that I'm poking a hornet's nest. If I had *any* legal grounds to take that place apart, I'd have the Watch in so fast, the man wouldn't have time to blink. But I don't. All I've got are some nasty coincidences and a hunch."

And a message to *start trouble so we have an excuse.* Though raiding the Atlan diplomatic residence was probably more trouble than even General Bones had had in mind....

I don't care. The Slaves think they can destroy my city. I'll do what it takes to stop them.

And it had to be flashy, and it had to be *fast.* This combination of sacred signs with the Slaves' elemental cycle would have their high priests drooling with bloodlust. The only way to derail their murderous plans was to get their attention.

Give them a more tempting target. They're not politicians, they're religious fanatics. And you can't bait a Slave with more religious ecstasy than the chance to kill an infidel female Flame.

And if they missed, and Caldera had to execute her afterward to soothe ruffled Atlan feathers... no one would care.

Probably especially not the street girl whose breath was hot with mistrust. "And you want *my* help."

"Actually, I want to hire you," Shane corrected her. "Contract and everything. Kay can witness. If you're assisting me for a salary, instead of a favor, then you're covered. If something goes wrong, the judge will have to book me to book you - and believe me, most of them won't."

"Yeah?" Tace challenged. "And why is that?"

Shane fished out her dog-tags, holding up the Flame for all to see. Let it drop, and bowed. "Flame Shane Redstone. Sorry we weren't properly introduced before, but I kind of wanted to treat that arm without you running away."

In the corner, one of the kids fainted.

"You're...." Tace swallowed hard. "Why *me?*"

"When you're hunting snakes, be sure your guide doesn't slither," Shane said flatly. "I trust you. There's not that many people I know I can trust. Not here. Not with what might be at stake." She held out an empty hand. "Are you interested?"

Warmth hesitated between them... then smaller fingers clasped hers. "And if it goes sour, you *want* me to run."

"Please," Shane said fervently. "I'm blind, Tace. I *can't see* what I'm targeting. If I'm pushed that far, everything I hit *will* die."

"You are crazy." But Tace shook on it, and the confidence was back in her voice. "So where's this place you want to hit?" Her words twisted a little, wry. "And you need my help because there's security, right? How are we going to sneak in their back door when you can't even see a tripwire?"

Shane grinned. "Who said we were going through a door?"

Chapter Nine

Wind shushed against the airship's sails, smoky with a hint of engine exhaust as it tried to pry loose a strand or two of Shane's tight braid. She breathed it in as she gripped the railing, quelling any trace of nerves. Her cane was already harnessed over her back for use inside, meaning she had to rely on her ears, toes, and the goodwill of the Fruit Bat Gliders' base crew to keep from pitching overboard. Better to hang onto the rail as long as possible.

"You're crazy," Tace blurted out, surrounded by the footsteps and zipping sounds of a couple of the gliders strapping her into the quick-release harness. "This is crazy. *I'm* crazy."

"It's my job," Shane noted. "And this isn't quite as crazy as you think. I checked. This is a residence, not an embassy."

"What's the sun-blasted difference? They shoot you just as dead!"

True enough. But even decades later, Shane could remember Strike Specialist Barquin's lecture like yesterday.

"The first thing you pups need for major lawbreaking is a little legal lesson. There is a distinct and lawful difference between an embassy and an ambassador's residence. They're both considered foreign soil, but the first is entitled to use all necessary force to maintain their country's security, just like any nation's border crossing. And if I ever hear about you trying to housebreak an embassy, I will box your ears. Literally. If there's enough ash left to put in boxes.

"A residence, now... that's also foreign soil, buuuuut both sides

recognize that it's somewhere you just can't fire off major munitions
without leaving big smoking holes in innocent civilians. Or worse."

Caldera fell under *or worse*. Because of all the wards keeping the
volcano calm, there were no embassies in Caldera City. She'd
checked.

"A residence means limited security," Shane summed up for the
scared girl. "All we have to deal with is human security and direct
Workings. I can handle the second... and we're going to avoid the
first."

"You can't see how far down it is!" A gulp. "...We're gonna *die*."

"No, we're not." Shane thumped one foot on the deck, checking
her position as best as she could. "I've made jumps like this before.
From gliders, even. We're going down on a rope, you get to pick when
to cut us free at a good falling distance, and we're going to thump
right down into one of their holes in security."

At least it ought to be a hole. Based on the plans she'd gotten, and
her best reading of them with Trillian's help.

"The second thing you need is a little military lesson," Barquin
had gone on. *"Every sane commander makes sure there's compiled*
background information and a plan to invade any piece of foreign soil.
Any. Piece.

"You just need to know who to ask...."

Master Sergeant Trillian had known who to ask. And who to ask,
to know who else to ask.

I love blueprints.

Of course there was always the chance that the Atlan
ambassadorial residence had done some off-the-books remodeling. So
the floorplans they'd gone over might not be *quite* accurate.

In which case, I *do some remodeling.*

Hopefully not. Flashy was important, but hopefully the attention
would only kick in after she got the info she was looking for.

Roof, attic, dumbwaiter, study, Shane ran over her plan of attack as
she walked over to Tace and held out half-gloved hands to take her

own harness. "I appreciate this, Captain Starer."

Shane couldn't see the airship captain grin, but she heard the grim chuckle. "Oh, our flyers have been *itching* to buzz these arm-gnawers again."

"That sounds personal." Shane busied her hands with buckles and straps; this she could do blindfolded and under a moonless midnight. "Not that I have any room to talk. As someone who does have an ax to grind, though - don't take any risks you don't have to. Revenge is much better if you're alive to laugh at their graves."

The low breath wasn't quite a growl. "My great-uncle didn't get a grave."

Tace gulped, but her voice was almost street-confident. "W-what happened to him?"

"Atlans caught a patrol too far from the lines," Starer bit out. "One of his squadmates said he blew his brains out with a rod before their Air-Worker could strangle him unconscious. Grandma still prays he wasn't lying."

"He... what...?"

Shane tested a buckle, lifted her fingers away. "You probably weren't in school long enough to hear your Religion lectures on the old Atlan jaguar-demons. Their higher powers demand flesh, not bread and wine. And the congregation is supposed to *share*."

"And we're going in there?"

"Oh, they say they've quit that, since we made it one of the terms of their surrender," Shane said cheerfully. "Of course, they've said that about five other times in the past two centuries, too. This is *just* about the right time for enough of the common folk who remember what we did to them to have mostly died off, and for the nobles to think they might be able to revive the old ways again. Shame."

Starer gripped her harness, clipping it onto the line that should hopefully carry them down. "We should Spirit-Work cacao so it'll grow up here, and burn the country to the ground."

"I second the first, but as someone who'd be doing the burning, careful what you wish for," Shane said soberly. "If Atlan attacks us again, yes, we stop them. Hard. But Fire is a bad way to die. Not the worst, but... it's not good for the soul." She tried to make her voice soothing, the way Terry would; knowing she didn't have a chance in the starry desert of pulling it off. "Keep your head, and stick to letting your gang friends distract the guards. If I'm right, and we find what I'm looking for, it'll hurt the nobles worse than any attack ever could. They'll *lose face*."

"Lose face, and have to explain to the High Jaguar himself." Starer let out a long, deliberate exhalation. "That would be good. That would be *perfect*."

"Uh." Tace shuffled nearer, almost bumping Shane's side to whisper. "Is that like losing face on the street?"

"Worse," Shane murmured back. "And usually permanent."

"...And we're going in there?"

"Tace." Shane took a breath. "This isn't safe. If you want out, just say so. But there's someone out there trying to blow up this city. And you have my word, if it all goes south, I'll blow a wall out so you can get clear." She let her voice lighten. "After all, if you don't tell Helle what happened, he'll never get to tell me *I told you so*."

That won her a shaky laugh. "Okay. Okay, let's - just do this."

"Relax," Shane advised, as Starer's second mate made sure they were latched on. "We let the gliders draw the residence's attention, Captain Starer sneaks in to the leeward, and then it's going to be just like judging a roof jump. All you have to do is gage as safe landing distance, and hit the release."

That earned her a less shaky snort. "*You* jumped roofs."

Ouch. But more than fair. "This time, I can't afford to miss." Shane cocked her head at the chatter; the first rush of air under silk as gliders started jumping from the deck. "Here they go...."

Thump and swoosh; the roar of coal engines, and catcalls into the wind. It was achingly familiar.

But this isn't a glider unit, Shane reminded herself. *These are civilians. Civilians who'd risk their own necks for a thrill anyway, but... I'm probably going to be in trouble for this.*

Not that she could let that matter. The Slaves didn't believe in civilians.

Breathe in. Breathe out. Get ready....

The airship banked, engine cutting out for silence as Captain Starer used Air-Worked sails to circle around to an empty patch of sky. In the distance Shane could hear the high whoops as the Fruit Bats buzzed the front of the residence, the outraged yells of security and even a few locals down in the street who didn't fancy being mostly innocent bystanders.

Shane swallowed nausea. Oh, this was *so much worse* than a night jump.

Don't throw up. Nothing hurts a kid's morale like seeing the grownups lose it-

"Ready?" Captain Starer called out.

No, no, can I go back to bed, a bed that doesn't move- "Ready," Shane answered, stepping onto the launch deck with Tace.

"Just like a roof jump?" Tace's voice was pitched a little higher than usual.

"Just like," Shane assured her yet again. "Pick the height you'd jump from, hit the release there."

"Set!" the captain called.

Tace groaned. "And people do this for fun?"

"It's an acquired taste," Shane admitted.

"Go!"

A shove, and there was no more wood underfoot.

Trust the rope, trust the harness, trust they're thrill-seekers but not idiots, they know what they're doing-

It wasn't the free-fall of a launched glider. Gravity had a definite down, the rope had a tug up as the airship moved, and Tace was solid and trying not to shake as the kid cursed under her breath at stupid Inspectors, stupid stunts, stupid roof tiles swinging around, couldn't the ship stay still-?

Click-click.

Hitting her release as she heard Tace's click free, Shane went limp, reaching out with Fire-sense for the heat of a sun-warmed roof. It should be five feet below, maybe ten-

There!

Night drops let her hit and not *break*; though Sunlit, she'd be feeling this in the morning. The cane wasn't standard equipment, it threw the angle of her roll off, where was the edge-?

Air and cool under her left fingers.

Shane lunged right, hand and legs flinging out and down to grip hot tiles like grim death.

Breathe. Don't move. Breathe.

Her braid was dangling free in air. Shane held her position, listening hard. That hadn't been her worst airdrop ever, but it definitely hadn't been *quiet*.

Give credit to Tace; the kid moved over the roof to her with no more noise than an anole skittering through leaves. "You okay?" Tace breathed.

"Ow," Shane said succinctly, listening to the ruckus at the front of the residence get even louder as someone brought out an Air-wand to start taking potshots at glider wings. "Anyone spot us?"

Tace went silent, little shifts of her heat making it clear the kid was doing her own listen-check. "Don't think so. But the gang's sheering off."

"Can't expect them to risk broken necks." Shane carefully rolled right, got to hands and knees. "If they did, some of the guards might get suspicious. Which way is north?"

Tace gripped one of her hands, moved it to the right point on the compass. "This way."

Quick and quiet, they ghosted over the roof. *According to the blueprints, clearest spot above the attic ought to be... here.*

Crouched, Shane lifted one hand in a moment's silent meditation.

Setting the roof on fire would be child's play, Worked-in water or not. A quiet break-in was significantly trickier.

Single-point. Focus. Use the Fire as heat, like focused sunlight. Don't let it spread a hair more than necessary.

With her finger she first bored four holes, to fit the spring-loaded grapple Tace had brought in her gear. The kid latched on the tool with just a whispered swear, lifting the counterweighted rope out of her pouch and setting it down yards away with a breath of relief.

Can't blame her. That was heavy.

But necessary. Fire-sense wasn't picking up any body-heat below them, but between the water Worked into the tiles and the roof's own heat, she couldn't be sure. Meaning they'd better not have a cut bit of roof fall on top of a stray residence bystander.

And now, cut.

Ceramic tiles with pockets of worked Water; someone knew just what kind of force Calderans were likely to throw at enemy territory. It'd stop a Journeyman. Maybe even a Master.

But not me.

Shane traced what looked like straight lines on the roof, a square wide enough for them to slip through easily. Under the surface the cut *rippled*, Fire burning through tiles less than a hair away from Water.

Two sides cut. Half through the third Shane had to stop, and shake out her hand. Whoever had installed this roof had known what they were doing.

"They're *flying away*," Tace whispered.

Shane kept her lips closed, though she wanted to bare her teeth. Right. No time.

The fourth line cut through, and the square lurched an inch down. Ear to the roof, Shane listened.

Silence.

"Okay," Shane breathed, prying up one edge enough to get a grip. A foot away, she heard Tace drop to one knee, and felt the tiles shift as the kid got her own hold. "On three. One, two-"

The slide and thump wasn't as loud as her landing. Shane still grimaced.

Worry about it later. Doesn't matter what they find, as long as they find it after you're out.

No sound or heat below. Time to take her chances.

Hands gripping the glassy edges, Shane dropped.

...Going to feel that one tomorrow, too.

Damned rich nobles and vaulted ceilings. This was supposed to be an attic-

Clamping her lips together, Shane thumped the back of her hand into her nose, cutting off the impulse to sneeze.

Dust. Lots of dust. Definitely an attic.

Tace dropped down more gracefully, stifling a cough. "Ooo... so many *goodies*...."

Shane cleared her throat.

"Yeah, yeah, I'm hired," Tace huffed. "'Sides, most of this stuff is too big to lift."

"And most of this *stuff* will be diplomatic gifts from one nation or another." Shane gave her a raised eyebrow. "Which means all *kinds* of spy and trace Workings on it."

"Oh." Tace gulped. "Um. Not good?"

"Very," Shane agreed, taking the cane off her back. Silence around her, though she could still hear muffled sounds of Air-blasts harrying the gliders. She could risk this.

Thump.

Echoes of stacks of stuff, slightly more hollow on one side. Which should be the right direction, from the blueprints.

"Couldn't fence it without getting cheated anyway...." Tace followed her toward the hollow sound, stopped short. "Wow. Never seen one from the top before."

"They like to put the motors in the attic. Less noise, and the nobles don't have to look at someone actually maintaining the gears." Shane kept her voice low, hiding her relief that so far the blueprints were right. "And since most motors work with charged Fire... Atlans favor Air. They really don't like Worked Fire near them."

Tace advanced a step, almost brushing her shoulder. "Um. If this goes down through the building, and *anybody* could open the doors...."

Spoken like a sensible lifter. "There are usually security Workings meant to keep anything alive from going down the shaft," Shane agreed, moving her hand within inches of the access panel. "But those are a lot more complicated than people think, especially in a kitchen dumbwaiter. Technically *sprouts* are alive." And this was a noble residence. No chef would provide anything less than the absolutely freshest meal. It'd be the death of them. In an Atlan residence, quite literally.

Tace drew in a breath. "And where people make things all tangled...."

"There are loopholes." Smart kid. Good. "And human nature being innately sinful, a friend of mine showed me an *interesting* trick."

Say what you wanted about Terry, and officers had said plenty about Terry, but he'd known how to get a girl in and out of *any* secure area. Which included finding every last way someone else snuck girls in. And Ambassador Salloum was known for having wandering hands.

Got you.

She might not be able to pick out the intricacies of the security Working, but she could feel the shape of the hole in it. The Atlan security was meant to keep out living things by stopping their breath. But some living things had to be allowed to breathe....

And from familiar twists that echoed of Water and Earth, the category *human female* had been added to that hole. "We're in."

Tace swallowed, but went right to work on the simple lock on the access hatch. "You better be right, Red."

Shane stifled a hiss. That *hurt*.

"Be right about this, Red."

"Oh man, oh man, this had better work...."

"We know you've got us covered, Red."

She'd been right, that last time. She'd been *right*. And it still hadn't made a damn bit of difference.

Shane closed her eyes a moment, sparking red going to darker red. Now was no time to remember that Geistan hell-Work. The dead were dead. The living needed her *here*.

Clack.

Tace huffed a sigh of relief as the hatch popped open. Waited a moment in case the sound or light drew unsuspected attention; then warmth angled down as she peeked. "Empty."

Good. "Can you see the platform?"

"Uh-uh."

Had to be at least a level or two down, then. Shane slung her cane back over her shoulder, reached out to brush the pull-rope aside, and gripped the central cable.

Down we go.

Ram would have just lowered her on their own rope, holding her weight and Tace's like they were bundles of feathers. Shane had to rely on her own muscle and the prayer that the cable would hold.

It ought to. Smuggling in girls. Not to mention, ambassadorial paperwork.

Leather half-gloves kept her grip from slipping on the covered cable, but her arms were already complaining. Blasted rehab. Sure, get a wounded soldier able to navigate streets; why couldn't they have thrown in a regular obstacle course for good old-fashioned exercise?

Grip. Shift. Release.

"U-um...."

Hearing that quaver, feeling the vibration in the cable above her, Shane mouthed a soundless curse. *Idiot. You couldn't see she was hurt, so you forgot.* "Ease down toward me. Rest your feet on my shoulders."

"But-!"

"There's nothing wrong with my arms." Shane gripped the cable between her legs, halting. "Come on. I hired you for eyes, not muscle."

Inch by jerky inch, Tace shuddered her way down. Shane braced herself as the teen's weight hit her shoulders, one foot digging into a bruise from the roof.

Breathe through it. Like Erastus always said - it's only pain. "Set? We're going to move down together. I'll take most of the weight; you just make sure you hang onto the cable."

A gulp. "Okay...."

Down. And hurry. Sooner or later someone might get the bright idea to check the roof-

The cable thrummed under her hands.

...Or use the dumbwaiter.

Tace squeaked. "It's gonna-!"

Close enough, then. "Let go," Shane ordered. "On one, two, *three.*"

She slid downward, a crook of fingers shunting friction's heat from the cable before it could sear her jeans. *Can't just drop, floor can probably take our weight, but the ceiling-*

Her foot struck no-doubt elegant wood with an ominous *creak.*

Yeah, thought so. Shane gripped on hard again, flattening herself as much as she could. "Keep your weight on the cable," she murmured. Breathed in a waft of air coming up through the new crack in the dumbwaiter's ceiling. Cotton, perfume, a few other unmistakable scents. "Laundry. Good."

"Good?" Tace hissed in her ear, shoulders cringing as the kid obviously imagined being squashed like a bug.

"Means it'll get sent back." Instead of a meal going down, or the remnants going up; either of which would mean people in the ambassador's office. Which would be more headache than she wanted to deal with.

Headache versus aching arms and legs, though... rehab had taken more out of her than she'd realized. She'd trained every day with her team; eight months ago, if someone had asked her if she could hold her weight and Tace's as long as it took, she'd have had no doubt.

Now her hands ached, her shoulders *hurt*, and her arms had a fine tremble that was not good at all.

Hang on. Breathe in, keep focused, breathe out. It'll stop soon-

Wood jarred under her feet. Shane held position, feeling Tace twitch. Probably at light leaking through the crack they'd put in the dumbwaiter ceiling.

Let's hope it's not big enough to notice.

Thuds of moving cloth, enough weight to vibrate the cable. Even with their weight dampening it.

Oh hell. The staff know this rig. If they realize it didn't move right-!

Shane held on, reviewing blueprints in her head. The shaft they were in would make a perfect chimney, if it came to burning this place to the ground.

Let's not, if we can. I hate taking out civilians. Even Atlan ones.

Minutes seemed to stretch forever. But at last she heard the rattle of the doors closing, and the dumbwaiter sank once more.

Just a little longer, if this is the standard design it'll go back to ground level to save wear and tear on the brakes....

Thump. And a breath of air that smelled faintly of fur, papers, and expensive sealing wax.

No heat sources she could sense, beyond the usual lamp so servants could tidy up without breaking their necks. Hopefully that meant no one was using the office. "Hear anything?" Shane murmured.

Tace let a few fast heartbeats pass. "Sounds clear." She sniffed, some of a street kid's bravado coming back as she finally shifted her weight off Shane. "So if the high-class slime is using this rig to smuggle in streetwalkers, there ought to be a door in this top somewhere around...."

Click.

"Gotcha."

Tace did have a good lifter's touch. Shane was listening, and she still barely heard the scrape of wood on wood as Tace opened the panel and dropped through.

Shouldn't be her, should be me-!

Shane gritted her teeth against that stupid, stubborn impulse. She'd already checked for any danger she could without eyes. Now it was time to let Tace do her part, and keep them from running into something like, say, a spider-silk tripwire.

Because that would be a stupid, stupid way to die.

Footsteps. And one back, that almost stumbled. "Come on. Um - careful, though. There's this... weird leather rug. With *teeth*."

Shane breathed out one more time; stray flames right now would leave evidence. More importantly, they might destroy evidence, if the ambassador had left any lying around.

Stepping down and out, she felt with her cane, carefully outlining the long, lean shape that haunted Atla's rivers. "Ah. Crocodile."

"...You mean that thing is real?" Tace gulped. "Not something Worked up for a lightshow?"

"Real, and nasty," Shane confirmed, remembering a nerve-wracking swim that had turned very bloody. For the other side. "You can keep their jaws closed, but prying them open? That takes help." Centering herself, she tapped down.

Softer and harder echoes; a few more fancy rugs, walls with bookcases, and if that angle was the window overlooking the conservatory then the desk should be... there. "See any interesting papers out?"

"The morning *Boiling Pot*," Tace said after a moment. "Somebody got their clothes pressed up special... huh, grocery list. Corn, flour, annato, intestines of long- *hurk*."

Shane clapped a hand across the kid's mouth before shock could kick in. "Think about mint. Cool and sharp and *clean*."

"Ugh. Uh...." Tace swallowed hard, turning away from the desk. "W-why? Why would *anyone?*"

"Atlan nobles." Shane kept her snarl low and cold. "They think it keeps the sun shining." She rubbed a circle on the kid's bony back.

"Odds are it's regular pork, here. They know if we caught even an ambassador at one of those rituals, we'd execute everyone we could prove was involved." And probably burn the residence to the ground, to boot. The Sunlit Lord forbade human sacrifice, and Calderans would hold to that faith as long as life lasted.

Sometimes I wish Caldera was bigger. All we can do is strike our enemies and leave. We just don't have the people to grind out these rituals for good.

"Forget the desk," Shane stated. Anything related to carnage and terrorism wouldn't be left lying out, anyway. Even an ambassador wasn't *that* stupid. "We need to find the safe."

"Got it." Tace tapped wood, then walls; Shane breathed a touch of heat into the air, searching for a mass of metal that would drink it in.

Tace stopped tapping a moment before Shane fixed where heat was leaching away. "Ah, c'mon, behind a painting's so *old*...." Wood and leather creaked open over one of the walls, and Tace froze.

Shane raised her head, searching heat and air for any trace of what had stopped Tace cold. "What is it?"

"...I can't do this one."

Shane nodded once. "Combination lock?"

"I can do the cheap ones but *this*, it's got three dials and that fancy I know there's got to be at least four numbers on each of 'em and we don't have time-!"

"Stay calm," Shane advised, even as her own heart-rate picked up. Cracking safes had always been Paul Resen's job. The Journeyman Water-Worker had known how to slip just a trickle of water into almost any mechanism, feeling the combination from the inside out. He'd have a safe like this open in minutes; a half-hour, tops.

We won't have that long.

"This one's mine," Shane said flatly. "And after this, we're going to have to run."

Tace sucked in a breath. "You can punch it?"

"A friend taught me." Shane slung her cane, and worked her

fingers, resting the bare tips near the dials. *Think it through.*
Residence, so the ambassador can probably afford the best; walls are
probably composite hardplate, keep any normal drill or Earth-
Working out for an hour. But it's a safe for an ambassador, *not a*
security expert. So someone has to be able to break in, in case
someone's too drunk or kicked out of the country or assassinated to
hand over the combination. There has to be a drill-point... there.

One weak spot that didn't absorb heat quite like the rest. Shane
touched it with one hand; lifted and flexed the other, switched hands
and repeated. "Keep your eyes open. I have to concentrate."

One finger to heat. One hand to gesture.

Even controlled, heat rippled through the air as Shane bored
through the spot of regular steel. Her free hand knitted intricate
patterns, confining Fire to that one point. The last thing they needed
was to set off any hidden Workings meant to damp Fire before it
burned the papers....

The rest of her hand hit the safe, and she felt a breath of cooler air
escape past her finger. The locks clicked softly.

Drawing her finger out, Shane tugged the door open.

"...Whoa."

"Practice," Shane said modestly, feeling at the air and papers
inside. Not a hint of scorching. Good. "Okay, you're up. Take a read."
Anything kept in secret like this would probably be exactly what they
needed-

"Um. Is this... supposed to be writing? It's all little pictures."

And a Calderan city street rat couldn't read Atlan glyphs. Right.
Could the day get any worse?

Across the room, brass rattled. Shane didn't need Tace's
whispered curse to know that had to be the doorknob.

Should've known.

No Strike Specialist broke in without a plan to break out. Smooth
and silent, Shane closed the painting back over the safe, and gestured
Tace over to her as she ran her fingers just above the interior

windowsill. If the ambassador loved his plants enough to make them the centerpiece of his office view, odds were he wouldn't have allowed anything annoying to keep him from fully enjoying the view. Like, say, alarms on the window-latch.

Hah. None. Figured he'd jump out here when the paperwork got too much.

Nothing *Worked*, at least. She touched Tace's shoulder.

"Looks clear," the girl muttered, shoving a few last papers in her pack as the rattling turned to a silence that had to be someone digging for a key. "But if they've got something fancy-"

Shane shrugged. Grinned. Gripped the latch, and *yanked*.

No alarms. Hands on the sill, Shane vaulted up and through, into swampy air that smelled more like Riparia than anywhere in Caldera had the right to. *Thank the Sunlit for arrogant noble privilege.*

The *squish* coming through her boots felt like Riparia, too. Grrr.

Tace splashed down beside her; less quiet anole, more oversized bullfrog. Glass and wood slid closed; only then did the street kid let out a whispered, *"Eww."*

"Keep low," Shane murmured, already crouched. "Get us out of the line of sight of the window. Without smashing any of the plants we don't have to. Someone will notice."

"In a *swamp?*"

"Especially in a swamp." Shane wet her lips as Tace took her hand, drawing in scents as they moved. Muck, the buzz of a midge across the tip of her nose, a trace of raw chestnut and something not-quite-vanilla....

Dark-twist. I'm in the right place.

"This is the ambassador's own playground," Shane murmured. "I wonder if we'll get a chance to *talk* to him?"

"Ambassador Adas Salloum will see you now, Inspector," the butler reported serenely. "Walk this way."

With an effort, Allen bit back the old Calderan joke, and followed.

Without mimicking the man's steps in any shape, form, or fashion. No need to start off a polite inquiry with sarcasm. Yet.

And right now, it was just a polite inquiry, no matter what they'd dragged out of Father Jacobsson. The Atlan ambassador was supposedly a model of civility and circumspect behavior; as befit the representative of a nation Calderan forces had walked all over with cleats six times in the past two centuries. For the last forty-nine years, they'd been allies. Supposedly. All those rumors of lingering jaguar-demon worship and cannibalistic feasts among the nobles was just baseless slander. Everyone said so.

...Damn it, Shane's paranoia was catching.

Are you sure *she's paranoid? She was right about the bomb. She was right about the snake. She was right about Jacobsson's being* told *what she was - by a guy who just* happened *to turn up for the first time since Marcus Wright's murder, right before Inspector Sorenson died.*

One Fred Aman, currently attached to the ambassador's staff under the innocuous title of delivery driver. With more than a few black marks on his record; though no surprise there, this was the Atlan residence and Calderans held grudges the way bankers hoarded gold. Of *course* the residence could only get sketchy applicants, to any outside job. And if deliveries just *happened* to be a convenient job for traveling all over Caldera with odd items and odder people, with nobody batting an eye....

If Shane was paranoid, she had a lot of company.

With a step over the threshold, they went from a tastefully appointed suite of rugs and rich furnishings to the mist-thick, warm air of a tropical greenhouse. Allen raised a brow, noting the subtlety of Air- and Water-Wards worked into the threshold.

And the *green*. So much green.

Miniature cypress trees, knees sticking up out of a pool bubbling with a waist-high fountain. Midges, hovering in gray clouds. Vines and bromeliads clinging to every branch, hosting the soft *creaks* of tree frogs. Ferns, water-lilies, and given pride of place as they rounded a corner on the damp stone path-

Allen eyed the green-cupped mound of a dark-twist tree, and tried not to react.

"Ambassador Salloum," the butler said formally, "Inspector Helleson, of the Caldera City Watch."

The ambassador finished patting a new sprout into soggy soil, and brushed dirt off gloved fingers. "Ah yes. Our good officer of the local law." He followed Allen's gaze. "Magnificent, isn't it? So very difficult to grow, here. Water, soil, nutrients - everything must be just so. And that was after all the formalities to import such a fragile beauty in the first place.... You had questions, Inspector? Of course, I and my staff are always willing to help with a Watch inquiry. Though I don't see why one of my people visiting one of your nation's churches is a cause for concern. Religious freedom, after all." He paused, too long to be anything but deliberate. "Well, for *your* religion."

Of course for our religion. There's nowhere else in the world our faith is safe. "A policy I imagine some in Caldera might consider modifying, if your people would stop firebombing our co-religionists' churches in your own country," Allen said, with the same dry civility. He wasn't allowed to truth-read an ambassador on residence soil, but he still had his mundane training. Any Inspector worth his badge couldn't miss that veiled hostility. *He wants a fight. Why?* "We'd just like to ascertain Mr. Aman's whereabouts on certain dates. And ask a few questions. Is he available?"

Movement, out of the corner of his eye. Allen glanced toward a neatly-dressed gardener, carefully snipping off a leaf-cupped twig for an elaborate vase.

"I'm sure he is," the ambassador said blandly. "Somewhere. Now, where could he be... Master Perello? Have you seen Aman anywhere?"

"Out." The gardener set the vase down on the path before applying a white paste to the clipped wound. "Sent him for lime. Soil around here stinks."

Allen quelled the automatic impulse to bristle; Calderan soil might be tricky to work with for someone used to barren jungle clays or the drifts of windswept plains, and it certainly wasn't meant for Riparian swamp plants, but no one who'd ever tried to work it for *food* instead of hothouse frivolities would slander it like that-

And that was wrong. Swamp soils were *acid*; he'd listened to enough of his friends and neighbors farming in Waycross to know that, bone-deep. Even more acid than the rawest soil cracked from Caldera's lava, with a poverty of certain minerals that made swamp plants vicious enough to eat animals to get them. Lime was one of the least of the things you added to swampy soil to grow crops. If you were trying to create a swamp, you'd keep lime away from it like a heretic shunned the Book.

Any gardener would know that.

The ambassador was lying to his face. Either he was counting on the fact that Allen was a city Watch officer, and ignorant of plants as most farmers were of skyscraper girders... or he just didn't care.

Diplomatic immunity. I can't take him downtown unless he chooses to go. And how likely is that?

"Well, I'm sure if you leave your address, Aman can call on you when he's back-" the ambassador started.

"Master Perello, is it?" Allen said levelly. *Upper-class Atlans never see servants.* "I'd like to talk to you."

"Whatever for?" Salloum sputtered. "If you had cause to investigate Aman due to a *mere* mention in an investigation, that would be acceptable. But to disrupt my entire embassy on a *whim-*"

"Residence," Allen cut him off. "And it's a common misconception, to think lime helps a body decay faster."

Silence, rippling like the water.

"Where is he, Perello?"

Glancing his way, the gardener slowly smiled.

Intent - no chant, but he's Working-!

Earth snapped around Allen like crocodile jaws.

Can't move - can't scribe a symbol - focus, get up and out-!

Yet the concentration he needed for a 'port fell apart with every squeeze of lethal muck. How - how did anyone focus enough to Work through something like this....

There were no screams. That terrified him. If the ambassador and the butler were in on this - if the whole residence staff was in on this-

Only maybe they weren't, because when Allen managed to crane his head through the mud's grasp, only mounds of disturbed earth remained.

"I wonder," Perello said dryly, "just how much you think you know."

"Enough to see you all hang." Allen shuddered, as swamp muck threatened neck and mouth.

"Oh, I doubt that. I very much doubt that, Inspector. Or you wouldn't be alone-"

Earth and air exploded.

Instinct made Allen flinch from the pulse of heat lacing down the sides of his prison. Reason made him push back, breaking through mud flash-baked to strengthless dry dust. He fell out of the earthen mound, trying not to listen to sudden screams; the ambassador could yell all he wanted, if Perello wasn't stopped they'd *all* be buried. Again.

Already dirt was trembling, answering to unseen will-

Fire roared up from a dozen spots, fusing earth to glass.

Hand on cooling slickness, Allen stared. He couldn't see anyone. But he knew only one Worker who shaped Fire like this. *"Shane?"*

"Don't just stand there, Helleson - catch the bastard!"

"Easy for you to say!" He hit the ground, as levitating glass shards splintered around him like daggers-

Ground. Earth. Bad idea-

Soil *shivered*, liquid as a fathomless well.

Hold your breath. Hold it!

Impossible, with earth squeezing his chest, muck pressing into his nose....

The morass pulsed into blistering hot ash, swirling underneath a shell of cooler earth to force him *up* and *out-*

Allen coughed out dust, and wondered when the world had gone insane.

"Helle!"

Tace, here, where no street urchin should have been able to sneak past the residence guards. Here anyway; a trusted hand yanking him upright, eyes wide and awed. "Come on!"

"I'm all right," Allen coughed, peering through veils of dust and heat-haze. Ribs definitely bruised, if not broken - but he was breathing, which had to be a plus. "Where is he?"

"Dunno!" Tace let go, eyes darting here and there for the next attack. "But Shane says he knows where *we* are-"

"Indeed." Dust swirled, and Perello raised his hands....

Flames exploded between them.

"Not so easy to read earth when it's burning, is it?" The Flame's voice was calm, matter-of-fact - and oddly echoing, as if she were in two places at once.

Can't be right, where is-?

Allen caught himself before his Spirit-sense reached beyond Tace. And swallowed hard. *No. Redstone can track traces of other elements. Maybe he can too. If I knew where she was - it's not worth it.*

But what can I do? Shane's blind. She can't fight an Earth-Worker alone, not when she risks hitting-

Oh.

"I could snuff you out in a heartbeat, Perello," Shane went on. "Surrender, and you may only face civil justice."

"I've an alternative," Perello sneered back. "Yield, and face a quick death."

Snagging Tace's wrist, Allen started scribing. This was going to be complicated.

The Flame snorted, still with that odd echo. "Don't make me

laugh, *Slave*. Your master would never let a *woman* have a quick death."

"How true." A shift of Perello's arm, and earth erupted.

Fell back again, crumbling like crusted sugar.

Shane cleared her throat. "Is that the best you can do? I think you meant something more like... *this*."

Fire leapt up in a slash at Perello's feet, searing clothes and hair before earth quenched it. The Earth-Worker swore, and struck-

Earth shattered in three places, erupting pillars to the ceiling.

"Pathetic."

He couldn't get outside the walls. A residence had enough Spirit-wards to make any short-jump through the perimeter a grisly death. But people were Spirit in flesh, and any ward where living souls worked had to allow for that. Allen pictured the residence hallway he'd walked through distracted by politics; close enough to jump to, and he stood a chance of intercepting any security before they could start blasting rods. There was the foyer, the awkward steps down, the ugly woven onion-yellow and cactus scarlet-dyed corn-husk tapestry thing on the wall....

"Where are you?"

"Hello?" A double and triple-echo. "Do I *look* that stupid?"

"You're a *dead bitch!*"

"Not for lack of your *trying*, I'm sure." Shane's words were light, careless; salt on an open wound of pride. "Such a shame. All a Mountain's power in your hands, and you can't even kill one blind, *made* Worker? A *woman?* Your grave will drown in the endless frozen sea, your lost body sinking into eternal ice, and the demons who serve what *you* call a god will laugh at your pathetic, powerless excuse for a soul."

Screaming incoherently, Petrello whirled on Allen-

Who'd had just enough breath to grab Tace, do the fastest chanting of his *life*, and scribe them *elsewhere*.

Out of the line of fire. Finally.

One hand braced on her cane, Shane twitched a finger to keep hot air swirling dust and haze between herself and her enemy. He shouldn't look this way, not if he followed the sound of her voice - but she wasn't going to count on that.

There's a reason Strikers study other elements, Helleson. And that reason... is now.

Fire mingled with air around her, altering the sound of her voice in a twisting spiral that led listeners in circles. More heat pulsed into the ground beneath her feet, damping the vibrations of her movement.

Shane grinned. *Who's blind now, Petrello?*

Body-heat, she could sense. And now only one body stood upright.

End this now.

There were plenty of ways for a Flame to kill a man. Burned to a crisp was simplest. That didn't always work against another Worker; someone fast and skilled enough could summon their own element to blunt the blast. As she had, letting swathes of Fire take the brunt of the Earth-strike that would have killed her. Baking him alive, charring a heart as it beat, superheating air until it burst from the lungs....

Plenty of ways to kill a man. Keeping him alive - that was tricky.

Centering herself, Shane reached out to the heat within Perello, and *pulled.*

Come to me.

Jets of warmth skirled out of his skin, dropping his temperature faster than a dip in a winter sea. Fast, she had to work fast; peeling off heat without *killing* him took concentration, and the more she focused, the more chance her concealment would slip-

Earth trembled under her feet.

Stay still. Stay still! He doesn't know where you are, he's trying to flush you out-

A rumble farther away, and someone screamed.

Stay still.

"Do you want them to die?" Perello challenged, teeth chattering.

Frankly, Slave, I do not give a damn.

Shane would hate it if they died. She would. But they were not her people.

And if Bones was right, this man might be the key to finding those who meant to destroy her city.

You should have spent less time threatening, Slave, and more time-

More screams. "Gods, why are you *doing* this?" someone cried out.

Good question, Shane thought. *You know I'm not over there,* or *there, so why bother- oh, hell!*

She sprinted, outracing crumbling soil, as where she'd stood gaped into an echoing pit.

Damn it! She'd spent too much concentration trying to take him alive; she couldn't juggle controlled hypothermia, clouding her presence, and heat-sensing her surroundings. *Used vibrations to triangulate - figured out where I was by where the ground wasn't shaking right....*

And now she'd lost momentum, and lost her bearings; all she could do was jump and roll and hope to hell she didn't-

Glass. Very, very hard. Greenhouse wall, fortunately; the *good* kind of glass, like high-rise windows, too tough to break just because a body'd slammed right into it.

Or maybe not fortunate at all, as it stretched like taffy, cutting off all but one last gulp of air.

Glass is Earth and *Fire.*

It took all her will to breathe *out*, trusting pinpoint control of Fire to melt open holes over ears and nose. And in, and out, falling limp to the ground....

Come here, you bastard. Come and gloat over the infidel, just as your holy texts demand.

Footsteps. Chattering teeth. Glass pulling away from her chest and neck, sliding into a razor edge that burned pain against her throat. More glass, pulling away from her hands....

Good as a confession.

"And when Ba'al has delivered them into your power, smite them down! Smite off their devilish heads, and strike off their accursed fingertips-"

A harsh breath sheathed her in pure Fire, melted away glass as searing rain. Hand wreathed in flames, she *struck*-

The Earth-shield stopped her Fire. It did nothing to stop her knife.

Choking, he fell.

"Sunlit damn it," Shane breathed raggedly, lying exhausted on the ground as the heat within Perello began to die. "Sometimes training sucks."

Helleson was right. She had no place in an investigation. Not if they wanted the suspects alive.

One breath to steady herself - a breath that hitched surprisingly like a sob - and Shane dragged herself to her feet. Swept a pulse of heat through earth and cooling flesh and steaming water, and found the solidity of ironwood. Picked up her cane, brushed off earth and drops of glass-

-Not blood; never blood again after her first close kill. Decades ago an older Striker had shown her that useful *twist* of Fire as skin was pierced - you couldn't walk back out through enemy security as if nothing had happened with bloodstains on you-

-And squared her shoulders.

Time to face the music.

Chapter Ten

"Oh. My. Lord." Captain Mason stopped dead in the soot-stained doorway. Glass crackled under his boots as he stared around what had been a lush swamp garden, just hours before.

"Somehow, I don't think the Sunlit had anything to do with this," Callie muttered.

Allen ignored them, walking over to where Shane leaned on her cane, dirt-stained and weary. "Are you all right?"

"Hell, no," the Flame grumbled. Her nose wrinkled in irritation. "I was trying to take him alive."

"How?" Allen sputtered, feeling again that strangling clutch as boggy earth opened and swallowed him. "You said the man was a *Mountain*. How on earth did you think you could-?"

"With a trained team, you can do it." Shane hesitated. "Sometimes. Are *you* all right? Did you get checked over? Dirt in the lungs can turn into an infection faster than you'd believe."

"I can take care of that much, thanks," Allen said defensively. He'd already started, running the self-healing meditation in his head while he waited for more of the Watch to show up. The residence personnel weren't going anywhere. Not with a cranky Calderan Fire-Worker ready to wreak even more havoc. "How did you - and you didn't hit *anybody* in the ground, and-" He waved empty hands, utterly flabbergasted. He'd guessed she could do it, he'd counted on that when he'd jumped himself and Tace away, but it was something else entirely to *see* it.

"Because they were *in* the ground." Shane tapped her cane, raising a puff of heat-dried dust. "Different heat signature. Thanks for getting yourself and Tace out of here. With you gone, the only heat standing was him." The Flame smiled grimly. "Even blind, I couldn't miss that."

She counted on me to do that. She believed I'd make the right call. Allen stared. *Damn it, Shane - do you have to believe in me that much?*

"Time of death...." Dr. Justin Stiller, one of the Watch's more steady coroners, pulled his thermometer out of dead flesh. Frowned. "Well, certainly *not* six hours ago."

"Sorry, that's my fault," Shane called out, more or less facing Stiller's direction. "I chilled him to incapacitate him, but I couldn't manage it quick enough. He was hypothermic and shaking, but still coherent when he got me with a glass wall. At which point he came a little *too* close to killing me, and, well-" She grimaced. "I'm not going to get my knife back any time soon, am I?"

"I imagine not." Dr. Stiller glanced at Allen. *Is she serious?* that arched brow all but shouted.

Allen nodded. *Serious as death.*

"Hmm." Stiller prodded cool flesh again. "You *made* him hypothermic? I've heard of Water-Workers doing so, but never Fire."

"Similar principle." Shane tapped the ground again, voice ragged. "A Water-Worker makes ice by shaping water. If they know what they're doing, they can get it to dump heat and solidify for real. With Fire, I can freeze anything living. All I have to do is pull heat *away*."

Dead silence.

"Why is everyone so surprised?" Shane grumbled. "The only way you get to be in my line of work is by being good at your job." Her blind gaze seemed to fix on Allen. "What do you mean when you say you're good at *your* jobs?"

Not this, Allen admitted to himself.

"Well, excuse *us* if our jobs don't exactly include mass destruction, Flame," Callie said sourly. "Plus twenty ways to kill people with Fire nobody's ever heard of."

"Just twenty?" Shane lifted pale brows. "Stretch your imagination, Inspector Freeport. You might find it interesting." She waved a hand, as if batting away a pesky fly. "This wasn't anywhere near mass destruction. Hell, we didn't even collapse the building."

It was the casual way she said it that chilled him. Allen could see it in his mind's eye; Shane walking out of the residence as it crumpled in flames, a mild look in blind eyes and the sharpest grin on her face. "How did you even get *in* here?" he gritted out.

"Well," Shane drew out the word, "given that you didn't need my help to drag information out of Father Jacobsson...."

The captain gave Allen a sour look. Turned one even more acid on Shane. "With all *due* respect, Flame Redstone-"

Allen stifled a hysterical giggle. Blind or not, Shane could apparently pick up on *justifiably annoyed superior officer* as easily as she could a lit flame. She straightened, humor wiped off her face like rain-swept ash.

"-This was a civilian murder investigation," Captain Mason stated. "You're not a sworn officer of the Watch. You're barely a concerned citizen. The Father has his rights, like anyone else in this city, and that includes not having an invalided-out Flame breathing down his neck while he's being questioned. Inspector Helleson looked for you the minute he was free, but you were already gone. Given what he'd told me about your drive to *take the initiative*-"

Oof, the captain was steamed. So to speak. Allen tried not to snicker, all too aware it might turn into panicked shaking. So *close.*

"-He advised me you were probably up to something. Not that I would have ever guessed you'd be up to this. A residence, Flame Redstone? A *residence?* This... is not going to go *well.*"

Shane's lips thinned, pale. But she said nothing. Only nodded once, silent.

"We had to move on what the Father told us before any of his names realized we were looking," the captain went on. "So here we are. One barbecued residence. Several manhandled diplomats who aren't likely to talk for love, or even money. And a dead murder suspect. I don't know how to *thank you*."

Allen winced. He wasn't the target, and the sarcasm still ate at him like acid.

"Noted, Captain." Shane's voice was very quiet. "Apparently I'm not as familiar with civilian law enforcement as I thought."

The captain growled. "If that's-"

"No excuse, sir." Shane's face was carved ice. "Only the facts. I- the subtleties of working in quieter environments-" Knuckles whitened on her cane. "My team handled that. And they're gone."

"Flame...." Captain Mason sighed, as if the young rookies on the Watch had filled his office with pink balloons to start a new year off right. "Why is Command letting you run around loose?"

"Yesterday I thought I knew." Shane's face was still cold. "If you want my current best guess? Bait."

That stopped Allen cold. *What?*

Stopped the captain, too; Mason gave her a long look. "Explain."

"It wouldn't be the first time." Fingers rubbed polished wood, as if memorizing the grain. "Wounded Elementals attract those with ill intent who are looking for an easier target." She took a breath. "If someone had asked me, I would have told them it was a bad idea. My specialty isn't *subtle*." A bitter smile. "Of course, for some in Command, that might make it even better. The files on me make it clear I'm not subtle. How could I be anything but what I look like? One blind, *easy* kill. So easy to add to your to-do list, while you're looking to inflict other harm on the city."

Mason's eyes narrowed-

"Sir," Allen stepped in, drawn to the sincerity hidden in rough-edged words. "I know what it sounds like, but she's serious." He looked directly at Shane. "You know something. Something that makes you think people knew there was a problem before the Watch ever caught wind of it."

"Not when I left your station. Now? I think so." Shane sighed. "Given I wasn't able to assist directly, I decided it'd be best if I went looking for alternative sources of information." She shrugged. "Ambassador Salloum moved up the short list of people to keep an eye on a few weeks ago, due to importing a creature of great theological significance to the Slaves of Ba'al. Politics, money, a useful patsy with yen for importing exotics - he seemed like a good bet to check out." She laughed once, short and bitter. "And if *I* could find that out, Inspectors, Captain... someone knew there was trouble brewing."

And didn't tell the Watch. Allen swallowed dryly. *But - is she* serious? *We were after Riparians; there hasn't been an attack by Ba'al-worshippers in Caldera City for decades!*

"Oh my," Dr. Stiller murmured, face very grave indeed. "Do you believe the deceased gentleman was of that ilk?"

"I can pretty much guarantee it." Shane's lips skinned back from white teeth. "No one quotes scroll seventy-nine, verse five, just off the top of their head when they're about to kill someone."

"And when almighty Ba'al has delivered them into your power, smite them down! Smite off their demon-tainted heads, and strike off their fingertips, which are anathema," Dr. Stiller said thoughtfully.

"Halter's translation," Shane nodded. "He was quoting the Goss Vulgate version. Which is more favored in...." She quirked an eyebrow Allen's direction, with a hint of a smile.

That, he knew. All Hellesons knew the texts of their enemies' cruel faith. "Riparia."

Shane gave him a thumbs-up.

"I'll look for the ritual scarring," Dr. Stiller growled. "The age should give us an idea when he converted. That anyone chooses to mutilate a perfectly good body before it's even dead...."

Shane huffed a frustrated breath. "Young, or he was born into the faith, would be my guess."

"Ah?" Stiller straightened, curious. "Based on what, if I may ask?"

Shane held up a finger at a time. "First, when you mix Fire and Water-Workers, if you get elemental power at all, Earth is a pretty common result. I'm guessing his mother was Riparian, and his father... well." She grimaced. "Second, he didn't know how to *fight* a Flame. Even if he hadn't been trained as a melee fighter - and he *was* - a little imagination should have let him skewer me a lot quicker. But among the Slaves, Flames are supreme; no one would dare challenge them. He didn't know how to fight me because he was never *allowed* to fight a Fire-Worker. He figured out a little on the fly, but it wasn't nearly enough."

"Call it a hunch, but I don't think everybody's got your kind of imagination," Callie grumbled.

Shane frowned. Lifted her cane a little, set it down too gentle to raise a puff of dust. "What do you mean?"

"She means," Allen stepped in, putting the most diplomatic slant possible on the situation, "that we're looking at all this, and... Flame, I was *here* for half of it, and I can't figure out what happened!"

"A report would be helpful," Captain Mason acknowledged. "If it's not-"

"Classified?" Shane smiled ruefully. "You said it yourself, Captain. I'm a civilian. Besides, if Command doesn't put all of you under oath anyway, they've lost serious brains since I left."

Allen hid his grin. In one breath Mason had managed to establish his authority and calm a still fighting-raw Flame down. The man was captain for a reason.

Shane poked about for the most solid ground, planted her cane, and waved toward the far end of the blasted swamp. "Leaving aside the details on security - if I had help, they were working for *me*, and they're going to get a lot of legal leeway for that - I entered the residence. Given all the other places with potential for investigation, this seemed the most likely to tie in to the leads we had. Including, potentially, Inspector Sorenson's death."

"What?" Callie burst out.

Shane pointed at a stump with some still-green branches. "Smell that? Orchids and burnt chestnut."

Allen squinted, picturing the conservatory before it'd gone up in flames. "That's what's left of the dark-twist."

Callie paled, speechless. "Bastards," Mason breathed.

"More than you know," Shane said soberly. "I suggest you call in an excavation team, Dr. Stiller. Because under there-" she pointed, about thirty feet away, "-is a hollow in the earth that's far too hot. It fits, in fact, what I've seen in the field of buried bodies treated with lime."

"Aman," Allen bit out.

"More than likely. I wonder how many other skeletons are rattling around in here? That's what makes a swamp so useful; plenty of decay, and most of the vegetation doesn't react to rotting meat. Not like forest trees will."

The captain skewed an inquiring look his way. Allen nodded, remembering country crime scenes. "You can find old bodies that way. Seeing where the trees won't grow."

"Huh. Saw that in a few park burials," Mason mused. "Good to know trees are trees anywhere."

"So. Perello was tending the plants, I was over there," Shane pointed again, "being rather small and quiet, when the Inspector and his escort entered. Helleson challenged Perello on Aman's where-abouts; Perello entombed everyone else and earth-gripped Helleson, intending to interrogate him. At which point hiding was out."

"Was it, truly?" Dr. Stiller tilted his head up from the body to eye her. "I admit the stereotypes of Fire-Workers as aggressive combatants have all too much basis in fact, but I know your aunt. Surely she taught you the value of strategic caution. And backup. If you suspected he was a powerful Earth-Worker... well, Flame. You knew *he* wasn't blind."

Shane shook her head once. Winced. "They didn't have time for me to be careful. If he meant them to suffocate, they could have lasted a minute or two, but if he was actively *forcing* earth into their throats - I had to assume the worst."

"How'd you know?" the captain jumped in. "You didn't see them sink."

"I didn't have to see them." Shane's fingers curled on wood, as if seeking every trace of vibration in the soil below. "I've fought Earth-Workers before. I know what it means when heat sources are suddenly blocked. I set up some concealment, scooped out the lids-"

"That you did," Allen muttered; resigned, and almost amused. How many other impossibilities was Shane going to pull out of a hat? "I felt heat, and then Earth moved." Which should be impossible for a Fire-Worker, Flame or not.

"Think sideways." Shane smiled. "Heat makes things expand. If you keep heat from moving one way, and force it another - I heated up air around them, made the earth over them dry to powder, and pulled the hot air up. Same to break his grip on you. Hot air, wet air, a little dust; concealing haze. Push and pull heat into the earth to numb the vibrations from anyone moving. Heat and chill air again - echo-maze even a Storm has trouble tracking to the core." She spread an empty hand. "See? Simple."

Right. Simple as a Helleson rhetorical essay, flensing the reader's soul with the keen reality of eternal damnation. Oh, if he introduced her to his family the sparks would *fly*. "Until it wasn't," Allen guessed.

A resigned huff. "Fair enough," the Flame grumbled. "I'm used to letting sight guide me when I'm doing tricky heat-work. Juggling that and keeping track of people - I fumbled."

Ouch.

The three inspectors looked at each other. Captain Mason shook his head, amazed. "Keep talking."

"I'd hoped Inspector Helleson could bring Perello down, but once Perello sucked Helleson under *again*, I knew he was at least a Master, not just a Journeyman with pre-set Warded traps," Shane said frankly.

"I sent my assistant to the inspector, so they could both get out while I distracted Perello. It worked, I had a clear field, and I tried to chill him so you'd have a prisoner to question. That... didn't work out so well."

"You did drive him hypothermic," Dr. Stiller pointed out, listening as intently as the rest of them.

"Not before he triangulated where the earth was too still." Shane grimaced. "I got turned around dodging, ran into the wall...." She waved at a missing pane of glass. "He was trained enough to know that *would* work - he grabbed me too quickly to have thought that up on the spot. I fell down, made sure I had some breathing holes, and-" She sighed. "He spoke the verse, and I... reacted."

"You killed a man because of a *reaction?*" Callie rocked back on her heels.

"I would," Allen murmured.

Captain Mason gave him a look as if he'd suddenly confessed to juggling goat kids with razor blades. "Helleson!"

"That's the execution verse, sir," Allen said gravely. "They chant that, the knife is coming down. *Imminent* threat of death. Or worse."

"Exactly." Pale hair glinted in the sun as Shane took a slow breath, strands slipping over slumped shoulders. "We're trained *not* to be taken. He was a Slave of Ba'al, he'd already almost killed me, and I had no chance of backup arriving in time. Not backup that could hold a Mountain. Yes. I *reacted.*"

"My word!" Dr. Stiller looked startled; from the man who'd seen just about every form of death Caldera City had to offer, that was beyond unusual. "Young lady, are you saying it's possible for an Earth-Worker to smother a victim with a sheet of glass?"

"I've seen it done. First time it's ever happened to me." Shane squinted, then huffed, as if she'd tried and failed to pick out the glassy fragments half-buried in ravaged soil. "Very effective. If your target isn't an Elemental, they're helpless - they can't chant, and glass locked around you makes it almost impossible to scribe." She raised an eyebrow. "Do you have a rash of unexplained smotherings with no detectable murder weapon?"

"One or two, indeed," Dr. Stiller said darkly. "I believe I'll be spending considerable time in the morgue records. After we've finished finding all the other poor bones in this abattoir." He gave the corpse a very narrow look. "You are very, very fortunate, Flame Redstone. For fate to allow you to free yourself in time, blind...."

"Fate had nothing to do with it." Shane shrugged; casual, save for the white knuckles on her cane. "Glass is Earth and Fire. A ghost of Fire, once it's been cooled solid - but enough for me to know it *is* glass." A hair-fine shudder. "You see someone die that way, you think long and hard on *exactly* what you're going to do if it happens to you."

Again, the three inspectors glanced at each other. Mason looked pointedly at Callie, and inclined his head toward the door. "We'll start on the survivors. Helleson?"

"Sir?"

"Keep Dr. Stiller company until we get some more uniforms past residence security. After that, I should have twisted the ambassador's arm enough to let you search. *Especially* his records." Mason paused. "Flame Redstone?"

"Yes, Captain?"

"Mind staying with them for now? In case somebody in the staff hasn't tipped his hand yet."

"Certainly."

Now that, was too *easy*, Allen thought suspiciously as his fellow inspectors left. "Just *what* did you think you were- Shane?"

Shane flopped down on a piece of dry ground that had been a meandering path, and drew a deep breath. "I'm all right. Just... tired." Fishing in her pocket, she brought out a battered piece of chocolate, and carefully nibbled it down. "How's our mutual acquaintance?"

"Split, like a sane person," Allen said tersely. "How could you bring Tace into this?"

"I needed someone I could trust."

Ow, that stung. "What am I, scattered sand? You broke into a *residence!*"

"*You* weren't available." Shane blew out a breath, and squared her shoulders. "I helped you get that hypocrite to tip his hand, and then you shut me *out*."

Allen glanced at Dr. Stiller. Who was apparently focused on the corpse at hand, making notes with a soft mutter under his breath. Until the silence stretched a little too long, and Dr. Stiller gave him a pointed look.

"I'm sorry," Allen said at last. "I should have made sure you got home alright."

Were it not for his gloves, the coroner looked distinctly like he would smack himself in the forehead. Or, preferably, Allen.

"*Wrong* reason," Shane bit out. "You really don't know what I did for a living, do you?"

"You're a Strike Specialist," Allen said impatiently. "Command gives you a target, you blow it up-"

"Command gives our teams *problems*. So-and-so has been kidnapped. Somewhere in area X, we think there's a munitions plant. Stretch Echo of the border is busy; why? Are there any stretches that are *too* quiet? Oh, and yes, we'd *very* much like certain people working for our enemies neutralized." Fingers curled on her cane. "Sometimes these come with available intelligence. Sometimes, they don't. No matter what happens, we *always* have to search out conditions on the ground ourselves. I am not a walking fireblast, damn it. I may be lousy with people, and I suck at subtle, but I *find things out*." Her breath snarled; tiny licks of flame curled around her knuckles. "I'm a civilian, and I'm blind, but I'm *here*. Bones asked me to see what I could find. I don't *care* if you think I ought to be wrapped up in swaddling and shoved in a closet while the *real inspectors* work. I'll set your damn closet on fire if I have to. They want to *kill our city!*"

"That would be Strike General Bones, if I'm not mistaken," Dr. Stiller put in. "The Black Flag is rather infamous in some circles.

Flame Redstone, if she believes you've reason to pursue this course, she must have good cause. But we are the Watch. Do you have any evidence?"

"Not yet." Shane's voice was iron. "But I found this place, and you found it, and between Aman, his safe, and Petrello, there's got to be something we can use." Flames flickered out. "Who were they? Where did they come from? Where did they *say* they came from? What have they done here? Who have they contacted?"

Allen nodded, making mental notes. "I'm going to be looking at all that...." Wait a minute. "His safe?"

"It's open," Shane said dryly. "Full of documents."

Oh. And ouch. "That you can't read."

Shane winced. And inclined her head. "I screwed up."

Allen blinked, bemused. "You break into a residence, set it on fire, terrify the ambassador and half the staff, and not reading the secret files is screwing up?"

"Yes," Shane bit out. "Because if you hadn't been here, they'd know the safe was punched and we'd have gotten *nothing*. The Slaves would have dropped their contacts like a cut anchor, and we'd have no way to track them."

Allen considered that truth, and Shane's bitter anger. "...I'd like your help."

"Why?" she shot back. "I told you. I screwed up." *Again*, her Spirit raged.

Damn. How many sharp edges did this woman have?

She lost her team, her job, her mission in life. Now she might lose her city. That's four broken places right there.

And it was a Spirit's job to fix what was broken. "Because you're rude, pushy, and jumpy as a cat in a room made of needles," Allen said plainly, "but you're right. I know homicide, not terrorism."

Huh. She'd flinched at *rude*, but she hadn't argued. She'd even grinned a little at *jumpy*, with the kind of resigned half-shrug that said *well, who wouldn't be?*

"I've seen people kill each other because they're drunk, because they're in love, because someone's not," Allen went on. "They panic, they just didn't know their own strength... Sunlit Lord, so many reasons. So many excuses. But this-" He had to stop, and shake his head, feeling helpless. "If it was war, I could understand. I wouldn't like it, but - we're at *peace*. And they're going after *innocent people*...."

"No. They're not. Not by their standards." Shane folded her legs into a more comfortable seat, and tapped fingers on her cane. "You're Orthodox, and Spirit-Gifted. What were you taught about the Slaves of Ba'al?"

"They're the bad guys?"

She threw a clump of dirt at him.

He blocked it with an arm, finally able to smile. It'd just been too good to resist. "The usual. They think we're raving deluded heretics, denying the elements their own divinity. They revere Fire above all, as Ba'al, and consider dragons to be demons who rebelled against his reign and cooled the earth so it could be polluted by human life. People with the Fire-Gift are honored, if they're male. I always wondered what happened to the girls...."

"You *wondered?*" Shane said sourly. "Who do you think tops the list when they practice ritual infanticide?"

Historically, yes, but- "We stopped that," Allen argued.

"We stopped it *here*. By wiping out any cult members we find inside Caldera's boundaries. Any Slave past the age of two can either leave, or die."

"All of them?" Dr. Stiller frowned. "Even the girls?"

Blind eyes winced shut.

I can't leave this on her. "They have Spirit-Workers as well," Allen stepped in. "And one of the tenets of their faith is that there is no compulsion in religion."

The coroner lifted a hand as if to scratch his head; laid it back down. "I'm sorry, I don't follow? That sounds as though it would be a good thing."

"Oh, it *sounds* wonderful," Allen said dryly. Hellesons had been fighting that battle for centuries, why were people still fooled by pretty words?

Probably the same reason everyone in Waycross shuts up. Why make it your problem, when it's only the criminals who get hurt?

Funny, how people always seemed to think *they'd* never be criminals.

"If you read their main scripture, without the glosses on how Ba'al wants them to show their faith in the world, it sounds good, upright, and noble," Allen went on. "What it *means* is, any Working they do - including warping someone's Spirit until they think fire is wet - *isn't considered compulsion*. It's for their faith. So it can't possibly be evil."

Dr. Stiller looked at him askance. "Young man, I know the Orthodox are very stern in their teachings-"

"So?" Shane cut him off. "Orthodox are extreme. They're hidebound. They think most of us who stick with Reform are going to end up wandering the starry desert as lost souls. But about this? *They're not wrong.*" Her breath hissed. "You think this is carnage? Try walking into a home where they converted one of the teenage boys. And every other throat is cut." Her knuckles whitened. "And he's standing there so *proud*, because they were his kin, but they were unbelievers, and now he'll go to Paradise." Fingers flexed on ironwood. "Doctor. Why do you think Elementals have the right to *kill* someone who tries to kidnap us?"

Color drained from the coroner's face. "You're serious."

"Deadly serious, Doctor," Allen said quietly. "That's exactly why it's the law. It takes a Star to warp an Elemental's Spirit - but sometimes the Slaves *have* Stars. And they use them. Other nations don't like to talk about it, but I can show you where to look to find some of the current incidents."

Shane drew a breath. "Oh. About the girls. Just so you know, Fire-Gifted babies aren't always sacrificed. Some of the smarter priests keep them alive, but untrained. Breeding stock."

A chill shivered down Allen's spine. No one could be that cruel. No one could be that *stupid*. "But an untrained Fire-Worker-"

"Inferno waiting to happen," Shane snapped. "So? A girl burns herself to ashes, what's it matter? They take any male children with Fire from her right after birth. Wouldn't do to have him *sympathize* with his *mother*."

"You hate them," Allen breathed, finally pinning that shift of Spirit down. It was concealed, like a sniper draped in forest cammo; hidden under flickers of pain, nightmare, and stubborn fury. But under that pain-dazzle the hate was palpable; the sick, angry determination he'd felt from farmers putting down a rabid wolf.

What insane Spirit-Healer let her walk loose bleeding like that?

"You'd better believe I hate them." Shane's fingers gripped the head of her cane, feeling the curve as if she meant to tear the hook into a vulnerable throat. "I've seen what they do. The lives they've ruined. I've seen the *heads*, Inspector. Almost everyone I've ever cared for in my *life* is dead because of them, or nations they instigated to act against us. That's what they *do* when they don't have the power to fight us directly; plot and lie and tempt other people into hating us. Because to a Slave of Ba'al, outside their own sick cult, *there are no innocents*."

Maybe it wasn't an insane healer, Allen realized, chilled to the bone. *Just a military one.* Because Shane's hate and pain was channeled, *controlled*; honed, like her Fire, to a deadly weapon against her enemies.

A weapon that can turn in the hand, and kill its own bearer-

No; this was no time to find a military-grade Spirit-Healer and start kicking their ass. After they'd run these murdering bastards to earth, then he'd slap someone. The job came before his family's calling.

Although the first thing I need to handle has some of both.
"Doctor? Would you mind-?"

He wasn't sure what the coroner saw on his face. But Dr. Stiller inclined his head. "I believe I should probe for bodies at the far end of this morass for a while. Mark possible sites while this is still a fresh scene."

"Thank you," Allen said gravely.

Shane tilted her head, following the coroner's footsteps as he headed for the far side of the conservatory. Evened out her own breathing, from that tightness of *hate*. "Something your captain doesn't want leaking out of the investigation?"

"Something I'd rather not talk about to most people," Allen said quietly. "You know, if I'd heard that verse, I'd have killed him too." *Tried to, anyway. But even a Mountain's flesh and blood. I might have gotten lucky.*

"I'm glad you didn't have to." Shane kept her voice just as low. "You're no killer."

That was jarring as hands slammed on an organ keyboard. "The men in that warehouse would argue the point."

"They'd be wrong," the Flame said calmly. "You're a Watch officer. You use lethal force when you have no choice." She shrugged. "You're not a killer."

And you think you are. Which at least gave him another thread to start unraveling this knot. "But I would have had to face him anyway," Allen observed. "No one quotes that verse for fun. When someone's got you down, and they're trying to kill you - you stop them. Any way you can."

Shane took a breath, let it sigh out. "I think I hear a *but*."

"This is not a foreign battlefield, and you are not an active striker," Allen stated. *Blunt. Keep it blunt. Pity is acid to the soul.* "You *should not have been here.*"

Knuckles paled on wood.

"I joined the Watch for a lot of reasons." Allen braced himself, and told the truth. "Back in Waycross... I won't give you names, because I can't prove it. I can't prove *any* of it. But there was a man, abusing the Spirit he was given. And I think my family stopped him." Breathe in. Breathe out. And try not to see the haunted faces left behind. "Permanently."

Slowly, Shane nodded. "That's important to you. The law."

"Without it, what are we?" Warm as it was, he wanted to shiver. "Don't walk that road. I love my family. And I left them. Because *I can't trust them.* They broke the law, for what they think are good reasons. What happens when they do it for a bad one? Because no one - *no one* - is going to call out a *Helleson* in *Waycross*."

"So you came here," Shane said quietly. "Where no one cares. Where... someone would stop you."

He tried to nod; flinched, struck all over again by that betrayal in his family's eyes. "Yes."

Shane took a deep breath. "I shouldn't have done that to you."

Augh. "You're missing the *point-*"

Her head bent. "Allen. Please."

Blinking, Allen cut himself off.

"I hear you. I swear. And... you're right," Shane said grudgingly. "But I'm a striker. I don't feel about laws the same way you do. I can't." Now she was the one wincing. "Believe me, Jehanna and I have had our knock-down drag-out fights about the difference. But I am a Calderan. And you're right. What I did was tactically unsound. And wrong."

Allen heaved a sigh. *I can guess which one is more important.*

"I've lived at the tip of the spear. I'm... not used to the idea that someone else might be working the problem." Her voice dropped. "And I'm angry. When I try to tell people what the Slaves are after, what they'd be willing to do to kill us all - they *don't listen*."

Now that, he could believe. "I'm listening."

"You do." Her head lifted. "Zavvan listened like that, too...."

She knew someone named Terror? Allen almost asked- but kept the words behind his teeth, sensing a whisper of grief through that cloaked Spirit. *Not a name. Nickname. You know Watch nicknames; he was probably the sweetest guy on her team.*

Grief, and fear.

She lost her family. She lost her sister. She lost her team. And if her aunt can't even agree to disagree on the morality of law and war - who does she have left?

"You think anyone who gets close to you is going to die." Allen grimaced, and shook his head. "No wonder you jumped in here first. If you went to the Watch - you thought we would come, and we would die, and it'd be all your fault."

No wonder she'd gone to Tace; who had no loyalty to her, or to anyone. Tace was a *street kid.* If the situation went south Tace would have run like hell, and left the Flame to crash and burn.

That's what Shane wanted.

It didn't make this mess anywhere near right. But Sunlit, at least he *understood.*

Survivor guilt. I am going to find *a military Spirit-healer and... damn, I have no idea. Yet.*

Best to put it away to think on later, nights he couldn't sleep. A debacle this extreme deserved a *careful and considered* response. The kind that left *other* people staring petrified at the ceiling.

Those of Spirit are meant to be patient, kind, and understanding. Allen hid a sharp-edged smile. *Until we're not.* "Well, too late, Flame Redstone, the Watch is already involved. Dead bodies are our job. And even if it wasn't...." He winced, recalling years of cold, razor-edged lectures from his family on any faith that wasn't Orthodox. "I learned about the Slaves. *Any* Calderan is fair game, down to babes in arms." He sighed. "Even if I could never grasp it. How can anyone live that way?"

"It's all they know." Shane rolled ironwood between her fingers. "We teach our children to think. They teach theirs to hate. And our *allies-*" the word dripped irony, "-don't have any problems harboring the bastards, because they're such charming, *friendly* neighbors. Until there's enough of them to take over a neighborhood, or a city, or half your country. Then, all of a sudden, they're not friendly at all. Which is just what their scrolls tell them to do: deceive the unbelievers until you're strong, then offer them the *choice* of conversion or death. Or *slavery*." Shane snorted. "Kings, queens, merchant princes - don't tell me they don't know what the Slaves of Ba'al are. And they harbor them anyway. Because if they want to start trouble with us, they don't even have to get their hands dirty. All they have to do is leave an *anonymous* donation at a fire-pit temple, and we'll have all the trouble we can handle."

"Interesting theological question, there," Allen mused, recalling long nights of debates and the finer points of scripture. "Who's the more evil; those who murder, or those willing to use them?" He shrugged. "I decided a long time ago it didn't matter. Cold and at a distance, or up close and personal with the blood on your hands; death is death. And hate is hate." He met blind eyes; at the least, she should hear the determination in his voice. "If you let hate rule what you do, you really will be lost."

"...Sometimes hate's the only thing that keeps you alive."

With everyone else lost to her? He could believe it. "Then let it keep you alive," Allen said bluntly. "*Don't* let it decide what you do."

Her lips bent at one corner; the ghost of a wry smile. "You're a very odd inspector."

"I guess I am," Allen admitted after a long moment. "I'd rather deal with murder than using people. It's cleaner."

"It is," Shane agreed, hate sinking to bleak exhaustion. "Murderers have reasons. Lousy reasons, but reasons. You're in my way, I won't let you talk, you remind me of my stepfather. Whatever it is, they still see *you*. A Slave of Ba'al... they kill you because you *exist*."

Not that different from Father Jacobsson, hating a Flame who'd gone against the Sunlit Lord's plan to gain unnatural power. Only Allen was pretty sure the good Father had never actually wanted to kill someone.

But Marcus Wright did.

If he wanted Shane's expertise.... "Marcus Wright had a grudge against made Fire-Workers," Allen stated. "Jacobsson overheard him speaking with those 'not of the Church' on several occasions. He tried to talk to him; counsel him, to remember vengeance was Sunlit's and those that defied the divine plan would suffer eternal consequences. Wright wouldn't listen. One night Father Jacobsson overheard him mentioning sacrificial fires, and that was the last straw. He gave Wright an earful about imperiling his very soul. The man was dead two hours later."

Shane took a slow breath, and nodded. "Aman was one of the names he knew?"

Allen nodded in return. *Damn it. Blind.* "Yes."

"Is the good father still in custody?"

"Oh, yes," Allen said dryly. "Wouldn't want him to have an *accident.* Like Inspector Sorenson did."

"Hope you told him just that way," Shane smiled, dark and grim. "Heads up, friendly."

Allen glanced that way, nodding as Dr. Stiller carefully drifted back their direction. The coroner might have been too far away to hear their words, but he'd bet the older man could read stance and tone and know the crisis was past. For now. "If Jacobsson had come forward years ago, instead of deciding Wright deserved to die - we'd have a lot less dead people for the good doctor to examine."

"A fate I can assure you I would welcome," Dr. Stiller said dryly, placing another marker where they'd have to dig. "What an odd business we're all in, hmm? Wishing we could join the ranks of the permanently unemployed, no more useful than the makers of buggy whips."

"We may have mentioned the possibility of becoming an accessory after the fact," Allen admitted. "Once or twice." He let a breath pass. "Or five or six times...."

"Good."

There was a darkness in Shane's growl Allen didn't understand. Hoped he *never* understood. "Tell me how I can help."

"You are helping." The darkness was gone, replaced by something oddly fragile; delicate as the thin blue flames that edged her fingertips, then vanished. "That's why I went looking for Tace. Why I want to work with you. I *hate* them, Helle. I hate them so much, it burns."

Allen swallowed dryly. With a Flame, you couldn't assume that was a figure of speech.

"I always had my team to ground me, before. To remind me not to do something *stupid*. Because other people were depending on me. But if I'm alone...." Shane shuddered. "I'm *not* suicidal, Inspector. I want to live. But I hate them so much."

Spirit-counsel under fire. It was one of the few things in his family's repertoire of Spirit-learning he could actually apply. *If you can't get a wounded soul to take care of themselves - find someone they need to take care of, so they have a reason to stay alive.* "You need someone to look after," Allen realized.

"Ironic, isn't it? I'm *blind*. I can't look after anyone. They'd have to be able to look after themselves." A bitter smile. "Kind of defeats the purpose."

At least she knows she's got a problem. Allen brushed off stray crumbs of dirt, thinking. "I don't know. You did pretty well with me."

She waved it off. "You'd have handled it, if he hadn't been an Elemental."

"You might give me too much credit," Allen admitted, looking down at earth dug in under his nails. "I'm not combat-trained, Flame Redstone. Self-defense, sure; taking down suspects, definitely. Killing people who've already decided they're going to kill me, and anyone around me? No." He shook his head, looking over the shattered greenhouse. "I didn't realize how much of a difference there was."

"No one ever does," Shane said soberly. Shifted her head. "I think that's your backup coming."

"Hopefully with the team I requested." Dr. Stiller glared at yet another spot of suspicious ground. "Go on, then. Find whoever's behind this slaughter. I'll alert you if the older bodies show anything of interest." He cast a glance back at Perello's shrouded body. "You certainly don't need me to tell you how *this* one died."

Shane looked hopeful. "In that case-"

"No, you may *not* have the knife back," Dr. Stiller said with great dignity; only slightly spoiled by dropping Allen a subtle wink. *Firecracker, isn't she?* "It's still evidence."

"Darn."

Chapter Eleven

"...Arggh."

"Sit still," Shane advised the frustrated inspector, kneading the back of his neck with warmed fingers. Surprising he'd let her get that close after he'd seen her kill, but - well, either he meant what he said about wanting her help, or his muscles were just that sore. "Heavy-duty reading on top of packing and hauling is always a pain."

"Mmph." Allen ruffled sheets of paper, searching for the one elusive bit that might get them somewhere. At least by this time the snarky remarks and honest bewilderment that the *country Orthodox inspector* could read Atlan glyphs had died down.

Shane tried not to smirk too visibly. Apparently Hellesons took their theological duties *seriously*. Which included knowing how to read the deviltries of the jaguar-demon worshippers, the better to root them out and destroy them.

Know thine enemy. Damn, they did a good job.

Which made Shane take that carefully not detailed story of some Hellesons dealing out extra-legal justice very seriously indeed. Allen believed in his faith, in his training, in behaving as an upright and moral soul. Only a terrible shock would have driven him to walk away from those he loved.

Have to look into that, later. For now, I'm just glad he's here, where we need him.

Allen's fingers thumped on the pages Tace had snuck out for them.

"Do you think we found everything?"

"Hard to say. Depends on how much tradecraft he was taught," Shane reflected. She'd spent years learning how to blend in a dozen kingdoms; or at least look like just another foreigner passing through. All of it useless now. Who could miss a blonde, blind foreigner with Fire?

Don't think about what you can't *do. The problem is here, and now.*

"Based on these records, Perello got by here in the city for five years, so - he probably knew some," Shane stated. "Or, he could just be really dedicated."

"Dedicated- oh. Right. Holy duty to lie to the infidel." Allen shuddered under her fingers. "How any soul could cling to a faith that calls its god the 'Father of Lies'...."

"Don't think of them in terms of sane or insane," Shane advised. "You'll just make your head hurt."

"Holy slayers." Allen looked like he'd sipped raw vinegar. "I know."

Shane grimaced herself. At least Allen *knew*. She didn't have to explain. She'd tried, to some civilians; she really had. But unless you'd gone tooth and nail with them, it was hard to even imagine the mindset of those raised to believe *everyone* went to hell, unless a holy slayer in their family died killing the infidel.

Which made their acts of terror, murder, and horror *entirely* sane. Who wanted to condemn their family to hell by not acting?

Allen was silent a minute, breathing slow and thoughtful. "It's just hard to accept that they have *reasons*."

"Who said anything about accepting it?" Shane said flatly. "All their reasons are a horrible, awful lie."

"You sound certain." Wary, that.

"You might say I have faith." Shane let her voice drop. "Sometimes, it's the only thing I have faith in anymore." Holy words, sacred books - she'd seen too many so-called priests leave wrecked lives behind.

The bright curve of dragon-shells in dancing flames, little lives trusted to the hands of human allies. Great wings of fire and air and water beating above the battlefield, or earth erupting from it, when all seemed lost. Those she could believe in. She didn't care if the Slaves called them demons.

Their reasons are a lie. Their faith is a lie. They kill and rape and enslave innocent people, and they enjoy *it.*

It won't happen here. I won't let it.

"I wish I had as much faith that we'll be able to keep all this long enough to read it," Allen griped, flipping another page. "As soon as someone higher up in Intelligence finds out we gate-crashed a residence-"

"Redstone!" a too-familiar voice snarled.

"Speak of the Opponent," Allen muttered under his breath.

Shane elbowed him. "Be polite," she muttered back. "Even to a devil. You can always throw holy oil on him later." She raised her voice. "Captain Stewart. Always interesting, hearing your sweet and vibrant tones."

The captain's footsteps were a solid tramp of doom. Allen tensed; shoved his chair back from his desk, standing-

Shane read the sudden silence, and the patterns of heat, and nudged him again.

Clearing his throat, Allen stepped forward, and took the offered hand.

"Good job," Stewart said grudgingly. Turned slightly; voice clearer in the way rehab had taught her meant someone was facing her. "I told certain personages that this was a bad idea. I informed them clearly, subtlety and respect for diplomatic niceties were not only not in your vocabulary, you would actively snipe them from a distance. I was, in turn, specifically instructed that they were well aware of that, and of the magnitude of the impending threat, and this was - I quote - *the best bad idea we've got.*" He sighed. "I suppose it'll do,

Redstone."

"Thank you." Shane bowed.

"Good job?" Allen echoed warily, as Stewart took one step back and assumed a formal at-ease, hands behind his back. "The diplomatic fallout has to be-"

"Has to be what, Inspector?" Stewart said dryly. "I can tell you *exactly* what Command will say, when Atla lodges a formal complaint. Unless the Flame would care to?"

"Oh no, Captain, you go right ahead." Shane tried to hide her grin. "I wouldn't dream of infringing on the privileges of our active military."

Stewart snorted, then cleared his throat. "Who did you say breached your residence security again, Mr. Secretary? Security that is supposed to protect all the diplomatic negotiations your ambassador carries out, for both our nations? A street urchin, and a *blind* woman?"

"Shame, shame, shame," Shane sing-songed, right along with Stewart. *What do you know? There's a human being in there after all.*

"You're serious," Allen managed.

"I have no sense of humor. I had it surgically removed." Stewart's voice shifted more towards her. "Or so the rumor mill says."

"Amazing what grinds through there, isn't it?" Shane lifted a shoulder, let it fall. Stewart in a helpful mood was nothing to sneer at. "How can we help? It'd better be fast - I must have looked like a perfect target for earning a ticket out of hell, price one murder, but I doubt Perello would have tried to kill Inspector Helleson *and* the ambassador if things weren't going to be happening *very* soon. Nasty, fiery, blowing-up things."

"I know," Stewart said flatly. "That's why I brought help."

Shane grinned, sensing more heat out in the hall. "My, my; are those the pattering sounds of little private feet?"

"We need to find this operation and shut it down," Stewart said bluntly. "Which means taking all the local help I can get that's not compromised. Sunlit help me, *you* fall under that classification,

Redstone. If I have to have the entire local class of Army translators read you every last bit of paperwork, *I will*."

"You say the sweetest things." Shane kept her face serious, aware how much this had to be costing him. "Thank you, Captain."

"Don't make me regret it," he growled.

"Too late for that, I think," Allen murmured. And cleared his throat, at what was undoubtedly a venomous look. "What? Just stating the obvious."

"Back to work," Shane advised.

"Slave-driver."

"...Ugh." The Flame's head thumped onto the only clear spot on her desk. The nervous private beside her took the moment to grab his cup, chugging coffee like the last water in the desert.

"More coffee?" Allen offered, feeling the wee hours of the morning drag at his bones. Hours poring over Atlan documents and every paper in the late Perello's lodgings, and he wasn't sure they were any closer to finding a fanatical plot than when they'd started. Stewart had kept his snark on the lighter side of acid, Shane hadn't set anything on fire; that was probably the best working relationship between them he could hope for.

"Nrgh. Urk. Bad idea." Shane slurped water instead, absently coiling a strand of blonde hair around her finger. Released pale hairs, drummed her fingers on the spare folding table they'd set up in one of the meeting rooms, and stood. "Blackboard. Chalk."

"Two words that strike fear into the heart of every bureaucrat," Stewart said dryly from his corner of the evidence, as Shane was guided to one and handed the other. "Find something?"

"Maybe. Sometimes, you have to take a step back from the details." Shane tapped her fingers against the slate. "Forget specifics. What, in *general*, have we found?"

"Bookkeeping," one of the privates groaned. "Lots and lots of bookkeeping."

"Never knock expense sheets," Allen stated. "Where money moves, so does information. These people were his contacts."

Shane gave him a thumbs-up.

"Inspector," Stewart said coolly, "they can't all be in on it."

Pale hair shook; stopped, with a tired wince. "Of course not. He said they were *contacts*. Willing, unwilling, unknowing - these are people Perello knew, or Aman knew, or both. Which makes them possible sources of tools, or information. You've already seen what he managed to get the ambassador to order, all in the name of exotic plants and fostering closer ties to Caldera."

"Lethal plants, lethal animals," Allen nodded, "one tiger of theological significance...."

There was more; a lot more. Not nearly as much as he felt there should be, given the tension driving spikes into his shoulders, but the paperwork had given them a sizeable pile of contacts, resources, and info whoever he'd been working with would have on potential targets. Shane scrawled each as he spoke, one hand on the board to keep her writing level. Moved it down about an inch, as they got from the legal and aboveboard to names and places and eatery receipts that hinted where Perello had dipped into the city's own shadows. *Skin and Water* hadn't made the list, but there was a warehouse down at the airship docks he knew Customs was side-eyeing, the *Last Coin Inn* did a thriving business in fake IDs, and the less said about deals made in the smoky backrooms of the *Bucket of Blood* for anything up to and including murder, the better.

And there were more. Too many more.

Allen walked up to the board to stare, as if the shift of angle would change reality. Bit back an *argh*, wishing he could act like a spoiled child and bang his head on chalked stone. "Sunlit, it's going to take forever to talk to all of them!"

Shane felt at green slate, dust staining her fingers pale. "We don't have to. What kind of information did they think was important to *personally* keep on hand?"

"Maps," Allen said uneasily. "Street, power, water, subways - you think they were compositing?"

"Which implies they're looking for something not on the maps," Shane nodded, scribbling.

"We know that," Stewart sighed. "They targeted a lava-Ward."

"They put a bomb over a lava-Ward, and it was *probably* a target," Shane corrected. "But it's not big enough."

"Thousands of people would have died!"

"And we have over two *million* here in Caldera City." Shane's fingers clenched, white dust sifting down. "This series of signs - this time when the years and the elements are right - only comes at three points in their sixty-year cycle. The last one was twenty-four years ago. Remember *that?*"

Every local in the room went quiet. Allen felt a chill, remembering what he'd read just this evening of prior bombs involving Redstone. Twenty-four years ago an underage girl had had a Fire-Pearl grafted into her heart, because it would *increase* her chances of survival. Given the less than cheerful survival rate of perfectly healthy people going into that operation - he didn't want to think what her injuries had been like.

"I read the reports," Stewart managed.

"I remember it," Shane said bleakly. "I was there." She blew out a breath. "They didn't target just one lava-Ward last time. Stop thinking small, Captain. They mean to *wipe us out.*"

"And they're after made Workers," Allen realized, a jumble of pieces finally fitting together. "That's our weapon against them. That's why Wright helped them - whatever they've planned, it's going to hit our elemental surgery."

"My Lord," Stewart breathed, as Shane's fingers stilled on the board. "Do you really think-?"

"Yeah," Shane said softly. "Yeah, that's just about big enough." Clouded gray eyes scanned the room, grim as death's own angel. "They're after the Points."

Chapter Twelve

I'm going to die, Allen thought starkly, staring into simmering air just outside the protective wall. *I'm going to be seared into ashes, and they won't even find a finger-bone.*

"Slow breaths," Shane advised, hand on his arm. "Try to relax."

Relax. Right. When Army Intelligence and every spare Watch officer was heading toward the other four elemental Points as fast as they could. Quietly, because so long as the Slaves thought their plans to destroy the pearl-crafting workshops were going to schedule, the Watch had a chance of getting in to disarm whatever explosives had been smuggled in before everything went boom. And in force, because even if Caldera's pearl-shaping Masters and Elementals weren't combat trained, the Slaves would have brought all the overkill they could scrape together.

In force, except for one. The Fire Point was Shane's.

Which makes sense, Allen told his terrified brain. *She's an Elemental. She's combat-trained. And if she has to get nasty against our enemies... the Fire Point is reinforced against, well,* Fire.

Right. Perfect sense. Now if only he could persuade his heart to climb back up from his shoes. Allen tore his gaze from shimmering air, and tried not to gulp. "Isn't there a safer way to get there?"

"Absolutely," Shane nodded. "Where *someone* will have set up surveillance. It's what I'd do. As much as we want the Points warned, we need our enemies *not to know*." She gave him a moment. "Can you trust me?"

Do I have a choice?

But that was the point. He did. She'd let him back out, here and now. And go in herself. Blind.

I think that was Rule 5 on General Bones' Care and Maintenance of Strike Specialists, Flame: Do not let her go off alone, unless you have a thousand-acre tract you want flattened.

Sunlit, the *looks* he'd gotten after that light-letter had shown up at the station. The Black Flag apparently hadn't cared that a high-level government transmission would draw eyes already sworn to secrecy; not when all of Caldera was on alert, hunting for Slaves.

But even if they didn't know the contents, half the station knew he'd gotten it. Which was going to make for very *interesting* gossip to deal with. If they lived.

Based on her report, Inspector Helleson, Shane seems to trust you and *think you have a sense of self-preservation*, the general had written. *Stick to her like glue. These guidelines should help.*

Help *terrify* him, certainly. If that mess in the conservatory had been a brick between the eyes, Bones' matter-of-fact list of circumstances under which he ought to *run like hell* were a gut-stab of *exactly* how much power had casually tapped its way through his city.

Now he was going to walk into Caldera's sea of molten lava, with only Shane's will to protect him.

Well. The family always said joining the Watch was the first sign I'd cracked. "So." He tried to swallow, throat dry. "How do we do this?"

"Just hold my hand, and walk with me," Shane advised. "Well, you don't have to hold my hand, but stay close. The smaller the bubble I have to keep cool, the better."

"Close. Got it." Allen gripped her hand. Loosened it a hair, at her polite cough. "Okay."

Breathing out, Shane stepped through the wall.

Oh Sunlit Lord, I'm really going to do this-

Heat prickled over his skin like a furnace draft, before Shane waved it away. Air around them simmered, hot as summer asphalt; ice-cool compared to the shimmering atmosphere outside. Especially given they were heading toward the shore of glowing red stone....

Allen forced himself to keep walking, as Shane advanced on the molten sea. Her brass-shod cane came down on liquid lava-

Touched black stone, rippling out in a frozen wave. Shane nodded, and stepped onto the hardened surface. "Come on."

Allen swallowed. Cleared his throat. Stepped forward. It *felt* solid, at least. "I've heard of Water-Workers parting the sea, but this...."

"Doesn't get so much mention," Shane agreed. More lava solidified in front of them as she walked; behind, their link to the shore was already melting away. "This is how Caldera was first built. Fire-Workers containing the eruption before it could destroy our clans. Channeling the worst of it away-"

"And raining fire on those who would destroy us," Allen finished, remembering one of the first histories he'd been taught as a child. "The Flames of Ba'al roused the very mountains to destroy us, but by the grace of sunlit skies-"

"And a hell of a lot of hard work," Shane stuck in.

"-We turned the very flames against them, and destroyed them." Allen shook his head. "It always sounded like a fairytale."

"Read some of the histories still lying around from the founding," Shane advised. "Not as fantastic as you'd think. A lot of death. A lot of near-misses." She grinned. "But every once in a while, I have to imagine what Ba'al's army thought, when the fiery clouds started heading *their* way."

"Ouch," Allen agreed wryly.

"We're far enough out now." Shane closed her eyes. One slow, ritual breath, prepping for near-trance as she slung her cane over her back. "Let go, but stay close. I need two free hands."

"Right." *Now if I could just convince my* nerves *it's all right-*

"We're moving!"

"Of course we are." Shane swooped one hand, then the other, for all the world like steering oars, as their fragment of hardened lava crunched loose and floated into the fiery sea. "This is faster than walking."

"I was *fine* with walking," Allen muttered, eyeing splashes of heat-glowing red-black against the outer edges of their refuge. "Shane, you get *turned around* on a *city street!*"

"Yes. Because there's about the same amount of Fire everywhere," the Flame said frankly. "We're heading for a Worked cool spot in the middle of an inferno. It's hard to miss." Both hands moved like a theater dancer miming swimming; together and push, together and push. Lava reacted, swirling apart to draw their hard patch forward, again and again.

It's not going to kill me, Allen told himself yet again. This time, he believed it. Shane was here, and the world bowed to her command, even though it should be *impossible*. "That's rock. Earth. How can you Work it?"

"I don't." Shane never slowed. "I Work the heat around it. Heat, Fire... it's not like most people think."

"So what is it like?" Sunlit, he really had cracked. Standing in lava, in the middle of the caldera, air shimmering like glass - and he almost felt *safe*.

No one's going to be sneaking up on us out here, that's for sure. He shivered suddenly. *Unless they've got a Flame, too....*

"It's like... water that can run uphill." Shane frowned, hunting for words. "Fire needs air, and fuel, but aside from that - it *flows*. Pushes. Pulls. Like blood in your veins; hot and needy and angry, if it's blocked. Earth-Workers move metal by moving bits of Earth in it; I can move objects by moving the heat in them. Lava. Glass. Even water, if I move fast enough. It's not perfect, but I *can* do it."

"Earth, Air, Water," Allen said thoughtfully. "What can you do with Spirit?"

Pausing a moment, she flicked a thumb toward her sunglasses.

"Not too damn much. Or I wouldn't be like this."

"Sorry." He struggled for words. "I just thought - that cycle you mentioned-"

"Nobody ever said the Slaves of Ba'al were *scientific*," Shane said dryly. "There's a reason they call it metal, not Spirit. Some of their splinter sects don't even *have* Spirit-Workers. It's 'unholy'. Then again, so are dogs, bells, and dragons."

"That's why they started hating us," Allen nodded. "Our people were born Spirit-Workers."

"Maybe then. Now?" Her voice had that abstracted tone he'd first heard as she Worked Fire out of a bomb; all facts, no room for clouding fury. "They hate us because we *exist*. Because we're *not them*. Because we build, and create - and all they can do is raid us and take it away. They hate what we *are*. If our priests were Water-Workers, they'd march on the sea instead."

Sobering thought. But- "Why *us*?" Allen repeated. Anything, to distract himself from the inferno outside Shane's will. "Why not Geist? Or Riparia? They've got Spirit-Workers too."

"*They* didn't wipe out the Prophet of Ba'al in a blasphemous firestorm," Shane said dryly.

True enough. A firestorm Caldera still sang hymns about to this day; though usually not outside Covenant Day festivals. Still. "Five hundred *years*."

"We're not the only people with long memories," she shrugged. "I don't know how to explain it any better, Allen. They hate *what we are*. They say everything happens as Ba'al wills. We say the Sunlit Lord has a plan, but you've got to go out and work for it to happen. You have to make yourself better. You have to be *responsible*." A low snarl. "A slave is never responsible for anything."

"'He made me do it,'" Allen quoted. "Murderers always have the same story. If he hadn't held out on the cash. If she hadn't slept with somebody else. If the kid had just shut up-" He cut himself off, wincing at the memory. Murder was bad. Child-murder kept you up nights, wondering how the Sunlit could love humans at all.

"Exactly." Shane's voice held a chill this fiery sea would never know. "We *make* them kill us. Because we won't do what we're *supposed* to do: convert, lie down and die, or toil for them like good little pagan slaves, always ready to be raped and murdered if they feel a little put out with the world."

"That's crazy."

"That's Ba'al. And crazy doesn't mean stupid."

"Too bad," Allen grumbled, side-eyeing a blurp of lava, droplets spattering into cracked obsidian as they hit cooler air. It was too true. Watch officers who made that mistake, didn't live long. "So how likely is it they've already gotten something inside?"

"Very." Shane hesitated. "Or not. It all depends on how they're trying to hit the Points. If that first bomb was part of this, they're going from the outside, with a countering element."

Right. Unbeknownst to him until Stewart had read him in an hour ago, that warehouse wasn't just above a lava-Ward. It was fairly close to the hidden Point of Water, and if it'd unleashed Fire, it would have been in immediate opposition to the Water portal. Very, very messy. Possibly even worse than breaching the lava-Ward - not just from the amount of destruction, but the time and resources Caldera would have to spend rebuilding. With *no* new Water-pearls for made Workers until that was done. If it *could* be done.

If we had a sudden shortage of Water-Workers - oh, Riparia would love to take advantage of that.

Then again... Shane didn't throw around *if* lightly. "You think it wasn't." Allen grimaced. "A huge bomb. Master's work for a *year*, Aster said. And you don't think it was part of this."

"Not part of the direct assault. And don't get hung up on one year. They've had twenty-four to pull this together." Shane swiped her fingers through the shimmering where cold air held off hot, came back with a handful of fire. "What happens when a building burns?"

Odd, how that fire was so much easier to look at than the natural lava around them. Or maybe not; Shane controlled these flames. "Fire Department puts it out."

"And what can you *see* when that happens?" Fire split to tip each of her fingers in flame; blazed and twisted back together, one bright ball. "Think like an enemy. If the Fire Department *was* your enemy - if the lives of your family depended on that building *burning to the ground*. Better yet, not that building, but the *next* one."

"You'd see how many people they have," Allen realized. "How fast they can move, what they've got to fight the fire with... are you saying we nearly *died* because of a *test run?*"

"Chaos would have made it easier to attack the other Points." Shane didn't shrug, every movement controlled. "All the dying, the dead; lava and poisonous gases reaching into the city itself... they *want* us to die, Allen. Horribly, and in pain."

So he'd learned as a child. But he hadn't *felt* it before. "So they could be inside already. They breed for Fire-Workers, they could get to the Point just like we are-"

"Not that easily," Shane smirked. And arched one brow up.

Allen looked, and his jaw dropped.

It doesn't look like the light-paintings....

Worked Air could never capture the sheer *reality* hovering overhead, shimmering in all the colors of flame.

It's... big....

Fire burned in strands of a mane, from heavy horns to the base of great, five-fingered batwings. More blazed in tufts along the long tail, booted each taloned claw and hand. And they *were* hands, if long-clawed as eagle talons. Assuming eagles got fifty feet long.

But the eyes weren't fiery. The eyes were silver as the moon, diamond-white as winter stars. They drew him in, and he was falling-

Shane's hand on his shoulder stopped him. "Allen."

He shuddered, like surfacing from deep water. *Inches* from the protective barrier.

"Why do you guard him, Flame?"

It crackled like fire; it *was* Fire, burning in his mind. Shane's fingers pressed in, pulling him from that blaze.

A white blink. *"If he is not strong enough to bear us, he should not have come."*

"But it pleases me to travel with him," Shane said easily.

"Does it?" A slow beat of glimmering wings, bearing the dragon in a long circle about them. *"We have heard of your wounding."*

"News travels fast," Allen said, trying for a light tone.

"Do not speak, small creature."

Crushing - soul - *heart-*

Fire, racing through his veins to heat and pry and tear....

He was gasping on his knees, barely feeling hot stone. Shane crouched beside him, cursing under her breath, cane a one-handed barrier as she pressed warm fingers over his heart. "-Don't you die on me, Allen, don't you dare-!"

"Not yet," he croaked. "Oh Sunlit, that hurt." Still did, shimmering inside in a way that just - shook him. He *knew* his Gift. Had known it for years. Now - he felt like a stranger in his own flesh.

"You're on your own for that. I just hit all the Spirit I could handle." Fingers felt his pulse; she breathed a sigh of relief. Stood, and rapped her cane on stone.

Waves of molten lava rose to either side of them, hanging like an executioner's blade.

"Do you threaten me, Flame?" The massive head tilted, as if drowning in lava were a matter of mild interest. *"If it pleases you to bring him among us, it pleases us to know him."*

"You could have killed him." Shane's voice was level. Angry, but contained.

"Perhaps." The dragon backwinged, landing on lava itself; walking firm as if it were dry land. *"What brings you among us without warning, with one so frail as to need protection from us?"*

"The Points are being attacked." Shane lowered her voice. "Don't say anything, Allen. Dragons *test* people. Speak, he acknowledges you're there, he gets to poke at you again."

Great. Now *you tell me this?* Allen thought darkly. Sure, everything he'd read warned that dragons weren't *safe*, but they were supposed to be allies!

"That would explain much," the dragon murmured, soft as burning paper.

"Explain what?" Shane said sharply.

Teeth gleamed like whitest flame; the dragon's neck curved, trying to catch Allen's gaze. *"Would you risk my touch again, little Spirit? This Flame is known to us, and I sense the warp of her wyrd knotting us all. You have need for haste, and surprise, or all may be lost."*

"What do you know?" Shane demanded.

"I know that I am here, because I sensed the wyrd, and found it intriguing, where others of my kind find it warning. They remain within Fire, or elsewhere. I came through the Point, and left it, and enjoyed the flight in this world of All. I knew you would come. Or not." Starlight gazed at Allen. *"What will you risk, for that which those of your kind hold dear?"*

"Humans?" Allen dared.

"Calderans." A crackling chuckle. *"Most humans are boring. Your kind are the only ones who dare to become as we. After a fashion."*

"I don't understand," Allen admitted.

"Do you not?" White eyes blazed at Shane.

"This is considered need to know," the Flame mused. "Apparently a dragon thinks you need to know. Helleson. They're not all born with pearls, either."

For a moment, Allen was sure he couldn't have heard that right. Dragons were the ultimate elemental creatures. They *lived* on the Elemental Planes, only entering reality when it amused them. And some of them hatched out pearl-less as a human?

They'd die. Quick, and horribly.

"Human hands are nimble; human surgeons, determined.

Calderans are our allies." Rising onto his haunches, the dragon spread great, clawed hands. *"Come."*

"Lend us your name," Shane requested.

"You may call me Candle."

Shane's shoulders relaxed a hair. "Your call. You're the one who's at risk."

"What kind of risk?" Allen's heart beat fast. *Wyrd... we're running out of time.*

"A dragon's all five elements. If you had no pearl, this *would* kill you. As it stands... they're elemental power, Allen. I'm a Flame; I can handle it. You'll be stuck in a feedback loop of your own power, as long as he's touching you." Her voice was taut. "Like I just dragged you out of."

"That didn't kill me," he reminded her, even as his mind shied from the memory of pain. "If we need to go - let's do it." Bracing himself, Allen walked into the claw.

It was like being seared by sunlight.

Dimly he felt forge-hot air slide over him, barely cooled enough to breathe as it whipped into his throat. The great fiery sea spread below, Caldera's protective wall shimmering in the distance; ahead, an odd circle of a building surrounded a sphere of pure Fire-

A wingbeat, and they plunged into flames.

The Point. The gate to the elemental plane of Fire. We're inside *Fire.*

Humans can't live here....

Everything went white.

Cold stone. Candle's hot breath over her head. A too-hot body in front of her as Shane knelt, pounding on a heart knocked horribly out of rhythm.

Breathe, damn it, keep breathing - you stop and I'll never *fix this-*

No use yelling at the dragon. All these centuries, and they still couldn't understand how fragile humans truly were.

Remember your training. The pearl will *stabilize the heartbeat, if it can - you just have to give it a chance.*

The only chance she had. She *wasn't* a healer. Heat *that* node of muscle to interrupt the pattern, cool another to slow it, and *strike-*

His heart stopped.

Please, please... Sunlit Lord, Allen....

Power rippled under her fingers. Gathered. *Considered.*

Flexed inside him, heart thumping back into rhythm as if it'd never left.

Lord, oh Lord. Shane drew in a relieved breath, and sat back on her haunches.

"*You may not wish,*" Candle's voice sizzled at her, "*to put your hand there.*"

Shane froze. Drew in another taste of air, senses stabilizing back to the real world, away from that overwhelming Fire.

Bright copper, bitter on her tongue. Blood. A lot of it.

Allen coughed, muscles spasming. Shane grabbed him, muffling noise as much as she could and still let him breathe. "Dead people," she hissed.

That got through; he made a mumbled sound of assent, leaning against her to dampen his shudders.

"*So the lines of wyrd were true.*" A roar of flames; she'd never been so glad to know dragons spoke Spirit to Spirit, and never human words at all. "*I will deal with this* thing *they mean to defile our gateway.*"

She felt it like a cold knot in her skull; Water and Spirit and metal all tied together into a device that would blast Fire with its scourging opposite.

"*You, Flame... you* shall deal with the defilers.*"

"You can't expect-" Allen started to protest.

"*Are you Calderans? Are you our allies? You carry our strength within you. Use it!*"

The inspector tensed at that incandescent fury; Shane held up a hand before he could protest. "Look at the Fire, Allen," she whispered. "*Look* at it."

He was silent then, and she knew what he saw. What he *sensed*. *Little lives, sleeping in the flames....*

"Not all dragons are born with pearls," Shane murmured.

"We're a refuge," Allen whispered back. "The Points. Here. I never knew."

"They don't talk about it. He won't leave them, Allen." She got to her feet, and bowed silently to Candle.

"May your wyrd twist well," rumbled back.

"You're blind," Allen whispered, hand seeking hers again.

"Yes." And their enemies must not hear them coming. She pulled the cane's strap over her shoulder, already missing the shape-painting echo. "But I trust you."

Hand on his shoulder, Shane followed him through carnage.

The heads. Sunlit, where are the heads?

He feared he knew, from history he'd prayed had been resigned to the past. Caldera had driven them back again and again; Caldera would live in peace with all its neighbors, if only they would let her. Why couldn't the Slaves just stop?

And when they had slaughtered the unbelievers, they piled the heads in front of the Prophet, so he might rejoice. And he did cry aloud to the skies, thanking Ba'al and his Consorts that the unbelievers had been slain, and their women and children taken as slaves... and he did seize the infidel's head by the hair, and scattered the blood on his warriors as blessing....

"They hate what we *are*," Shane had said. As all his clan had said.

But from her, it was heavy as iron.

Focus, he told himself. *She's counting on you.*

Shane's steps weren't soundless; without sight, they couldn't be. But she was nearly as quiet, sneaking, as he was.

He stopped, and leaned down to whisper in her ear. "I've never been in a Point. What are we looking for?"

"We came in by dragon. That was the Nest," Shane breathed back.
"It's built in a circle. The first quarter is the secure gateway... was,
anyway. After that are the workshops, and the operating rooms.
Deepfire, I hope no one was scheduled for today.... Last quarter is the
Nest. So someone has to get through all the Point personnel to threaten
the eggs."

Which they had. Allen shook his head. "No rod blasts. Just knife
wounds, really big ones-"

"Swords," Shane nodded. "My guess? The Thanes."

So legendary assassins. Terrific.

"Think about it," Shane murmured. "Most rods you can get in
Caldera are Fire. Most of the people here *Worked* Fire. Swords and
knives... most surgical Fire-Workers don't learn how to warp metal.
Not fast enough to keep them alive-"

Something *boomed.*

"Someone must have made it to a safe room," Shane muttered.

Oh good, someone else alive. "Think it'll hold?"

"Most of the pearls are *kept* in safe rooms," Shane said flatly.
"You think they'll stop?"

"No," Allen admitted. "Hold onto me."

They crept up quietly, sacrificing speed for stealth as the
explosions went on. It hurt his heart, but - they were all the backup
there was, here and now. Even if Captain Stewart had told them
everything about a Point's security precautions, about the forces that
were being sent - that could take an hour. And all the blood was fresh.

The corridor curved; he stopped while the bend still gave them
cover. "What do we do?"

Shane's teeth lightly gripped her lower lip. "Have you followed
someone else's elemental sense before?"

Allen hesitated, tamping down bad memories. "With other Spirit-
Workers."

"Do it with mine." Shane stared ahead, as if she could peer through rock like an Earth-Worker. "Odds are, everybody beyond that bend is an enemy. But I'd hate to fry a hostage by accident."

So would he. But. "What good will that do if I'm not looking?"

"You're a truth-reader." Shane squinted, as if trying to clear blind eyes. "You're *good* at it. You don't need to chant or scribe; either you've got a lot more Gift than you've let on to anyone, or you were *really* motivated." Her smile was wry. "I think I can guess which."

Allen winced. And wondered. "Not sure I can. It burns."

"Dragons aren't for the faint of heart. You'll hurt, but you're alive. Now I need you to do yourself one better. I need you to read a question right off their Spirit, *without* speaking. 'Are you a child of Caldera?'" She sighed, face cold. "Anyone who isn't, I deal with."

Oh. "What if there's another Elemental?"

"Oh, I'm betting there is." Shane's lip curled. "I'll *handle* them, Allen. But odds are, that Elemental *will* block some of my attack. They've got numbers on their side. If I know who I *shouldn't* target, I can focus - and those numbers will go down." She gripped his hand. "I'm counting on you to keep the survivors off me long enough."

Scary thought. "Have you ever seen someone do this?" Allen demanded.

"Yes," Shane answered, unflinching. "A Star." She gripped harder. "You survived a dragon's touch, Allen. You're stronger than you know."

"Not like you," he admitted. *Not the way I've seen you take life, and just keep going.*

"You'd be surprised," Shane smiled. "I was a rookie once, too." The smile slipped away. "We're only going to get one shot. Ready?"

"Let's do it." Allen rested his left hand on her shoulder, rod already in his right. A whisper of Fire sliced outward.

He swept after it with his own sense, startled how easy it was. Fire had always burned, but this- this almost seemed like kin. That, or the dragon had scorched him so fiercely he was numb.

Heat and heat and more heat, human spirits reading clear as lights on a darkened sea. All to be weighed, tested, *asked-*

Are you one of us? Are you ours?

Hate! Denial! Negation!

A whip of water, slicing through curved stone in an arc that should have taken their heads off, if Shane hadn't jerked him aside.

Bleeding. The bright splash of red on her arm was a horror. *What the hell was-*

He felt the strength facing them, and he knew.

Not one elemental. Two.

Shane swiped fingers in a hiss of burning blood, sealing the slash before it could weaken her. The same sweep of fingers sliced air, fire bursting into being and *slamming* down the hall-

Allen steeled his heart against the screams, following even as his brain caught up with *why* she was still attacking.

If they're screaming, they're not dead.

No shouted warnings, no thoughts about getting a suspect down and in cuffs - just shoot and dodge and try not to think-

A half-dozen bodies flamed on the floor. Others, singed and smoking, charged him, swords lifted-

Steel melted, in one twist of Shane's hand.

They came on anyway.

Sunlit, I don't want to do this-

Cold swallowed him.

Water. Everywhere.

It pounded his ears, twisting up and down, hitting so hard he didn't dare open his eyes. Already his lungs ached, as water fought to get past sealed lips. More yanked at his pinched nose, crushing life and light-

Water-Worker - kept some of them from burning - I don't want to be here!

Light blazed.

He was *behind* a man; dripping, but breathing. The dark-garbed enemy whirled, lashing out with another whip of water.

Allen shot.

The first Fire-bolt missed center of mass, but the bastard wouldn't be using his right arm again anytime soon. The second and third crashed into the shield of water suddenly *there*, as the Wave's face contorted in a snarl.

Water Elemental. I am so dead.

If he tackled the guy head-on, yes. He aimed bolts four through six at the others instead, taking down at least two of those heading Shane's way.

Not that she needed much help. Not for them.

Dancing hands spiraled flame around her; slow, fast, stuttering and starting so he could never tell which patch of air would be aflame next. Every blade that neared her melted. Every limb that crossed that spiral *seared*, as if eaten by molten lava. Death walked wreathed in flames, and nothing human could stand against it-

Flames stopped.

"*Die*, you abomination!"

Fire-Worker. Allen felt the flame inside the man, hot counterpoint to the cold arc snapping toward his own face. He didn't try to duck; just focused again on *elsewhere-*

A life snuffed out, as water lashed through where he'd been like a razor.

Allen stumbled behind Shane, resurfacing into *here* with enough presence of mind to shoot two who'd tried to slip through the now-still spiral. How had he done that, and why he wasn't out cold on the floor after two lurching jumps- *later.* "Are we in trouble?"

"Shoulder," Shane said tightly; sweating, hands flat against air as if holding back a crushing wall. "Trust me."

"I do," he muttered, gripping her shoulder, "but that Wave is-"

"Oh, yes." He *felt* the dark humor in that laugh. "He most certainly is."

He saw the Elementals' plan, sure as if he were truth-reading them in Interrogation. The Flame held Shane still, a prisoner of her own fires, while the Wave raised smug hands to smash a miniature tsunami through....

At the last moment, Shane's stance shifted; one subtle shimmy that swept half the flames into icy death. She slipped through the sudden gap, and he stepped with her, *freezing-*

Half the wave flashed into steam. The other hit the chill wreathing them, and froze into sculpted ice.

Their enemies stared.

"That's the problem-" Shane clapped her hands together; every man still standing erupted in flames. "-with treating Fire-Workers like gods!" She swept her hands upward, swirled them as if looping ribbons-

All but two of their foes collapsed, necks seared through by incandescent fire.

"If you don't take a few lumps, you never learn how to fight." Shane was breathing hard; he felt her tremble. But the look she shot the Elementals was nothing short of utter confidence. "Who's next?"

The Wave was pale, neck steaming from hastily-conjured ice to block her kill. The enemy Flame held the fire-ribbon in his own hands, struggling as if with a snake.

"I hate them so much," she'd whispered.

Allen cleared his throat. "Caldera City Watch," he said into crackling silence. "Surrender, and you'll get a fair trial-"

Freezing.

Heart seizing.

No!

He blazed his heart back into motion, deflecting the Wave's blood-freezing with a fluid move he'd seen Shane use to send Fire-bolts awry. It shouldn't have worked. He didn't know *anything* about Spirit-Gifts in combat. Though if he lived through this, he swore he was going to sit down in Shane's library and let her lecture him 'til her voice ran out.

It shouldn't have worked. But it did.

"I think," Shane stated, a ball of fire held protectively in front of her own heart, "that qualifies as a *no*."

All hell broke loose.

Their training might have sucked, but there *were* two of them. Damn; she hated a fair fight.

Allen was a rock, thank Sunlit. Never flinching, moving when she moved, ducking when she ducked. She had no idea if he could feel all the levels of the fight going on; the Flame trying to turn stone to lava under them, the Wave striving to freeze the blood in their veins.

Fire between us slows him down - he needs line of sight. But some of it's getting through, and every bit I spend to warm us....

Lucky the Flame was sloppy. Deflecting cost less power than countering. But more concentration. It came down to endurance, will, and sheer stubborn grit.

Which of us will cave faster?

They weren't scarred. They hadn't fought another Elemental this week.

Breathe. Keep your guard up. Think. Can't go forward. Can't flank them.

...Oh, what the hell. "Allen," Shane said tightly, "do you trust me?"

"You're insane," he coughed, waving away stray bits of steam. "But yes."

"Then *hang on*." Shane stamped down on stone; no longer holding it solid, but adding her strength to her enemy's, *pushing* it into lava. Pushing every last bit of warded rock under them back into the primal sea of fire-

She hugged him close, as they dropped into molten stone.

Make a shell, move the heat away - you can survive molten lead if it doesn't touch you-

The crust of lava was hot, torturously hot; filled with acrid stench as hair and cloth seared. But they weren't dead yet. She could live through burns. She could live through scars.

The aching pressure as hot air expanded - that *would* kill them. Shane breathed out, but there was only so much human lungs could exhale. Either air-sacs would pop and suffocate them, or expanding lungs would squeeze their hearts to a stop.

Seconds. They had seconds.

I trust you....

Searing heat vanished. Whisked away, as they coughed on the icy floor of a nesting room, under a dragon's watchful eye.

"Nice work," Shane managed.

"Thanks...."

Darkness rolled her under.

Chapter Thirteen

"Sunlit, you're alive."

Allen pried open one eye at a time, wondering exactly when the whole royal Aeolian wind orchestra had taken up residence in his head. "Callie?" Another blink; he recognized white ceiling tiles with subtle star-signs. Hospital. "Ugh."

"You can say that again." Still wan from venom, his Watch partner smirked. "You look worse than I do."

"Shane?" Allen lifted a hand, one finger at a time, but couldn't quite lift his trembling arm. "God, I hurt."

"Yeah, well, that's what happens, when you try to channel enough power for an Elemental," Callie said dryly. "Or so I hear." She shrugged. "Redstone's down the hall. They say she'll probably be out for another day. Lucky for her. You have no *idea* what kind of high-level screaming is going on about that hole through the Point's floor. *And* its lava-Wards. Nobody's supposed to be able to do that." Her voice had an edge of grudging respect. "Only I guess if you helped *build* the damn things, you know goddamn well how to unravel them."

"She helped build the lava-Wards?" Somehow, that made a lot of sense. Or none at all. Allen felt like he had after a near-lethal case of the flu; wrung out, and disconnected from the world. "What *happened?*"

"Well, they found the boxes the assassins shipped themselves in."

"Boxes?" Allen echoed, lost.

"I kid you not." Callie helped him sit up to sip water; he was suddenly, desperately thirsty. "That warehouse in Perello's contacts? They got to people who normally shipped stuff to the Points, and then-" she shrugged. "They're insane. No two ways about it."

"Don't think I'll ever hear that word the same again," Allen managed. "You stopped the others?"

"Us, that Captain Stewart, a bunch of other people." Her fingers clenched hard on his, before Callie made herself let go. "Lord, they killed so many people."

"Who did we lose?" Allen asked, dreading the answer.

She started to speak, then shook her head. "I shouldn't be in here, the docs said not to stress you-"

"Tell me."

Which *hurt*, deep inside, in a way he'd never felt hurt before. Aching, burning-

Cooling power, soothing like balm from the touch of a stern-eyed doctor lady who felt of Spirit's starlight and glared at them both impartially. "You," she said bluntly, "are in no shape to truth-read *anyone*, Inspector. And *you* should have told me he was awake."

"Yes, ma'am," Allen managed. "Mind...." *Breathe.* "Telling me why?"

"I could bore you to sleep with the long explanation, but given you already know a Flame... sane people do *not* get an elemental boost from dragons and then charge right into combat. It's not a good idea."

Allen stared at her, nonplussed. "What?"

"Ask Flame Redstone. When she wakes up."

Worse and worse. "And when is that going to be?"

The doctor was grimly silent.

Chapter Fourteen

Cold. Oh, so achingly cold.

Points of warmth, resting on her wrist. A wash of *home*, and *welcome*, like aloe balm. "Hey."

Blinking, Shane tried to pierce the darkness-

Memory crashed in, and she just wanted to curl up and hide. *No more. No more, I'm so tired....*

"Shane?"

Allen. She reached out with Fire-sense; found a warm body, not another haunting ghost. "Did we win?"

"We're alive. The city's still in one piece." The heat of his body shifted in a shrug. "I think that counts."

"Good." She let her eyes close.

"Hey. You okay?"

"Tired," Shane admitted. "Unraveled the lava-Wards all the way under us." She gave him a crooked smile. "They're not supposed to come unraveled."

A *huh*. "That, and you melted all the stone between us and the caldera."

"That, too," Shane yawned.

"Did you know I'd be able to get us out of there?"

He's not going to let it lie. "I knew you'd be able to get out of there."

"You knew-" A sharp inhalation. "You keep telling me you *don't* want to die." Something ached in his voice, desperate and hurt; a man who'd almost seen something precious lost forever.

"I don't." Shane gripped his hand back. "I'm a Strike Specialist, Allen. Retired, yes; crippled, yes. But I swore an oath to Caldera. It's not my duty to *die*, Inspector. It's my duty to protect our people, no matter what it takes." She tried to shrug, lying down. "You'd do the same, and you know it."

"I wasn't sure." He cleared his throat. "I mean, about me. I don't- I'm not really... brave."

"Not fearless, you mean?" Shane snorted. "Good. Fearless people get themselves killed. Worse, they get *other* people killed. Nothing wrong with being afraid. I'm afraid a lot."

"You?" Stark disbelief.

"Oh yes," she said softly. "All the time." Coughed, and shook her head. "Is that water over there?"

He helped her sit up, steadying her shaking hands. "The doctors told me you'd be all right."

And you're not sure you believe them. "I will be," Shane said simply, gripping the cool mug. "In a few weeks. This - it's like running a marathon. You just have to crash for a while."

"Is that why Jehanna's not here?" he asked warily.

"Damn right. She knows I'm a horrible patient." Shane took a breath, glad not to smell blood. "I *will* be fine, Allen. In a few weeks."

"Good. I mean, that you will be...."

"Is something wrong?" Shane tried not to grab and *shake* it out of him. She'd spill everything. "Did we lose people? Is Inspector Freeport all right?"

"Callie?" A confused lilt. "Callie's fine. We're all fine... well. Most of us." A ragged sigh. "They killed so many people."

"Tell your captain not to let his guard down, just yet," Shane warned. "They *love* taking out first responders. Let the Foxes bat cleanup. Now that we've dug up the biggest rats, the rest should be easier to flush out."

"They're working on it." His voice was still taut. "Shane... how did you *know* I'd make it? I couldn't chant, I didn't have time to scribe-"

I'm a Flame. Of course I knew. "I sensed you teleport twice. I knew you could do it one more time."

"How?" His voice was raw, control over seething panic. "I did something *impossible* - and all the doctor says is dragons and elemental boosts and none of it makes any *sense!*"

Shane blinked. "It doesn't?"

Oh, damn it, Waycross.

Allen could run rings around her in theological history, but she knew darn well the country Orthodox went out of their way to avoid talking about Elemental surgery. He needed her history books, stat. "Of all the...." Shane leaned back against the pillow, cursing under her breath. "It's a wonder you're not twisting things up right now. Granted, you're probably almost as tapped out as I am, but that's no excuse-"

"Shane. *Tell me.*"

She crooked a finger, beckoning him closer. "Give me your hand." She tugged up the hospital gown closer to a modest neckline, then placed his palm over her heart. "Reach out with your Spirit-sense. What do you feel?"

"A volcano," Allen said softly. "Sleeping."

"Flatterer." She reached up to tap over his heart. "And what do you feel here?"

"...Light," Allen said at last. "Dim, but - it's *too much.*"

"Shh. It's all right. I promise." *I hope. If I can just talk you down. I really,* really *want to hurt someone. I don't care how much of a mess the other Points were! Why didn't anyone explain? He's wearing an* Orthodox coat. *Maybe singed, still smells like smoke, but his denomination's in his Watch records and Captain Mason should have throttled someone into talking. Leaving a Worker to wake up with power they've never had to chain down before - somebody could have gotten hurt, damn it!*

Which stirred up too many old, bad memories. She'd been twelve, traumatized, and in enough pain from broken ribs, broken *everything* to drive the strongest Spirit-healer on staff to get *himself* knocked out. The heat in her chest had been one more pinprick of agony, and when she'd flailed-

She didn't want to think about it. Those she'd seared had healed. Eventually. She'd been *lucky*.

Thank the Evening Star Allen was Journeyman-level.

He'd had practice. Training. Discipline. If his power had flared, he'd successfully sat on it. So far, at least.

Going to fix that. Starting now. "That light's what happens when you deal with dragons. If you survive."

"...Please tell me you're kidding."

"No." Shane squared her shoulders. "You wondered how someone becomes an Elemental. Training and practice, I told you, and that's true." She paused. "For those born with a strong enough pearl."

"I *wasn't*."

"So? Even those born with a strong Gift might never get to Elemental. It takes discipline, and years to build up your power to the point your pearl matures. *No* human is born with that. Workers can't be made as Elementals, either. The best pearl we can create is a Master-level. The body can't tolerate anything stronger, not without years of conditioning." She let a breath sigh out. "And for a made Worker, the pearl you're given is the pearl you live with. *Unless.* You do something terribly, terribly risky, and stake your life on your belief that your body can handle the energies." She shrugged, glancing aside. "Though it's not as dire a risk as people say. Dragons don't think like we do, but we are their allies. They usually won't touch us if they don't think we'll survive."

Allen sucked in a sharp breath. "So when Candle offered-"

"I knew you stood a good chance of making it," Shane said simply. "And no, I didn't tell you. I couldn't leave you there, Allen. Without my power, you would have died. And I *had* to get inside." She looked away.

"We both had to," Allen said at last. "So... what happens to me now?"

"Nothing, as far as I know." Shane blinked, puzzled. *Why would he think-?* "You haven't had Master-level training. You *have* to learn to manipulate your element, before you can do it reflexively. Teleports, truth-reading; anything you've already mastered, you can do. Anything else is up to you."

"But Elementals aren't ever civilians."

Now he realizes that. "You're already in service, Allen," Shane said patiently. "You're Watch."

"But-"

"Command is *not* going to scoop you up and dump you on the front lines," Shane cut him off. "The whole point of training an Elemental is massive, *controlled* power. Do you think any sane commander wants to ride herd on an Elemental who doesn't want to be there?"

"...Good point."

"Though someone might try to guilt-trip you into signing up," Shane acknowledged. "Say no. Unless you really want to be in uniform - and *not* catching murderers, which you're *good* at - say no. Captain Mason thinks highly of you, my aunt respects you, and you've got a partner willing to take on a Flame to keep you safe. These are good people. Stay with them. This city's going to need you." *Now more than ever.*

"Now you're starting to worry me," Allen said dryly.

"I hope so." Shane tapped her fingers against water-cool glass. "The year of the azure dragon's not over yet."

"...Oh, Lord. *Tell* me you're kidding."

"I wish," Shane sighed.

"We stopped them!"

"We stopped *this* attack." Glass warmed in her hands, a wisp of steam brushing her face. With an effort, Shane quelled it. "This is *holy war*, Allen. *This* group is shattered. But any other nest of Ba'al-worshippers can read the signs and decide this is the year Caldera's going down. And they *will*." She took a moment just to breathe, hating her weakness. "They've got most of a year to come up with something else."

A long silence. "That explains a lot," Allen said at last.

"Allen?" That didn't sound good. At all.

"I *had* a partner."

Definitely not good. "But you said Inspector Freeport-"

"Is fine. She is." Fingers gripped hers, as if seeking warmth. "But after what she saw, the reports that came back from the Fire Point...." A weary sigh. "She asked for a new partner."

Oh. Oh Sunlit, that had to hurt. "You think she's afraid of you."

"Spirit, remember?" A dry chuckle. "I *know* she's afraid of me."

Lousy excuse for a Watch officer, then. Not that Shane would say that. Not about a man's partner. Ex-partner. "But why? You never-"

"You never did anything to her, either." Allen leaned back. "Callie was my emergency contact. I think the doctor told her, when they weren't sure I would wake up... the lady wouldn't explain what happened, just to talk to you when *you* woke up, and Callie wouldn't even look me in the eye...." A ragged sigh. "No one should be above the law. We always agreed on that. If I'm an Elemental... why would anyone want a partner who's *allowed* to break the law?"

Reaching out, Shane smacked in the direction of his forehead.

"Ow!"

Cheekbone. Close enough. "We don't have the right to *break* the law. Idiot. The law's written to allow us aggravated self-defense. The *only* difference between that, and an ordinary citizen, is the legal recognition that if an Elemental's being threatened, it's not anything as petty as a mugger with a knife. Something that *deserves* being blown halfway to hell."

"But-"

"Yes, some Elementals have skipped out of charges they shouldn't have - though between you, me, and the wallpaper, people like that tend to end up dead of friendly fire. But most of the time? Allen, that law was written because of *Ba'al's assassins.* You get *one* shot to realize they're stabbing you. Or shooting you. Or sticking you with the old-fashioned poison needle. *One.*" Shane shook her head. "Welcome to my world, Allen. You're a target. For the rest of your life."

"But I'm not in the military-" He cut himself off. "They really don't believe in civilians."

"If you're an unbeliever, you can't be innocent. *By definition.*" Shane closed her eyes, trying not to look at bloody memories.

"Young, old, women, children - their own prophet cheered when a poet was murdered, suckling a babe at her breast," Allen murmured. "Because she'd laughed at him."

"Yes." Shane clenched her fingers. "They're not going to win. I'll fight them, as long as I draw breath. So long as Caldera stands, they *can't* win - because as long as we're alive, we're free."

"You won't be alone." Allen caught himself, voice turning a little more hesitant. "If you're interested, that is."

Shane raised an eyebrow. "Interested in what?"

"We got an *unusual* request, from Strike General Bones. Put together with Captain Stewart's report, it shook up some wool-heads at Command. Or so Master Sergeant Trillian said when he dropped by my room yesterday." Allen's voice turned rueful. "That is one tough old soldier. I want to put him in a room with my father and watch the sparks fly."

"Lectured you on the proper care and feeding of people who've watched your back, hmm?" Shane smiled.

"My ears are still ringing," Allen affirmed. "Anyway. The general mentioned what we'd found, and the casualties, and... well. If you want the job, you're hired."

Even through the gray fog of post-combat, that sounded intriguing. "What job?"

"Officially? Elemental liaison between the Points and the Watch's

Investigative Division. Civilian, but with the clearance to deal with Point security, and take a couple of us along with you."

Bones. Had done that. For her? Shane swallowed.

"Unofficially," Allen went on, "I think it was mentioned that everybody *knows* you're going to poke into weird things anyway, might as well limit the damage."

"Stalking horse," Shane grinned. "That's Bones, all right."

"You *want* to be a target?" Allen's voice rang with disbelief.

Setting the glass aside, Shane ticked off points on her fingers, one at a time. "Woman. Made Worker. *Flame.* I'll be a target as long as I live." She smirked. "This way, I get a chance to see it coming. So to speak."

"About that." He drew a quick breath. "Day to day stuff, you want to hire Tace, that's fine. But if it's going to get dangerous? Let me be your eyes."

Oh, *really.* "Is that part of the job description?"

"It does say, Watch officer to work with you," Allen admitted. "But you get to pick. As long as their superior officers are okay with it."

Uh-huh. "And Mason would be?"

"First time out, and you not only stop a terrorist attack, you help clear a cold case, *and* uncover an inspector's murder?" Allen said wryly. "Captain Mason thinks you're worth your weight in rods."

Did he, now. Though it wasn't Mason she was worried about. "And you want the job."

"I have never been so scared in my entire life," Allen said bluntly. "Dragons protect Caldera, everyone knows that - but you never hear about *why.* I never knew... I never *imagined* they had so much at stake." A soft breath; she sensed him shake his head. "They're not infallible. They're not all-powerful. They're just trying to get by, like we are...."

Shane let the silence stretch out, and nodded.

"I thought my country was strong, and safe, and powerful."

Allen's voice was thick, choked with threatening tears. "And it *is*. But it's so fragile... and I *never knew*, and - oh Sunlit Lord...."

"I know," Shane murmured, holding him when he leaned into her to silently, finally weep. "I love this city too."

A last gulp and scrub of tissues, and he leaned back again. "That's how you do it, isn't it? I couldn't understand... how you could live through what you have, still *want* to live...."

"Love. Yes. *And for the love of her people, Angharad sought out the dragons....* Not that I'm anywhere near that league," Shane added wryly. "Just a sinner like the rest of us, trying to limp by. But love... love can get you through things you'd never be strong enough to face alone." She chuckled. "Of course, old-fashioned grit doesn't hurt."

"No kidding," Allen muttered. Held out a hand. "So. Partners?" He cleared his throat. "Ah, my hand is-"

"I know." Grinning, she shook it. "This is going to be an interesting year."

"That's it," Allen muttered under his breath. "I'm doomed."

"Oh, definitely," Shane snickered. "So. You know theology. What say we put our heads together, and hash out what omens the Slaves are coming for next?"

Made in the USA
Monee, IL
09 February 2024

53158339R00152